★

We walked another fifty feet or so. The creek turned sharply away from us. Here was a downed tree and a sandy bank covered with debris that had come from the lake. I saw tangled fishing net and pieces of Styrofoam. As I stepped closer I even saw a fish—a huge fish, bloated and white.

Diane gasped and swung around, her hand over her mouth. Then she was retching and finally she vomited several times in a row.

"Are you—?"

"Don't look at it," she said between heaves.

I turned back around and stared at the large tangled fish, only this time I saw the blond hair matted to the head, and the form that was a body—swollen, white, with marks where something had nibbled at the bloated flesh.

We had found Leigh Greer.

★

Previously published Worldwide Mystery titles by
BARBARA BURNETT SMITH

MISTLETOE FROM PURPLE SAGE
CELEBRATION IN PURPLE SAGE
DUST DEVILS OF THE PURPLE SAGE
WRITERS OF THE PURPLE SAGE

BARBARA BURNETT SMITH

SKELETONS IN PURPLE SAGE

WORLDWIDE.®

TORONTO • NEW YORK • LONDON
AMSTERDAM • PARIS • SYDNEY • HAMBURG
STOCKHOLM • ATHENS • TOKYO • MILAN
MADRID • WARSAW • BUDAPEST • AUCKLAND

This one is for Doris, my "other" sister. With much love.

SKELETONS IN PURPLE SAGE

A Worldwide Mystery/January 2004

First published by St. Martin's Press LLC.

ISBN 0-373-26479-8

Printed in U.S.A.

Acknowledgments

Bits and pieces of every work of fiction come from real life, and this book is no exception. For that reason I would like to offer special thanks to Reverend Charles Meyer, a marvelous mystery writer who spent much of his life cleverly disguised as an Episcopal priest. Chuck was also an expert on, and was an advocate for, what he termed "a good death." He was the one who gave me the idea for the murder. Unfortunately, he died before he could give me all the help with research that I needed. Someday I'm going to discuss that with him.

I'd also like to thank another wonderful writer, Katharine Eliska Kimbriel. While her published books are fantasy and science fiction, she has also written a terrific mystery that hasn't yet found a home. Using that expertise, she pitched in at the last minute when I needed moral support and some expert editing. For that I am grateful.

Caroline Young Petrequin always reads for me, and offers the best feedback. I love the "ahas" and other comments that let me know if the story is on track. This time she even upped her technical expertise to help me out. I am blessed with dear friends who also happen to be marvelous writers. As always, I am in Caroline's debt.

Last but not least, many thanks to the members of our short-lived writers' group: Rob Lallier, Larry Brill, Janet Christian, Marsha Moyer, Geoff Leavenworth and Jan Grape.

ONE

THE LAST TIME I gave a big party we were hit with a tornado.

This time it was a flood. At some point people will ask me not to give any more parties.

The rains had started three days earlier, and by now much of the town was underwater. One small neighborhood had been evacuated and the residents were at a temporary shelter in the high school gym.

However, I couldn't call off this particular reception because it was to honor two people I considered the most special in Purple Sage. The first was Dr. Bill Marchak, who was retiring from the local hospital. Dr. Bill has only been in Purple Sage for two years, but he deserved more of a send-off than just a cake in the staff lounge. I haven't met many saints in my life, but to my mind, Dr. Bill qualifies.

The other honoree was Beverly Kendall, who'd come back to town after three years' absence. Bev was one of the initial members of my writers group and a woman who has given more, and received less in return, than anyone I know.

The reception was to be held at my best friend Diane Atwood's house, since both she and it are equipped for large crowds. We had announced it in the local paper.

Then the rains came.

Now the governor was coming.

As I stepped from my car onto Diane's wide circular drive I was acutely aware that at that very moment the governor and his wife were touring the water-ravaged downtown square, to be followed by the inspection of several other areas that had been hardest hit by the deluge. Once the tour was over, the couple would be arriving here for a brief respite and coffee before hurrying back to Austin for a formal dinner.

We'd planned that the governor would be gone before the party actually started, but Purple Sage is a small town, and word of the governor's attendance had spread faster than the floodwater. Instead of the fifty to seventy-five people we'd initially planned for, we were now expecting the number to swell into the hundreds.

We were prepared. I had walked out of Diane's front door barely an hour earlier to race home and change, then to pick up flowers. The house was ready for the party. *En fête* as the French might say. Her home was immaculate, the silver set out, and the coffee ready to brew.

I hurried toward her house carrying an enormous floral arrangement, one of the last things we had to put in place.

That's when I saw the water gushing over the front doorsill. All my forward momentum ended.

"Diane?" The door was already open and I could see a sheen of water that spread across the foyer tile and back onto the living room carpet. "Diane!" I placed the flowers on the porch, watching as water from the house ran across my shoes.

"Need a life preserver?" Diane appeared in the doorway, wearing a very wet sweatshirt with the sleeves cut off, and a pair of jeans that were soaked to the knees. Not usual attire for my very elegant friend.

"This can't be happening," I said. "Why didn't you call me? And what did happen?"

"I think it's a pipe. I turned off the valve at the main, and it seems to have helped. At least it's clean water. The ground must have shifted." It was the overload of rainwater causing pipes all over town to stress and break. "By the way, nice flowers; where do you think we should put them?"

"Who cares?" I sank against the doorjamb; I couldn't take it in. "What happened to your furniture?"

"The track team ran by here and they moved almost everything upstairs or into the garage."

"So, what are we going to do?"

"You could try a nervous breakdown. I've already had one, but it didn't do a damn bit of good. The water just kept coming, time refused to stop, and Trey still didn't answer his cell phone." Trey was her husband, who was also the current mayor of Purple Sage. It was he who was shepherding the governor and his wife.

"You've lost it," I said.

"It drowned."

A deep blue pickup truck pulled into the circular drive, and my sixteen-year-old son, Jeremy, jumped out. "Mom, the cake is in the back and we didn't get it wrapped very well. It's going to get—" He stopped on the porch, much as I had, and stared at both Diane and the water rolling over the front doorsill. "Oh, wow."

"Succinctly put," Diane said.

Jeremy shook his head, his eyes still fixed on the water. "The water is, I mean..."

"It's the newest in feng shui decorating—water flowing through the house."

Diane's nonchalance was a sham. While she is not given to panic, this behavior was much too cool even for her.

"I can't take any more calm," I said. "It's time to panic. If your furniture is safely upstairs, then we have to handle the reception. Where in the hell are we going to have it?"

"I have no fu—frigging idea." She gestured toward the pickup. "First things first. Let's at least get the cake in here, then we'll worry about where to put the people."

The drizzle was gathering forces to form droplets and I knew from recent experience that soon the gray skies would send another downpour.

"Okay," I said, my mind racing in a million directions at once. Better to focus on the next right action. "Jeremy, do you need any help?"

"A lot," he said. "The cake is in the bed."

"Jeremy! You knew it was going to rain."

"You haven't seen the size of this thing. It's huge."

Diane and I followed him to his pickup, and as I peered into the back of it, I saw what he was talking about. IdaMae Dorfman had made a sheet cake, beautiful, white, and massive. Actually it was composed of several sheet cakes. When I had called the Bakery that morning to say we might have hundreds of people attending, she had volunteered to put all the flat cakes she had side by side. I'd agreed, without realizing how immense the result would be.

"Oh my God..."

Diane asked, "Can we just slide this out?"

"Well, a, could we lift it just a little?" Jeremy asked. "I'd rather not scratch the paint, if you know what I mean."

"Of course; what was I thinking?"

This wasn't just a pickup truck to Jeremy. It was a gleaming chariot, or a passkey to a world he had never known before. Its official name was the Midnight Blue Beast, and usually it lived up to it, gleaming in every direction, only now it had streaks of a sticky, white coating of caliche mud.

Gently, so as not to damage the cake, the three of us lifted it just enough to get it to the end of the pickup bed, but once there we stopped. The board was too flimsy for the weight it was bearing; we needed one person on each corner and without that additional person the cake was going to land on the ground.

"Now what?" Jeremy asked. He set the edge of the board on the tailgate and slithered to the driveway, careful not to bounce the truck. He looked around, as I was doing, as if help might drop from the sky along with the rain.

It didn't happen quite that way, but help did arrive. Diane's next-door neighbor, Tom Greer, drove up and climbed out of his car.

"Tom," Diane called. "Could you give us a hand?"

He looked up, saw our predicament, and hurried over. "That's the biggest thing I've ever seen," he said, getting a grip on the board that held it.

Slowly, carefully, we shuffled toward the front door. I was mentally going over optional locations for the reception, but I couldn't come up with any. The high school gym was being used as a shelter, the community center was underwater, and the country club had suffered a fire caused by lightning.

As we stepped onto the porch Diane said, "Now, will this go through the door?"

"What in the world—?" It was the first Tom had seen of the flooding. "Why are we taking this in your house? And what are we going to put it on? I don't see any furniture. What's it for, anyway?" Then a look of comprehension spread across his face. "The reception for the governor and his wife?"

"It's not really for them, but that's not important, now." Diane looked at all of us. "What do you think?"

Tom spoke up. "I think it's a big waste of time taking this inside, because no one is going to be visiting you today, at least not by choice. What's plan B?"

"There isn't one," I said.

Jeremy shifted his hands on the board. "What about the Baptist church? They have a big basement."

"I called and it's flooded," Diane said. "And at the Episcopal church they're having a wedding. Actually, it's only the rehearsal dinner, but the hall is already decorated. I asked if they might work around our reception, but Father Matson said we didn't have a prayer."

"Not very holy of him," Tom said.

Jeremy was thinking hard. "What about our house?" he asked.

"Of course! That's what we'll have to do," I said. Our house was smaller and not as formal, but it was dry. "We'll just rotate people through, rather than allowing them to linger." The cake was getting heavy and even though we were under the two-story portico, it was damp and cold. "Let's put the cake back in your truck."

Diane shook her head. "Your place is too far away. It would take the governor twenty minutes to drive out there and twenty minutes back in the wrong direction from Austin. He'd be late to his own formal dinner. And where would you put all the cars?''

We live on a ranch outside of Purple Sage. It was my husband's family home, set over half a mile back from the highway on a white caliche road. Our guests couldn't walk the distance in the mud and rain, nor was there room for all the cars near the house.

My shoulders began to sag, both from the weight of the cake and from what seemed an insurmountable problem. "We'll just have to cancel," I said.

"No, you don't. This way," Tom said. He began walking and we had no choice but to move with him. He went straight to the end of the drive, into the street, then around the low brick wall that separated his property from Diane's.

"We can't!" I said.

Diane pulled back, jerking the cake ominously. "Tom, this isn't a good idea. Leigh isn't expecting company and certainly not over a hundred people." Not that Diane's refusal had a damn thing to do with Leigh.

"Leigh'll love having the reception. Come on." He started forward. We were having a tug-of-war with the cake board.

Diane held her ground as best she could. "Women see these things differently from men."

"You think she'll be worried about how the house looks, but that isn't a problem. We had a cleaning crew in last week and it's never looked better." He began to march us inexorably toward the front door.

Diane's face paled. Jeremy appeared stunned. I felt sick. We had good reason to be that way and it wasn't one that we should have to explain to Tom.

"Leigh will be happy to see y'all. She's missed you."

The man was oblivious to the fact that we were not friends of his wife's, and never had been. At least not friends with this wife.

Three years earlier Tom had divorced his first wife, Beverly. Beverly the honoree of the reception.

Divorces are rarely happy events, but in most cases, after

they are over, everyone gets on with their lives, including family and friends.

In Tom and Beverly's divorce, my husband, Matt, and I had been some of the friends, as had Diane and Trey. We had played cards, watched our kids' ball games, gone out to dinner, and had even taken weekend trips together.

When I had first arrived in Purple Sage, newly married to Matt with my then-twelve-year-old son in tow, Beverly had made me feel welcome. Special. Which is how she makes everyone feel.

Bev isn't a particularly beautiful woman, but she is an exquisitely beautiful person; she has an inner glow that radiates outward and draws people to her.

She had been one of the original members of our writers group, where we read each other's work and offered encouragement. Beverly was the best at that. No matter how bad a piece of writing was, Beverly found some reason to praise the writer. Reading her early work gave me the opportunity to really know her; we used to kid about seeing into each other's souls. Beverly's soul is glorious. And funny. And sometimes downright wicked.

When she called to tell me that she and Tom were divorcing I had been stunned. She didn't offer details, so I was blindsided when Tom showed up on our doorstep, holding hands with Leigh Burton. At the time, Leigh had been twenty-six years old, and according to Tom, the woman he had been searching for all his life. That was quite a shock to Beverly and the rest of us.

I don't believe in taking sides in a divorce, but in that case I had to make an exception. Not only did Leigh want Beverly's husband, whom she got, she also wanted Beverly's house, all the things in it, and Beverly's life. Tom saw no reason for her not to have them.

In a moment of disgust and anger, Beverly had named a price for her half of the house and furnishings, and Leigh had snapped at it.

Beverly packed her personal belongings and moved to Dal-

las. She landed a great job at one of the teaching hospitals.
She also did a little freelance writing on the side.

Leigh should have accepted her victory with grace, but she
wasn't finished. Having gotten Tom and his house, she then
wanted Beverly's friends. Bev and Tom had always hosted a
number of parties throughout the year, and Leigh attempted to
give those same parties with the identical guest lists. I came
down with a sinus infection at the time of the first one and
called in my regrets; I also vowed to my husband, Matt, that
while I would always be cordial to the couple, I would *never*
set foot in that house again.

It seemed ''never'' had arrived.

''Tom, we can't do this,'' I said. ''There has to be some
other place.''

''Why? Just not good enough for you, anymore?'' His response hit like a whiplash.

''No. No, of course not.''

''Bullshit, Jolie. You and Matt have avoided us for years.
It's obvious that any port in a storm doesn't hold here, because
mine won't do.''

''Tom—''

Diane spoke up, ''Look, Tom, it's not about you, it's about
Beverly.'' She shifted the weight of the cake slightly and said,
''We can't bring her here. That wouldn't be fair.''

Comprehension slid across his face. I felt relief. He did un-
derstand. ''God, is that all you're worried about? That's not a
problem! Bev and I have talked since she's been back in town.
I even took her a couple of boxes of pictures that she left.''
He dismissed our concerns. ''We're very civilized these days.
Bev won't mind a bit.''

We were under the canopy of his front porch and Tom hit
the doorbell with his elbow. He was being naive; I was sure
of it.

Leigh appeared in the door, a bright smile on her pretty face.
She was in tight, light blue jeans and tall, strappy high heels.

''Oh, wow,'' she said, ''it looks like a party on my doorstep!
Here, this way; bring that into the dining room before it gets

wet.'' She opened the double front doors, and started off through the foyer, then veered into the formal dining room. We followed.

A sense of déjà vu grabbed me hard. The room was almost exactly the way I remembered, with a beautiful round oak table in the center, a matching sideboard to the right, and on the far wall a fireplace that was also open to the kitchen. Above the mantel was an antique beveled mirror that Bev had bought at an auction in Austin. Diane and I had been with her at the time.

There were photographs on the mantel, and for one startling moment I thought they were the same pictures as four years before. They weren't; the frames were the same, but the pictures inside had been changed. In the ornate gilt frame that had held a wedding photo of Beverly in her flowing satin gown, there was now a wedding picture of Leigh. Another frame, turquoise and modern, held a photo of Leigh and Tom on a ski lift. I remembered it particularly because it had once contained a snapshot of Beverly, Diane, and me taken during one of our rare snowfalls.

It was eerie to the point of frightening.

''You have to tell me what the cake is for.'' Leigh studied it a moment, and said, ''Oh, I get it, this is for Dr. Bill's reception. Isn't the governor coming, too?'' She either didn't know or didn't choose to acknowledge that Beverly was being welcomed back to Purple Sage, as well. ''Diane, that's being held at your house, isn't it?''

''Except Diane has a broken pipe and a flooded downstairs,'' Tom explained.

''Oh, I'm so sorry.''

Tom said, ''I want to move the reception here.''

''Really?'' Leigh looked like a five-year-old who'd been given a present. She turned to Diane. ''Do you mean it? I get to have the reception? For the governor?''

''Not just the governor...''

''So, it's settled.'' Tom's expression was smug.

''No,'' I said. Someone had to have both feet planted firmly on the earth, even if it was wet ground. "Leigh, this is also to honor Dr. Marchak and Beverly."

Leigh took in the information, giving it serious thought.

Finally she nodded. "I see your concern. But Bev is a real trooper, and if this was still her house and the party was for me, she'd do the same thing I'm doing. So, what time is everyone arriving?"

A sick dread invaded my body. I looked at Diane, who was checking her watch. "Forty-eight minutes and counting," she said.

I was frantically trying to think of an alternative location.

Leigh opened a drawer of the sideboard to whip out a beautiful tablecloth with delicate bluebonnets embroidered around the edge. I'd swear it had been Beverly's. "Here, lift the cake and let me get this under it."

The matter was settled.

The party would be held as planned—except it would be in Beverly's old house.

TWO

THE FIRST WAVE of guests arrived even before we finished ferrying things back and forth between the houses. Either the citizens of Purple Sage had cabin fever from the rain, or they wanted good parking places.

Besides all the frenzied physical activity, mentally I was also doing gymnastics. How was I going to insulate Beverly from the shock, and pain, of being back in her old house? It was particularly difficult because everyone at the reception would be watching her, waiting to see how she reacted. My heart hurt just thinking about it.

Meanwhile, Leigh put on music at a deafening volume. Her choice was inappropriate, too—Eminem.

Diane whizzed through the dining room where I was arranging forks only slightly faster than the guests were picking them up. "Leigh's going to blow out hearing aids all over town," Diane said. The doorbell rang.

"You get the music; I'll get the door," I said. And while Diane went to tell Leigh to turn it off, diplomatically, I ran to answer the bell.

The double doors opened as I stepped onto the foyer tile. Unfortunately, the floor was slick with rain and I slid across it, grabbed for balance, and slammed into the doorjamb.

IdaMae Dorfman stood in the doorway watching me with interest. "That was quite a gymnastic routine," she said. "I'll give you a nine point seven. Your execution was off."

IdaMae is almost as old as the dirt in Purple Sage, yet she has more energy than I do. She owns the Bakery, which keeps her active, and it was she who had made the enormous cake for the reception.

"No extra points for artistic interpretation?" I asked, straightening up.

"Not unless you point your toes, although you did stick the landing. Oh, and by the way," she said, taking off her rain poncho. "The governor was just gettin' outta Trey's car. I figure they're coming up right behind me."

I had barely enough time to brush my fingers across my damp hair and smile before the governor stepped through the door. Following him was Diane's husband, Trey, our reluctant mayor.

Trey did the introductions. "Jolie Wyatt, let me introduce Governor Edward Rains."

With one eye on the door waiting for Beverly, I greeted the man whose face I'd seen so many times on television. I watched while he and his entourage went into the house, and flashes started going off. The citizenry had not only come to see the governor, they were armed. There must have been at least a dozen people with cameras, including Ute Roesner, who calls herself an amateur photographer, although she now works part-time for the *Sage Tribune*. Ute took several still shots, then reached for a video camera and began recording with that. All the while the governor was nodding, smiling, and shaking hands, yet still moving forward.

When I lost sight of them in the crowd the doorbell was once more ringing. I answered it quickly, but again it wasn't Beverly, and I ended up staying in the foyer to open the door again and again. It was like Halloween, only most of the trick-or-treaters were in their sixties. They were bundled up to their eyebrows and underneath their coats they wore their Sunday-go-to-meetin' finest.

I took coats, shook out umbrellas, and hugged more than a few of our guests. Finally, Diane appeared to take my place.

"It's freezing up here," she said.

"Yes, it is, and you're welcome to it. Oh, and keep an eye out for Beverly. God, I feel bad about bringing her here."

"I know, but I still don't see that we had any choice." The doorbell rang and she shooed me away. "I'll handle this; you go serve coffee. Make yourself a cup of tea while you're at it."

I intended to do just that, but I never found the time. By then the house was almost full, and still we didn't have either of our guests of honor. Maybe they were here and I'd just missed them. Perhaps they had come in the back door.

I scanned several rooms and spotted instead my handsome husband, Matt, working his way through the crowd. Matt is old Purple Sage and much adored, at least by the women of the community, so he had many to say hello to. When he finally reached me I could see that he was in jeans and work boots, and his smile was grim.

"Hi." He leaned down to give me a quick kiss. "I can't believe the party is here at Tom's."

"Some kind of bad karma," I said. "And I suspect it's mine, not Beverly's."

"I'm sure you did the best you could. Everyone seems to be having a good time."

I wondered if we would still be able to say that after Beverly arrived.

"So far."

Matt and I have only been married for a little over four years; sometimes I think he is my reward for the previous twelve years of my life. My first husband, Steve, left when my son, Jeremy, was just an infant. Steve never came back and he never sent child support, so I did what a woman does in that situation—I got a job, and became both mother and father to my son.

There are probably millions of women who are doing it better than I did. Some are better mothers, some better bread-winners, but I've finally come to accept that I did the best I could at the time.

Now Jeremy and I both have Matt. He is a wonderful adoptive father to Jeremy, and even in these troubling teen years they seem to be grateful for each other. Matt's not perfect, but much closer to it than I am—sometimes annoyingly so.

I looked down at Matt's clothes. "You're not staying."

"I'll be next door using a wet vac on their carpet." How he managed to find one in the current flood conditions is still a mystery, but typical of Matt. "Oh, and by the way, I asked Diane and Trey to stay with us until their house dries out. I hope you don't mind."

"Of course not," I said. "I should have thought of it. Have you got any help for next door?"

"Some of the high school kids are there, friends of Jeremy's, and as soon as Trey can shake loose from the governor, he's coming, too."

"If you need anything just call. We'll send cake or whatever." He was already making his way toward the door and I followed.

"Maybe later. You look great by the way." He grinned. "Even with the leaf in your hair." He pulled it out.

It was no doubt from my run between the houses.

"Wish someone had mentioned it before I met the governor."

"Don't worry, it looked like a decoration."

I smiled and he offered one more quick kiss before he opened the door. As usual there was someone on the other side of it—this time it was Dr. Bill's wife, Gretchen Marchak.

"Oh, Jolie, I'm late," she said.

Matt says that rain falls on everyone, but it affects us differently. I ended up with smudged mascara and leaves in my hair. Gretchen Marchak merely looked dewy and refreshed by it.

When she pulled off her plastic rain hat, her silver-white hair was still gently waved. She stuffed the plastic into the pocket of her beige raincoat. "I'm afraid Dr. Bill is going to be even later than I am. I called, but I couldn't pry him away from his precious hospital." She slipped off her trench coat to reveal a beautiful black and cream wool suit. With her elegance and poise Gretchen always reminds me of a senator's wife, or perhaps a senator herself. She smiled at me. "He promised me he'd be here in ten minutes."

"He'll make it," Matt said. "Here, let me handle that." He took her coat and found a spot for it on the rack, then shook out her umbrella and placed it on the porch with a dozen others. "Have a good time," he said in parting.

"Bye," I said.

Gretchen looked over the crowd. "Doesn't this look lovely."

I checked my watch. The reception had officially started fifteen minutes earlier and neither of the honorees had arrived. The dread I'd been feeling was getting stronger.

"Does someone need to go get him?" I asked.

"Oh, no. I gave him *what for* on the phone, so he should show up in a few minutes. He's got his own car, of course. My, the coffee smells wonderful."

I led her to the coffee, introduced her to the governor, and went back to the door to let in another wave of guests.

There were half a dozen people who hurried inside, where it was warmer and drier. I greeted each guest and held the door for the stragglers—Beverly and her father.

"You're here." Relief swept through me, followed by concern.

She gave me a hug. "I'm so sorry we're late. We had a few problems." She didn't elaborate, but helped her father into the house and began peeling off his London Fog overcoat. She didn't seem disturbed by the location of the reception. "Here, Daddy, put your arm down. That's good. Jolie, I can't believe you actually pulled off the party despite the rain and all the other impediments. Thank you so much."

"No problem, I'm just so sorry that we had to move it here...." Concern shifted to guilt.

"It was very kind of Tom and Leigh. I have to remember to thank them."

When her father's health deteriorated Bev had moved back to town and into his little house without a thought for her own career or needs. She had done so knowing how difficult the situation was going to be. It was then I had told her I would do everything I could to make it easier.

This time I had let her down.

Beverly's eyes went beyond me, taking in the scene inside the house. "Oh, my God, look at all these people."

"Sunday gawkers," her father said. Ever the patriarch, he went on, "We can't stand here by the door; there's a draft."

I closed the door, and Bev slid off her wet trench coat, then turned to face me. "How do I look?"

I wondered how many people would be comparing her to Leigh.

Earlier, Leigh had slipped upstairs to return in a simple black dress and high heels, with her blond hair piled up on her head. She had looked stunning. Beverly was not slim, not blond, and not stunning. She had a roundness that seems to find women in middle age, and her brown hair was plastered to her forehead from the rain. I reached over and wiped it with my sleeve then fluffed it off her forehead.

"You look terrific."

"You're sure?"

"Yes, and I especially like your outfit," I said. She was in a cobalt blue dress that had a gray band at the waist and on the wrists. The colors set off her large eyes.

Self-consciously she smoothed the skirt over her plump hips and smiled, but almost immediately her focus shifted to the house again. Her eyes took in the walls, with a framed picture of Tom and Leigh, to the wallpaper behind it that she had selected. How did it feel to see your home in the hands of a new woman? Her face gave no indication of her thoughts, but I saw her swallow hard before she turned back to her father.

"Come on, Dad, let's find a place for you to sit down."

I tried to escort Mr. Kendall through the crowd, but he pulled away, allowing only Bev to give him support.

As we moved into the living room I heard someone announce, "Beverly is here."

Everyone turned toward us as if they'd been magnetized. Suddenly we were surrounded by people all wanting to say hello and make Bev's entry back into Purple Sage society a little easier.

A young woman in her twenties gave Bev a huge hug. "I'm so glad you're here!"

"Me, too, Stacey! How are the kids?"

"Just great. They've missed you. Falon wanted to come tonight, but I told her it was just for grown-ups."

"She could have come. Give her a hug from me." Bev turned to the next guest. "Oh, IdaMae. I hope you made a cake for the party."

"I did. Several, all rolled into one great big one."

"Really? Then there should be leftovers for me to take home. When I was in Dallas I missed the Bakery. And you, too, of course."

"Of course."

Bev moved a few more steps and her eyes lit up. "Mildred! How are you feeling? Are you doing okay?"

"I'm pretty good." Mildred Segriff was fighting her way through another round of chemotherapy just weeks after a radical mastectomy.

"You look wonderful," Bev said.

"I feel better, but I sure am getting tired of doctors."

Beverly leaned forward and said softly in her ear, "Ask Dr. Baxter if he's heard the saying 'tit for tat.' You tell him he owes you a tat, and a great big one."

Mildred looked stunned, then her mouth opened and she began to laugh. It was the first time I'd seen Mildred laugh in months.

Beverly was proof again that beauty really does come from within.

I had watched the governor work the crowd, and while he was certainly a professional, he was nowhere near Bev's league. He led with his intellect, making contact superficially. Beverly led with her heart and somehow touched each person.

We continued moving, and as we did, Ute came over to take a couple of pictures. I smiled for the camera, then stepped aside.

"Jolie, it's all right. You are the hostess, you should be in the picture," Ute said, her sweet face in a smile. I smiled back. Some people consider my employer, KSGE radio, and her employer, the *Sage Tribune,* competitors, since we vie for the same advertising dollars. Ute and I agree, however, that until I can broadcast pictures and she can print sounds, we should work together. Still, you won't find my photograph in the paper very often.

"That's okay, Ute," I said. "Get a couple of Bev with her dad."

She did just that while I kept an eye out for Leigh and Tom. Neither was in sight.

Finally we moved on to the great room, and a place on the love seat was graciously offered to Bev's dad. "Thank you; this is perfect," Bev said.

Henry Kendall grunted agreement, and lowered himself stiffly. I took his cane and held it while Bev eased his sweater sleeves down over his thin arms.

Once a robust man with a fearsome reputation, Henry Kendall was now in his eighties, in that stage where our bodies begin to wither and diminish. Only his tone of voice still held some vestige of his powerful past.

He looked around the room, then turned to his daughter. "Beverly, what are we doin' here? I thought you didn't live here, anymore?"

"I don't live here," Bev explained, placing his cane across his knees. "We're here for a party. It's to honor me and the governor."

Why, I wondered, was everyone leaving off at least one of the honorees? Leigh had left off Bev, and now Bev was leaving off Dr. Bill.

"Governor Briscoe?" her father asked. "He's coming here?"

"Dolph Briscoe isn't governor, anymore," Beverly said. Nor had he been for more than twenty years. "It's Governor Edward Rains in office these days; you remember, I told you that. And he's already here. Would you like to meet him?"

"He a Democrat or a Republican?"

"I think he's a Republican."

"Then I got no use for him."

The corners of Bev's mouth twitched, although she didn't quite smile. "Can I get you anything before I say hello to everyone?"

"No, you go on. I can take care of myself."

"Okay, Daddy. If you need anything, let someone know. I'll be right in the other room." She touched her father's arm and bent over to kiss his cheek, then stood up and straightened her shoulders. "Okay, Jolie, I'm ready."

"Bev," I said, as we started off, "I can't apologize enough for having the reception here. Are you still going to speak to me?"

"Jolie, don't worry about it—you've done a wonderful job."

"We were stuck. There wasn't another place in town. Nothing." I stopped. "Damn! The hangar at the airport!"

"Now that would have been nice and cozy. This is lovely. Really." I watched her closely as we wove our way through the crowd, and the tension around her mouth seemed to lessen. Or perhaps I'd only imagined the tightness.

I didn't think she loved Tom any longer, but they held a history of life together—both romance and bad times. They had children. They had also shared the vision of growing old together and it had been ripped away from Beverly.

Now even her past had become a sham.

The memories of her old house, the place where she had been a young mother with a happy family, were being replaced by Leigh's vision.

I said, "How can I make this easier?"

"Jolie, everything is fine. Really," Bev said, turning to me. "But there is one thing you can do. Keep me away from Gretchen Marchak, okay?"

Dr. Bill's wife? I nodded, willing but confused. "Gretchen? But why—"

"You asked what you could do."

"No problem. I'll run interference."

She took a deep breath and let it out. "I can't believe how many people are here. I suppose most of them came to see the governor, but I'm going to pretend they wanted to see me, too."

"They did. And they do."

"So, where should I start?"

An impromptu receiving line had formed to allow all the guests to meet the governor. I had planned to take Beverly to the head of the line and introduce her, however I faltered when I saw that it was Leigh who was shaking hands with Governor Rains.

I needn't have been concerned. Standing next to him, no doubt coaching him, was Diane's husband, Trey, who may not like being mayor but is very good at it. He said something softly to the governor. Governor Rains smiled and made his way directly to us, his hand outstretched.

"You're our guest of honor," he said to Bev. "I understand I have crashed your party. Thank you for letting me come."

I let out a long breath, one I had been holding for quite some time.

I FELT LIKE a piece of crystal inside a very busy kaleidoscope. I manned the coffee bar, got shifted to cake detail, then found myself at the door waving good-bye to the governor. The apprehension I'd felt for a week should have dissipated, but it was still with me. At some point I spotted Leigh and Tom, separately working the party. Tom played the perfect host, a role I'd seen him in dozens of times. Leigh just floated, smiling sweetly.

Dr. Bill finally arrived and was greeted with a round of applause. He flushed with chagrin. He looked tired as he peeled off his raincoat, but then he wasn't young, and he'd put in a long day.

Ute appeared, her camera already aimed and ready. "Dr. Bill, please smile for me."

"On top of everything else you want me to smile? Ute, it would be a lot easier if someone would bring me a beer."

There was laughter, and then Gretchen joined him for more pictures. As soon as that was over, they were swamped with well-wishers.

I watched from a distance, wonderfully relieved that he had arrived. So why was I still so tense?

I went in search of Beverly and Diane and found both in the kitchen, just the way they might have been during a party years before. Bev was holding a dish towel and Diane was filling a huge trash bag with used napkins and paper plates.

"What are you two doing in here?" I asked. It was then I realized I had interrupted a serious discussion. I wasn't sure what it had been about, but Diane's mouth was pursed tightly and Bev's eyes were rimmed with red as if she might have been crying.

Diane and Beverly have known each other for a good twenty years longer than I have been part of the equation, so I didn't ask what they'd been discussing. There was also a part of me that felt responsible for Beverly's unhappiness, which I assumed had something to do with the party.

I made my tone light. "Aren't you supposed to be mingling?"

"I'm mingled out," Bev said, wiping what might have been tears from her cheek. "By the way, have you talked to my father recently?"

"Last time I saw him," I said, "he was fine. He seems to be holding up very well."

"Actually, it's not him I'm worried about. How are the guests doing? Has he tortured anyone?"

I smiled. "I'm sure he's been charming, but if you're concerned I'll check."

"Good, you do that," Diane said, closing the trash sack, and putting it by the back door. "It's time for Bev and me to visit with our guests."

Beverly put down the towel and straightened her shoulders.

"Okay." Her smile lacked credibility, but there was a great deal of effort in it. "We're off to see the wizard," she said.

"Right." I followed them into the crowd, hoping that Bev hadn't been crying, that I'd simply jumped to the wrong assumption.

As they began chatting with an elderly couple, I veered off toward the great room, where we'd left Mr. Kendall. He was still in the same spot. The elderly man's posture was straight and his hands held the cane in his lap. It was a deceptively peaceful pose that hid both his strong personality and his illness.

As I moved closer I saw that he wasn't alone. Leigh was standing beside him, a fresh cup of coffee in her hand, as she bent over to converse. Only it was Mr. Kendall who was talking.

"I told you before," he snapped, "you can't get me a thing. I am just fine." He saw me approaching and spoke as if no one else could hear him. "Jolie Wyatt, who is this girl that keeps pestering me?" He gestured in Leigh's direction.

I paused, not sure how to answer.

"Well?" he demanded again. "You going to tell me who she is?"

His conversation with Leigh hadn't yet attracted much attention from the other guests.

"Of course," I said, leaning toward him. "This is Leigh, and I'm sure you've met her." I smiled at Leigh, who merely seemed curious. "She used to be Leigh Burton when she worked at the electric co-op."

That statement was a masterpiece of obfuscation without ever bending the truth. Leigh had indeed been a Burton before she married Bev's husband, or rather, Bev's former husband. Now she didn't work at all.

"At the electric co-op?" Mr. Kendall asked. "Well, that's fine, but how come she's pestering me?"

"Leigh was just seeing if you needed anything. Do you? Need anything?"

"No. I'll just set here all peaceful like." He shot a sharp glance at Leigh. "If you think I won't be bothered anymore."

I took a long breath and glanced purposefully at Leigh. "I'm sure you won't."

Leigh patted him on the arm, much as Bev had done earlier, before waving a delicate hand at me and starting toward the kitchen.

Henry Kendall snorted. "I don't like skinny little girls." He gestured toward Bev who stood near the front door. "Women ought to be like my Beverly with a little meat on their bones. Now she's special."

At least on that I had to agree with Mr. Kendall. "Well," I said. "How about if I stay here and visit awhile?"

"Just go on," Henry Kendall snapped at me. "No need babysittin' me."

"Right." I felt even more compassion for Bev. Had her father been my responsibility, I would have sent him off somewhere, yet Beverly remained faithful to her dad, caring for him without any help.

I turned to see where I might be more useful, at least more welcome, and discovered Dr. Bill and Gretchen practically at my elbow.

"Jolie, I haven't had a chance to thank you," Dr. Bill said, his arm out to give me a hug. I slipped into it gratefully.

"You're quite welcome. Although I thought we were going to have to send a tracking party after you."

"Just some final details to be wrapped up at the hospital."

Up close I realized how much he had aged in the last few years. His small potbelly was now supported by thin legs and topped by slumping shoulders. His eyes were as mischievous a blue as ever, but there was the tiniest shake to his head as he spoke.

"This is quite some shindig."

"I'm glad you're having a good time," I said. "You deserve it."

"Yes, he does," Gretchen agreed. "He has given so much to people wherever he's been."

"He certainly did in Dallas." It was in Dallas that he had been my father's doctor right up to the moment when my dad died. "Where did you practice before that? Did I hear some story about Alaska?"

It was Gretchen who responded. "You did. He graduated from school at Baylor, but then he decided to give back to the world in general so he went to work with the Aleuts in Alaska. And he wasn't forced to go, either. It was all his choice." She added, "and this was way back in the bush. We were so far from civilization that our food was flown in every six months. It could have been a time of hardship in our lives, but Dr. Bill made it quite the adventure."

The twinkle in Dr. Bill's eyes was apparent even behind his glasses. "Now, Gretchen, you can't be saying too many nice things about me or people will suspect we aren't married. Spouses aren't supposed to be like that."

"That's how Matt talks about me," I said. "At least he'd better!"

Dr. Bill laughed. "Smart man that Matt Wyatt, grabbing you up like that."

It was because of Matt that Dr. Bill and Gretchen were living in my guest house, on some adjacent land, about a mile or so from our place.

They had been in the midst of a major renovation of their lovely old home when the first of the rains had drowned out their hopes for staying in the house during the remodel. The roof had leaked, a wall had collapsed, and pipes cracked. They had tried to flee, only to discover that there were no decent houses left in town for them to rent.

On hearing of their plight, Matt had graciously offered to let the Marchaks stay at the Hammond Place, which is now our guest house. Even though they were officially renters, I considered it a privilege to be able to help.

"You really have done an extraordinary job with the party," Gretchen was saying. "Especially under the circumstances. I mean, the rain and all."

"I enjoyed every minute of it." Gretchen looked doubtful

and Dr. Bill raised an eyebrow. "Well, okay, most of the time," I said.

"That's more like it," Dr. Bill said with a smile.

"Seriously though, you have always been so good to my family. I mean, up in Dallas. I can never pay you back for what you did, and it meant so much to me."

Dr. Bill's eyes turned soft. "When your father passed on. That was a sad time—he was just too young."

I swallowed. "Yes, he was."

At the time I had been living alone with my son, who was only ten. My mother had been living in a world of denial, ignoring the results of medical tests, glossing over symptoms, and somehow insisting that nothing was seriously wrong. But we all knew. And to be sure I called my father's doctor. Dr. Bill. I hadn't known him at the time, so I was surprised when my call was put through so quickly, and just as surprised at the honest, yet gentle, way he broke the news to me.

"I don't believe your father is in imminent danger."

My heart had lifted at his words. For an instant I had believed everything my mother had been saying and shared her optimism. Then he went on. "The long-term outlook isn't good, though. I would say he has a few months of quality time left to share with you."

The intense pain almost took my breath away. I could barely force out a question. "And after that?"

"It could be six to eight very difficult months. That's at best."

I had cried. I had railed at God, and even thrown things at the wall, but nothing eased the anguish except time and the many visits I made to Dallas. Those were hard months for us all, watching my father. His very spirit seemed to desert his cancer-ravaged flesh until there was little left but fragile skin and brittle bones.

At least then I knew the truth, so that when the phone call came, the one from my brother telling me to get to Dallas immediately, I was slightly better prepared.

I remember walking down the long hospital corridor that

seemed to be more cluttered with equipment than usual. My family was there, each one locked separately in their grief. My mother sat on the bench by the door, and she touched my arm briefly, but didn't stand to hold me. My brother paced the hall in his long athletic strides, his fists clenched as if waiting for a moment to use them. Elise, my younger sister, was quietly crying into a tissue, her creamy skin a blotchy red.

Dr. Bill stepped outside my father's room. I'd met him twice by then, and he recognized who I was, or perhaps he knew me by the expression on my face.

He said gently, "He waited for you to come and say good-bye."

That sentence said it all. I remember standing, rooted outside the door, as though my dad might not die if I didn't go in. Dr. Bill opened the door for me; he knew quite well that if I waited too long, my father might die before I saw him.

Afterward, it was Dr. Bill who held me as I cried.

That memory remains sharp, sometimes cutting at my heart.

"He died way too young," Dr. Bill said. "Much too young."

"HE IS GONE, I'm telling you. Completely gone!" It was Leigh's voice coming from the dining room, pitched high enough to be heard over the din of the now-pouring rain.

Diane and I were in the kitchen filling the dishwasher, and we exchanged a quick glance. Who was she talking about? Was something wrong?

"I'm sure he's here someplace." It was Tom responding in a soothing tone.

"He's *not* here someplace—I looked everywhere. He's gone."

"You probably just missed him—"

"I told you," Leigh was practically yelling now, "I looked in every room. It's an emergency—"

In one movement Diane and I whipped out the door. Most of the guests had left, with only Bev, Gretchen Marchak, and

IdaMae Dorfman remaining. They arrived in the dining room at the same time we did.

"Can we help?" Diane asked.

"Can you hear me?" Leigh asked.

Diane frowned. "Of course."

"Good. I thought maybe I'd died and my voice was only audible in the spirit world. You can relay my words to Tom."

"I'm not—"

"Tell him that he is gone. Missing. I checked every room in this house and he is *not* here. Just tell him, okay?"

"Who is gone?" Diane asked.

Leigh turned her head to search the room. When she spotted Beverly she said, "Her father. Her father is gone."

Beverly stepped forward, more puzzled than concerned. "I'm sure you just overlooked him. He can't leave without me—"

"Well, he did," Leigh snapped. "He is gone. G-O-N-E, gone. As in, not here. Why the hell won't anyone believe me?" She took a deep breath and said firmly, "Trust me—your father is missing."

THREE

AFTER A THOROUGH search of the house, it was determined that Mr. Kendall was indeed G-O-N-E, gone.

Beverly was logical. "I'm sure someone just gave him a ride home. It's not like he's incapable of being alone."

"Do you think he would have gone off, just like that?" Leigh asked. She was the most distraught, despite Mr. Kendall's rudeness to her earlier.

Beverly frowned. "I'll call the house and see if he's there."

A huge crack of thunder split the air and the lights flickered. Leigh screamed. The lights came back on.

As Bev left the room, I said, "For a minute there I thought we were trapped in some old Agatha Christie movie."

"What makes you think we aren't?" Diane asked.

Rain poured now, creating a background of steady pounding. It was punctuated by more thunder. Outside the window there was darkness shot with lightning.

"Nice weather," Tom said, gently stroking Leigh's arm. She jerked away and glared at him.

Because of my relationship with Beverly, I hadn't spent time with Leigh and Tom, but in a small town you still hear the gossip. People here are like planets in the same small galaxy—sometimes orbits cross, and sometimes we collide. Always there is proximity.

In the case of Leigh and Tom, there was an absence of gossip about their marriage, which usually means that the relationship is strong, but there were those rare instances when everything appears normal on the surface, while something is being hidden. There could be alcoholism or abuse or perhaps an illness a family wasn't ready to share with the rest of the community.

In this case I knew that there was no abuse or alcoholism because it would have shown up during the long years of marriage between Tom and Beverly. Still, the exchange between Leigh and Tom caught at me; I wondered if there was something not quite normal that the rest of us didn't know about.

I shook off the thought. I was probably wrong.

"I'll finish up the dishes," I said to Diane. "And you should go home. You need to check on your house."

She didn't take the excuse to leave. "Our husbands are over there vacuuming water even as we speak." She flashed a weary smile. "I figure the longer I'm here, the less I'll have to do there."

I glanced at my watch. "Yes, but we also need to get you packed. You're staying at our house until yours dries out."

"Oh, I have an idea—" Leigh began.

Before she could finish Beverly returned. "My dad didn't answer the phone. Of course, that doesn't mean anything. He could be in the shower. And sometimes he just ignores the telephone."

"He's certainly had time to get home," Tom said.

"I think we should call the sheriff," Leigh said. "Wait, Jolie, you work for the radio station—could we broadcast some kind of bulletin? You know, get everyone looking for him?"

"Good idea," Gretchen said. Dr. Bill Marchak had left earlier and Gretchen had stayed to help tidy up.

IdaMae snorted. "Sounds like pure foolishness to me," she said. "The man just had more socializing than he could take. Happens to all of us. Besides, everyone else left; you couldn't expect him to stay on."

"Yes," Leigh said, "but he's really old and I think we should get everyone in town started searching, so we'll find him faster."

Beverly shook her head. "He would hate broadcasting anything about him. Look, it's simple; I'll just run home and check on him. I'm sorry to leave the mess, but—''

"Do you want me to go with you?" Leigh asked.

"I'll go with her," Tom said. "Where's your coat, Bev?"

"No!" She softened the snap in her voice by adding, "I'll go alone. Let me just grab my purse."

Leigh stepped away from her, but stayed close as if waiting for the next opportunity to be of service.

"You will call, won't you?" Leigh pushed.

"Certainly."

Tom picked up Bev's purse and handed it to her. "Here. Let us know."

"I will."

IdaMae put on her rain poncho and turned to Gretchen Marchak. "You about ready? Beverly, we'll walk you out."

"Ready," Gretchen said, clasping an umbrella firmly. "Beverly, dear, walk close to me and we'll both use this."

"No, no," I said. I stepped in to get Beverly loose, but Gretchen was intent on doing good. Without Bev's help, I couldn't prevent it. "You're our guest, and you've already done too much—''

"Don't be silly," Gretchen said. "I don't mind a bit." She clasped Bev fiercely by the arm and headed out the front door, from the back just two anonymous beige raincoats.

Except they weren't, and the one request Beverly had made of me during this whole terrible evening was to keep Gretchen away from her. And I hadn't.

"What's wrong?" Diane asked.

"Nothing. I'll tell you later."

"Come on, and we'll finish up the kitchen," Diane said. I followed her.

I heard the front door close sharply, then Leigh and Tom started arguing again. Actually, Leigh argued, Tom tried to console her. I loaded dishes, banging them more than necessary to cover their words. Diane looked too tired to notice; she didn't even ask me why I was upset about Beverly and Gretchen leaving together.

"Fair?" Leigh demanded, her voice now rising so that I couldn't miss what she was saying. "A whole lot of things haven't been fair—"

"Leigh, you don't have to be so loud—"

"It's my house and for once I'll be as loud as I damn well please—"

The front door slammed again and I heard Bev say, "You won't believe this. My car is gone."

"Your car?" Leigh said. "Someone kidnapped your father and stole your car? Oh my God!"

By that time I was back in the dining room, Diane on my heels. "What's happened?" she asked.

"Crazy talk," IdaMae said, entering just behind Bev and Gretchen. "I'm bettin' that your daddy just got bored and took the car and drove it on home. Nothin' more logical." There was certainly nothing more logical for a woman who believed in, and lived, full independence for the elderly.

"Would he do that?" Gretchen asked. "Could he do that?"

Bev nodded, tight-lipped. "Not well, but he could and he would. He's got his own keys. Damn it. Sometimes he worries me. I can call a cab—"

"It's on my way," I said. "I was just leaving."

"Don't be ridiculous," Leigh said. "I was the hostess, so it's my responsibility. I'll take Beverly home."

Beverly didn't protest, which surprised me, and the two women started toward the door. It was Leigh who looked back at us. "We'll call."

Then they were gone and a voice at my elbow said, "Pushy broad." That from IdaMae. "I'll follow them," she said. "If Bev goes searching, someone ought to stay at her house and I can at least do that. Now where'd I put my keys?"

Diane shook her head. "What a screwed-up day," she said. "And my house is still wet." Her body, normally so elegant, slumped as she leaned against the wall for support.

"Good news is," IdaMae offered, "this, too, shall pass. And if it don't pass soon enough, you can take to heavy drink 'til it does. Oh, here they are. In my pocket."

I wanted to smile but I couldn't quite muster it. My own day had started at 5:30 a.m. I had worked until noon at KSGE, covering news, primarily the weather, then run what seemed like a hundred errands for the reception, and finally I had raced home to change clothes. It had been nonstop movement on a day that would have been better for cozying up in front of a fireplace with a good book.

IdaMae clutched her plastic poncho tightly before opening the door to find, as expected, wind and rain. "Sure would like to see clear skies sometime soon. Night."

In Purple Sage I sometimes find people who are close, not just in distance, but in ideas. I feel that way toward IdaMae. She is of the generation of my grandparents, while her soul lives and breathes with a much younger crowd.

I waved her on her way, then looked around the dining room to see what was left to do. The remains of the cake had been cleared away and the plates, clean and dirty, had been removed to the kitchen, along with the coffee cups and silverware.

"I've been thinking," Tom said to Diane, "why don't you and Trey move in with us for a couple of days? Until your house dries out."

I shook my head firmly. "Diane is coming home with me. You have already done more than enough." I gestured to the house around us. "It could take you days just to get everything put away from the reception. Besides, Jeremy would never forgive me if I didn't insist that Randy stay at our house." Randy is Diane's son and Jeremy's best friend.

A flash of anger showed on Tom's face and slid away as if it had never been there. "I'm sure you're right."

"We'll just finish the dishes," Diane said, "then leave you with the rest of it."

"You don't have to worry about cleaning," Tom said. "We'll get our regular woman to come in."

We argued about it for a few minutes but I didn't have the energy to both fight for the cleaning and do it, so Diane and I finally conceded then went to look for our own things.

I agreed with Diane, it had been a bizarre day and Beverly

didn't need this on top of everything else she had endured. Not only that, I shouldn't have let her go off with Leigh.

When the phone rang just minutes later, I grabbed it without thinking. Tom picked up an extension somewhere.

It was Bev. "Tom? Jolie? My dad's not here, and neither is my car."

"I'll come right over—" Tom began.

"That's not going to help." A sharp boom of thunder shook the house. "God! Did you hear that?" she asked. It was a rhetorical question; she was less than a mile away. "I just don't like the idea of him driving in this weather. There's no telling what could happen. Leigh already went out to look for him, but I'm going to call the sheriff."

"Good idea," I said. Mac Donelly was the sheriff of Wilmot County, and had been of great help to me more than once.

Tom agreed, as well. "Tell Mac that we'll all help. Have him call us here."

"I'll get back to you," Bev finished.

BETWEEN CRACKS of thunder and intermittent static, the announcer on KSGE said that tropical storms lined up along the coast were the source of our troubles. While that did account for the overabundance of rain, it didn't make clear why, or how, Henry Kendall had disappeared so thoroughly, and why Leigh Greer was so upset about it. Nor did it explain why I wouldn't give up and go home, instead of interminably driving over the same area of town. I'd been at it for more than an hour.

Maybe it was that I felt sorry for Bev—first losing her husband, then watching everything that had once been hers be claimed by someone else. Her house, her job, and her town—everything.

Purple Sage is small, and the influences of the Bible Belt are strong, so a divorced woman is considered a threat. People don't hand out scarlet letters, it's not the woman herself who is the problem, although she can be. Instead it seems the people fear the idea of divorce as if it could be contagious. If such a thing could happen to someone else, it could happen to you. Divorce threatens the fabric of a small, close-knit community.

Leaving Purple Sage after the divorce was wise on Bev's part. Coming back was, unfortunately, mandatory. And now, here she was taking care of an elderly and ailing parent. Especially difficult, since she was alone without family members for support.

If it would help Bev, I knew that I would stay out in the rain until the car flooded and I could no longer tread water.

I turned the corner of Palmetto. This was north of the square in a small residential area that was slowly being refurbished. Unfortunately the streets were narrow and lined with parked cars, as is the case in many older districts. No one had needed triple-car garages in the twenties and thirties when these houses had been built.

My driver's side window was leaking just enough to let in a periodic splash of cold water, while the lightning struck often enough to blind me the rest of the time.

Another flash of lightning, followed quickly by a crack of thunder, revealed a dark green Dodge Caravan, much like Bev's, parked on the side of the road. I hit the brake, sending the vehicle into skid, and had to do some quick wheel turns and brake pumping to get it halted. I know better, but I was stunned. This particular van hadn't been here on my last go-round.

I backed up to a spot behind the car and grabbed my cell phone to call the sheriff.

When he answered I said, "Mac, it's Jolie." I could almost see him running his fingers through his gray hair, his regulation khaki Stetson sitting on the desk in front of him. "There's a dark green Dodge Caravan on Palmetto. Want the license number?"

"I do," he said.

The raindrops looked like slashes of silver in my headlights and the license plate reflected the numbers clearly. I read them off.

"Sorry. Right car, wrong plate," he said.

"Oh. Darn." I knew that Bev would be getting more worried as time passed. "Anyone else found anything?" Gretchen Marchak, Leigh and Tom Greer in their separate vehicles, my husband, Matt, as well as Jeremy, Diane, and me. Even Beverly was out in her dad's old Lincoln while IdaMae manned the phone at Bev's house.

"No, but we've got most of the county covered. You might drive around the airport."

"Consider it done." And so, I headed across the highway. I was surprised at the number of vehicles out on this miserable night.

Rain in Texas is not like rain in Seattle. Here the drops are heavy and large, at times falling so fast that they become a solid sheet of water plummeting from the sky. My windshield wipers were on their highest speed and yet I had trouble seeing. This kind of rain makes me nervous, and with good cause. It's simply dangerous. I didn't like the thought of my son out in his Blue Beast, and I was also worried about Henry Kendall, although my concern was touched with annoyance. I knew Mr. Kendall no longer had the capacity for rational, adult thought, but I was tired and hungry, which may have altered *my* capacity for rational adult thought.

Still, for Bev's sake, I wanted him home safely.

Eventually I made it to Wilmot International Airport. Rumor has it that it bears the title "international" because once a plane flew in from Mexico. It is also said that the plane carried marijuana, but I can't get anyone to confirm either story.

Half listening to the radio, I went through the gate to get a closer look. The small airport building itself was completely dark. Apparently no planes were expected in the bad weather, and anyone who had already flown out would have to put down elsewhere. There were no cars in the parking lot.

Tyler Smith, the KSGE nighttime announcer, was talking about an upcoming livestock auction, but I could hardly make out the words through the static.

My cell phone rang. "Hello?" The phone beeped again of its own accord, signaling that the battery was playing out.

"Jolie, it's Mac. I've got some good news."

I felt my aching shoulder muscles begin to relax. "He's been found?"

"That's right."

"Mac?" Another beep from the phone. "Is he okay?"

"He's fine, although the car's not so good. He slid off the side of the road into the mud and got himself stuck. Matt found him."

"Where?"

"Out east of town. On FM 537."

My mind flashed to a hot summer afternoon and a police roadblock on FM 537 set up to catch an eighteen-year-old escaped convict. It had been a lonely area then and I imagined it was even worse in the dark and the rain.

"What was he doing out there?" Another beep. We were about to be cut off.

"Don't know," the sheriff said. "He seems pretty confused. I don't expect we'll ever know for sure, but I'll talk to him tomorrow after he's settled some."

"Thanks for calling, Mac." I leaned back in my seat, letting my tired body relax.

"I have a message from your husband. He said he'll be home in about an hour—he's going to check on Trey's house first and see about the water."

"Okay."

"Jolie, I got some more news—" The phone beeped a final time and went dead.

Whatever his news, it was gone, so I headed for home. The interminable day was finally over.

I caught a short burst of sound from the radio—the signal that a news bulletin was about to begin. I turned it up, expecting more information on Henry Kendall.

Thunder drowned out the first of it, then I heard the word *dead*. I turned up the radio and listened intently as Tyler said, "South…near…creek. Authorities…*pop*…identified the dead…*crackle*…a resident of Purple…"

There was a heart-stopping moment and then I heard clearly one word: "Marchak."

FOUR

HOW COULD THE WORDS dead and Marchak be in the same news bulletin? I had just left Gretchen and Dr. Bill. No, actually, Dr. Bill had left earlier, but still they had both been at the party.

I drove on automatic pilot, my mind futilely attempting to fill in the gaps in the news bulletin. I couldn't imagine what I'd missed. And who? Who was dead? How had it happened? A car wreck? Could there be another Marchak?

When I neared Hammond Lane, the tiny dirt road that leads to where Gretchen and Dr. Bill were staying, I found myself slowing, then turning into it. It was black as only a country night can be, my headlights showing me a small stretch of muddy road. Then there was a break in the trees and ageratum bushes so that I could see the front of the house. It's an old wooden house with a beautiful yard and a wide front porch. Usually the house seems welcoming, but tonight something was off-kilter. There was light blazing from every window, but no cars and no sounds.

Like a house hastily abandoned.

I turned around in their drive, then made my way back to the highway, which now seemed more an obstacle than a road.

Finally I passed through our ranch gates. When I could see my house, it, too, was brightly lit, only here there were cars. I recognized Diane's big silver Mercedes, but not the other two.

I parked, then ran through the white mud up onto the porch. Through the front windows I could see some women circled together in the living room. I kicked off my muddy shoes and stepped inside the house.

The women broke apart, and there in the center of the group was Gretchen Marchak, very much alive.

Diane turned toward me. "Jolie, I'm glad you're here."

I didn't move, and I couldn't speak.

Diane continued, "It's Dr. Bill. He's—"

"Dr.—?"

Gretchen's face distorted. "No!" She leaped at me, her hands grasping my shoulders. "Doesn't anybody get it?" Her fingers were like claws grinding into my flesh. "Dr. Bill isn't dead. He can't be. Jolie, they have the wrong body."

"They do?" A flash of relief.

A woman started toward us and I was surprised to realize it was my mother. She lives in Dallas and her infrequent visits are always planned.

"Mom?"

"Hi, honey. Now, Mrs. Marchak," my mother said, gently removing Gretchen's clutching fingers from my shoulders. "Let's get you something hot to drink." She led her toward the couch. "What would you like? Coffee or tea? I think some chamomile tea would be best, and I'm sure Diane will get it. With lots of sugar."

Gretchen fought her. "I don't want anything. I'm going to Jackson's Funeral Home." Jackson's Funeral Home serves as a morgue. "That is not Dr. Bill they found, and I need to prove it to someone. Jolie, come with me."

She lunged toward me again, even her fingers stretched in the effort. I couldn't move to protect myself, and luckily my mother held Gretchen back. "Jolie looks exhausted. Let's let her sit down for a minute."

"But, what about—" I was shushed and moved aside.

"Gretchen," Diane offered, "you probably need to eat something. I'll fix you some soup. Does that sound good?"

"Are you insane?" Gretchen jerked away, backing to the fireplace, her eyes wild. "Talking about food when people are saying my husband is dead? He isn't! I have to show you.

And I have to find Dr. Bill. He hasn't had his dinner—he needs me!''

She sounded so sure.

Diane's soft words hit hard. ''Gretchen, the sheriff wouldn't make that kind of mistake.'' A pain started around my heart. Not Dr. Bill.

''No!'' Gretchen threw her head side to side, as if searching for something. ''Where's my purse? My keys? I'm going into town.''

My mother took over. ''Gretchen you can't go without a coat, and you need something warm inside you, too.'' She took Gretchen's arm. ''Your skin is cold as ice. Diane, would you get Gretchen some hot, sweet tea, and Jolie, would you find her a coat?''

I nodded, but I couldn't move. My legs were leaden.

My mother went on, ''I'll go with you in a few minutes, Gretchen, but I want you warm first. Besides, I'm sure the funeral home is closed. Someone needs to call and tell them to expect us.''

Through my fog of shock I noticed my mother's competent nurturing. After my father's death, my mother, Irene Berenski, had broken out of her middle-class cocoon to become a butterfly, flitting around the world in pursuit of pleasure. Yet here she was, gently taking control. It jarred some fleeting memory of a distant past, but it was gone before I could catch it.

''Jolie. The coat.'' My mom looked at me pointedly.

''I'm sorry.'' I went to the front closet. Already the microwave was humming in the kitchen. I found a soft overcoat that had belonged to Matt's mother, along with a throw from the top shelf, and brought them back. Gretchen was on the couch now, her feet up.

''Put this over you, Gretchen,'' my mom said. ''You need to warm up.'' She was treating her for shock.

''Is someone calling Jackson's?'' Gretchen's whippet thin body began to relax, her eyes losing that crazed look.

''I'll do that,'' I said, turning for the kitchen.

I found Diane there taking chamomile tea bags from a box.

She glanced up. "You look beat."

"But I don't understand. About Dr. Bill. Is he really...?" The fact of his death floated in and out of my brain as other thoughts took precedence.

Diane's expression mirrored my own sorrow and bewilderment. "I don't know. I was putting things in the guest bedroom when your mom arrived."

"She was in Costa Rica."

"She flew in this afternoon—she said she wanted to go to Dr. Bill's reception, but she was late. Her flight. Because of the rain..."

I had mentioned the reception in an e-mail to my entire family, and of course my mother would want to attend; it was she who had leaned on Dr. Bill hardest when my father was dying.

"She drove in right after I did," Diane went on. "She hadn't been here three minutes when Gretchen arrived."

Apparently when Gretchen arrived home from the search she found a deputy waiting for her. He broke the news about Dr. Bill.

"But is it true?" I asked. Maybe answers would ease the hurt inside me. "It just can't be. How did he die? Was it a car wreck?"

"I don't know anything, Jolie. You heard Gretchen; she's not saying much that makes sense."

I nodded.

Dr. Bill was, had been, a wonderful man; someone who had cared deeply about others. I admired him greatly, revered him even, but hadn't spent near the quality time I'd wanted to with him or Gretchen during their two years in Purple Sage, and now I regretted it terribly. We traveled in different social circles. I didn't see Dr. Bill professionally, either, since Matt, Jeremy, and I went to Dr. Baxter, who had our loyalty after saving Jeremy's life.

I had been honored that Dr. Bill and Gretchen were staying in our guest house, and I had hoped it would allow us to see them more, but that hadn't happened. I caught them only in passing and now I found it hard to accept that the opportunity was gone.

Diane poured a cup of tea. "Let's get this to Gretchen. I don't think she's doing very well." She added some cold water to the mug along with three heaping spoonfuls of sugar.

I followed her into the living room. Gretchen was on the couch, staring at the fireplace. She kept shaking her head and making a soft sound that might have been a moan.

"Here you are," my mom said, taking the tea and holding it to Gretchen's lips. "Just sip a little to warm you up."

Gretchen drank obediently, her face now a confused blank. "Thank you."

"Is she going to be all right?" I asked.

"She'll be fine."

Diane went to the hallway and I followed, watching as she pulled her coat out of the closet.

"What are you doing?" I asked.

"I think I'll go back home—"

"No; you can't sleep in your house with all those wet floors. Please, Diane. We've got plenty of room."

"Not really. Not anymore. Don't worry, it's dry upstairs."

"But it will be cold—"

A voice interrupted us. "I arrived at a bad time," my mother said. She looked me up and down. "You look tired, honey. I didn't mean to cause you problems."

"There's no problem, really," I said. I wanted to reach out and put my arms around her, but we didn't have that kind of relationship. Besides, she was holding the tea. "Where's Gretchen?"

"She's in the bathroom," my mom said. "I gather that Diane and her family are staying here. That's going to fill the house, so I'll go to a hotel. Or a motel. A tourist court. Whatever Purple Sage has to offer."

"No, you can't. Besides, there's nothing at the moment," I said. "Everything is filled with people who've been flooded out. The high school gym has even been turned into a temporary shelter."

"Then that's where I'll go." She said it matter-of-factly, as if she went to shelters every day.

"No." Life was upside down, like an ugly Wonderland, but I wanted my mother to stay with us. I suddenly needed her. "The boys can sleep on the living room floor and you can have Jeremy's room."

"Or I can take the floor. Either way." She dismissed that topic to look more closely at me. "Jolie? Are you all right? You're swaying."

"I-I-I'm fine." I said the first thing I could think of. "I haven't eaten." It was true. "No one has."

"Why didn't you say so? I'll fix some food."

"I'll check on Gretchen," Diane said, and hurried off.

"What would work? Soup? Sandwiches?"

"Uh-huh. Look in the pantry." I realized I hadn't had anything to eat since early that morning, and the shock of Dr. Bill's death, on top of the reception, and Mr. Kendall disappearing—it seemed like a long string of shocks in a day that had come straight from hell with no detours.

My mother handed me something and the next thing I knew I was sitting at the bar with an almost-empty glass of cranberry juice in front of me. My mother was bustling around the kitchen heating soup and making sandwiches out of leftover roast.

"Feeling better?" she asked.

"Yes."

"Low blood sugar," she said simply. She pushed a sandwich toward me. "Here, eat this and when you're finished we'll go."

"Go?"

"To the funeral home."

"You mean, you think that Gretchen—that maybe there was some mistake?"

"I couldn't guess, but there's only one way to know for sure, and that's to view the body."

THE MOON SLID OUT from a break in the clouds and then back again. We walked along the sidewalk in front of Jackson's

Funeral Home, under the huge old oak tree. Each time the wind stirred the branches, they sent a shower of cold raindrops down on us.

The building is a three-story redbrick, with ivy covering two sides. The front door is heavy wood with Tudor-style paned windows. Gretchen led us toward it, while Diane, my mom, and I followed behind. I had pushed Diane to come with us, afraid that if we left her alone she'd pack up and go home. I hadn't taken very good care of Beverly and I wanted to do a better job with Diane.

The wind howled and I sidled closer to my mother as if a middle-aged woman could protect me. Of course she couldn't, and she wasn't middle-aged, either. At forty, I was middle-aged, and my mother was…well, older.

And it wasn't really the protection I wanted. I wanted some assurance that Dr. Bill wasn't dead and that everything was going to be all right.

My mother stepped away from me, her focus on Gretchen.

Gretchen's strong belief that Dr. Bill was alive had me creating scenarios that would support it. Maybe the deputy didn't know Dr. Bill very well. Elderly men did look something alike, so he could have made a mistake. Which deputy was it? And did he make the identification alone?

But if there was a mistake and Dr. Bill was alive, why wasn't he at home, and where exactly was he right now?

There was another fact that prevented my hopes from rising too high. If Mac Donelly, the sheriff, had been involved in the identification, there had been no mistake.

Gretchen reached the door and threw it open with such force that it banged against the wall. My mother took three quick steps and caught it before it shut again. Mom went in quickly, her tiny, plump feet in their woven sandals sounding loud on the plastic mat that protected the carpet. Diane and I followed. Despite the warm temperature of the room, I shivered.

A desk stood off to our left in front of an office; it was the place for a greeter during funeral services. A massive hallway went straight back from the door. It was at least twenty feet wide, with two small viewing rooms on each side of it. Only a few lights had been turned on, and the leftover scent of too many flowers clogged whatever other smells might have lingered. The whole place felt dark and lonely.

A man's voice came from behind me. "Mrs. Wyatt?"

I whirled to face him. "Oh, Skip. You startled me."

"I'm sorry. I was in the office—"

Before he could say another word Gretchen swung around and charged toward him. "Skip Jackson! There you are." Her voice was too loud—she was afraid. "Where is this body that is *not* Dr. Bill? And how could you make such a stupid mistake? I have a good mind to sue you, except I don't want to end up owning this place."

Skip was the model of funereal calm. "Mrs. Marchak. I'm so sorry that you're distressed. This can't have been easy for you." He moved in close to her, walking in step as if to offer physical support as well as moral. "We aren't quite ready for you, but…" His voice became softer as they moved toward the far end of the large hallway. "I want you to know that if we can help…"

When they were ready to enter one of the far viewing rooms I said, "Should we go with her?"

My mom touched my arm. "Give it a minute."

I watched as they entered the distant room, my muscles tense, hoping against hope, waiting. Then it came—a high-pitched keening that pierced the solemnity of the funeral home.

Dr. Bill was dead.

It hit me hard, like my father's death all over again. Beyond all the wonderful attributes of Dr. Bill, he was also a link to my father—a tiny piece of my dad had remained alive as long as he was around. Now the link was gone.

I moved closer to my mother, but she only patted me absently before moving slowly toward the room where Gretchen was. The sound coming from it faded to a horrible moan, then a series of pleas. "No, no! Dr. Bill. It can't be. Please, God!"

Behind us the front door opened. I turned and saw Sheriff Mac Donelly framed in the light.

FIVE

When Mac Donnelly took the oath of office to defend and protect, he was serious about it. I have known him since my first months in Purple Sage. He is in his early sixties. And has always been a source of knowledge and strength. Even now, knowing that there was nothing he could do to help us, I felt my tension lessening. He is simply one of the finest men in Wilmot County.

He shook off the rain, then stepped toward us.

"Jolie. Ms. Atwood," he said, nodding in our direction. His rugged face was tired.

Even in the presence of death, proprieties must be observed. "Mac," I said, "this is my mother, Irene Berenski. Mom, this is Sheriff Mac Donelly."

Mac took off his regulation gray Stetson to reveal mussed gray hair and a pale strip of forehead that never saw sunlight. I was reminded of an old Western as he said, "We've met. Pleasure to see you again, ma'am."

My mother was looking at the hat, which had a plastic rain covering, but finally her eyes came up and she nodded back at him, "Thank you, Sheriff."

Gretchen came stumbling out of the viewing room. "It's true; it's true. My husband is dead. Someone killed Dr. Bill."

"No, no, Mrs. Marchak," Skip said, following closely behind her. "I think he was in the creek—"

"No!" She swung around to Skip. "Don't you try to smooth mouth me! I saw those bruises on him. Someone hurt my Dr. Bill."

Someone hurt Dr. Bill? My shock-clogged brain heard the words but found them incomprehensible.

She continued toward us, once again with that wild-eyed look. When she spotted Mac she tensed. "You have some explaining to do, Sheriff," she said. "Dr. Bill was at the reception, and he left to go home. What was he doing at Cavalry Creek?" She had shifted her anger from Skip to Mac, as if Mac had been responsible for the doctor's death.

"I think you should sit down, Ms. Marchak."

"I don't want to sit down! Everyone's telling me to sit down when there are things to be done. Now, just why would he be at Cavalry Creek? And why would he go *in* the creek?"

"Ms. Marchak, I don't rightly know," Mac said.

"Was his car in the creek? Did he drive in? He would never do that. He wasn't one of those kids who try to drive over low-water crossings. Besides, there isn't a low-water crossing on Cavalry Creek. Is there? I thought there was just the bridge."

"Yes, ma'am. I mean, no, there isn't a low-water crossing, not for another mile or so, and that's downstream of where he was. His car was parked off the pavement beside the bridge. Just north of Fisher Road."

I tried to picture it. Cavalry Creek came out of Sage Lake and narrowed abruptly before it went under the highway. Next to the bridge there was room for cars to park, and in the summer, when the creek was a sleepy little stream, families picnicked there.

During drought times Cavalry Creek was nothing more than a trickle of water through a muddy bottom. However, now the heavy rain had turned it into a high, fast river, filled with dangerous debris. It was almost frightening just to look at it from the bridge—but Dr. Bill was in it?

"No! There's nothing to draw Dr. Bill out there. It's miles from the reception," Gretchen said. "And it's in the wrong direction of where he was going. He was coming home. He always came straight home to me, do you understand?"

"Yes, ma'am. Dr. Bill worked hard, and I know you two had a happy life together."

"Then what was going on? You can't tell me he just decided to drive out there. Not when he was tired! He needed to come home to rest and eat a good dinner. I make one for him every night."

"Yes, ma'am," Mac agreed. "Right now, Mrs. Marchak, we don't have answers to your questions. I sure wish we did."

Mac was so tired even his eyes were drooping, but there was something more on his face. I saw it in the tiny twitch near his mouth.

Mac Donnelly was lying.

But why? What was there to lie about in a man's death? I didn't understand, but there were a lot of things I couldn't take in at that moment.

Gretchen took a deep breath. "Maybe he just wanted to see how high the lake was. He might have done that. Did they find him in the creek; was that what happened? You think he fell in? Maybe slipped on the mud, and then the water was moving so fast he got swept downstream. Oh, how horrible! Is that what you think?"

"Yes, that's very probably what happened." Mac nodded, hiding the continuance of the lie. "Now, ma'am, what's real important, is that you start taking care of yourself. You need to go and get some rest. You've got some decisions coming up, and you can't be making those when you haven't had sleep."

"Go home?" She looked horrified. "No. I can't leave Dr. Bill!"

All of us responded, but it was my mother who became firm. "Mrs. Marchak, you can't stay here all night. I won't allow it. You are in shock, and you know that when someone is in shock they have to respect the greater wisdom of those around them. You are the one who told me that when my husband was so ill. My husband was Jolie's dad. Do you remember that, up in Dallas?"

"Yes, I mean, I remember him...."

"I'll tell you like you told me. You have to take care of yourself right now, and that means rest and regular meals. It was excellent advice, so *'Physician, heal thyself.'*"

The quote seemed to confuse Gretchen, as if there might be some code of honor she had to uphold. "Well, yes…I do think that. You know, I don't remember your name."

"That was thoughtless of me not to reintroduce myself. I'm Irene. Irene Berenski. Is there someone we can call for you?" My mother was being so kind and so gentle. Where had she learned to be that way? Why hadn't she taught me?

"No, no one. I'll just go on back to the house." Gretchen paused. "I don't mind. Not really." For the first time Gretchen Marchak looked frightened, as if she might not be able to handle this alone.

"I'd be happy to stay with you," my mother said. "You would actually be doing me a favor. The hotels are all full because of the rain."

"Really? We have a guest room. You're more than welcome to it."

"That's kind of you; I think that will work out very well." We cleared a path for them as they started toward the door.

I took the moment to touch Mac's arm lightly. "Mac?" We hung back from the others as I asked quietly, "Do you know something about Dr. Bill's death? Is there something…?"

He averted his face. "We can talk later. Right now Mrs. Marchak needs tending to." He slipped his hat on his head and strode to the door to hold it for the rest of us.

The lie remained between us, although I had no idea what it was and I couldn't understand the reason for it.

THE LONG DAY finally ended, but not easily. We took my mother to the Marchaks', where she located a medicine closet containing a full supply of drug samples. It was Gretchen who picked out what she took, and when Diane and I left she was resting quietly. We knew it wouldn't last forever, but the hope was that the chemically induced calm would give her a respite that would see her through the night.

Jeremy and Randy had taken my mother's things to her, and as soon as they were back we all closed our doors and went to bed.

I spent the night sleeping fitfully, holding tight to Matt. At least half a dozen times I woke up with an ache around my heart. Each time it took me a few seconds to remember the cause. Finally, at some early hour, Matt said quietly, "It's okay to cry. It might even help."

I nodded, but the tears wouldn't come and the pain wouldn't go away.

I kept thinking of all the things I should have said to Dr. Bill. I should have told him what a great person he was, and how much I admired him. I should have spent time with him and Gretchen.

When my father died Dr. Bill talked to me about death and dying, but he never talked about what comes afterward. Not for us, or for my father. Now I wish I'd asked him, because of all the people in the world, I think he could have told me.

I'm a spiritual person, but not religious. I believe strongly in God and that there is a purpose to all things, but I'm not wise enough to know what that purpose is. I almost think death is a reward. When you have done all the things you need to do, and learned all the lessons you need to learn, then you get to move on to some wonderful place beyond the everyday irritations and pain of life.

But I can never be positive.

I gave up trying to figure it out or to sleep and got ready for work. By that time Matt was sleeping soundly, so I kissed him good-bye gently, almost fearful of leaving him, and tiptoed down the stairs careful not to disturb my guests. When I reached the kitchen I discovered that not all of our guests were sleeping. Trey, Diane's husband, was already at the table in jeans and a sweatshirt, holding a hot cup of coffee in one hand and a soggy *Austin American-Statesmen* in the other.

"Morning," I said.

"Good morning," he said with a nod. "You look tired. Didn't sleep well?"

"No. How about you?"

"Like the dead." He stopped, and shook his head. "Sorry, I didn't mean that."

"I know."

"Usually I'm the only early riser in the house. I always get up before everyone else. My mother says it has something to do with being born at five in the morning. I guess you must have been born early, too."

I winced. Too much conversation. "No, at noon." I filled a cup with water and put it in the microwave. Trey was watching me and I realized I had sounded terse. "I'm sorry; I only get up early because of my job. Not a want-to, but a have-to."

Trey put down his paper. "Have to? Jolie, you know you don't really have to. Do you?"

Trey loves to discuss the ethereal and philosophical, rarely touching on what's real and now. At times in the past that has annoyed me, but at that moment, it seemed safe and far away from the emotions that were weighing heavy inside me. "No, of course I don't have to work," I said.

"Not with two of our companies going public last year." He was proud of that, as well he should be. He and Matt had backed winners, based not on luck but rather on research and skill. I was proud of them, too.

The ranch is only marginally profitable, and Matt has built his funds through wise investing. First in the stock market, and most recently he and Trey had been involved with some startup companies in Austin. This past year two of those companies did an IPO, and then the dollars really rolled in.

My name is on everything, all the stock, the ranch, all the bank accounts, but despite that I've never considered it my money. I came into the marriage with a small savings account and a smaller IRA. That is my money. I work part-time at the radio station, part-time writing advertising copy for a friend in Austin, and I've recently sold a book for a very small advance. To feel useful I put a portion of my income into our joint checking account, but I haven't added to my IRA.

"Do you want any of the paper?" Trey asked. "I brought it from the house last night, so it's not very current."

"No thanks." I made my tea and poured it in a travel mug. "Jolie, have you got any sugar?"

"Sure." I pulled some out of the pantry and gave it to him. It wasn't his presence in my house that bothered me; it was his presence in my time. I may not be an early riser by nature, but still I use that time to enjoy the silence and solitude of my own kitchen and to think about things. Trey had invaded that. Yet, even as I experienced the annoyance, I thought of Dr. Bill and felt a wave of guilt. Trey was probably Matt's best friend, while Diane was my closest friend. They are great people— warm, caring, and intelligent. I would do anything for them, and a part of me realized how fortunate I was to have Trey here.

"Trey, can I fix you breakfast?" I asked, putting aside my mug. "Bacon and eggs? Hot cereal? What can I get you?"

"No, thanks, Jolie. I don't eat this early. Matt and I can grab something at the café later."

I nodded. "I need to say something."

He looked up, puzzled. "Okay."

"Trey, I'm glad you're here," I said. "You and Diane are so terrific. Randy, too, of course. You mean so much to us."

Trey's face suddenly turned sad. "Thanks, Jolie." He paused, then said, "I'm sorry about Dr. Bill, too."

I HELD OFF crying all during my drive. I knew if I cried it would overwhelm me and I might not be able to stop. I let the ache remain and I tried to ignore it as I drove to the radio station. I had work to do. It wasn't life or death, but it was there.

I got out of my car in a drizzling rain, and hurried to the side door. The building is shaped like a U, with the receptionist and the main door at the far back, while the two sides hold the two different staffs—the office staff, manager, and sales on the right side, with programming, the control room, and news on the left. I went to my left, punched in the code, and entered.

At that time of morning the station is peopled only by the disk jockey, but there is always noise and light, the pulse of even a small-town radio station. A weather computer sat behind my desk and a mechanical voice routinely droned information, while music emanated from the control room, and intermittently I heard the announcer speak.

After I had done several on-air reports advising which streets, schools, and businesses would be closed because of high water, I placed a call to the sheriff's office.

"Mac?" I said when he answered his own phone. "Where is Relda?" Relda is his dispatcher.

"Can't get out of her ranch," he said curtly. "Water washed out the cattle guard."

"Oh. I'm sorry. Have you slept?"

He grunted in reply and waited for me to go on.

"I'm rewriting the story on Dr. Bill's death and all I have here is that he was found in Cavalry Creek at approximately eight-fifteen last night. People will want to know more; I'll take anything you have." I was slipping into reporter mode, no longer discussing a man who had done so many good things for me and my family, but an entity. I knew this dispassionate feeling wouldn't last long, sometimes I couldn't even achieve it, but for the moment I was grateful for the distance it put between my hurt and me. "Can you give me something more?" I asked.

"We don't know much right now."

"So, I just say that he drowned?"

"No, that's not correct."

"Wait. Wait a minute, last night you told Gretchen he'd drowned."

"No, Jolie, I don't believe I said anything of the kind," the sheriff responded. "We found him wedged in a tree, half in and half out of Cavalry Creek. He was wet and he was dead, but that don't mean he was drowned."

The words created a vivid and horrible picture of Dr. Bill's death. I took in some air and turned my focus to the ceiling—acoustical, with holes in the yellowed tiles. After a moment I was able to breathe normally, then I returned my attention to the sketchy news story before me.

"Sorry," I said, offering no explanation for my long pause. "What exactly are you saying?"

"We just don't have any details."

"When will you have some?"

"Couldn't say. I hope by tomorrow, but that depends."

Whatever he knew, he wasn't going to tell me, and certainly not for broadcast purposes. For the moment I allowed my frustration to push aside my upset. Perhaps that was Mac's intention, to distract me. Yet I was positive he had been lying the night before. "Was there something besides the water that could have caused his death?" When Mac didn't respond a second time, I said, "Like a rope around his neck? A bullet hole in him?"

I heard a sound come over the line that could have been a chuckle or a snort. "The portable DPS lab investigated the crime scene and the ME in Austin is doing an autopsy." He let out a breath. "Jolie, I don't have any idea what killed Dr. Bill. It looks like a drowning. The water is high and fast, with enough good-size chunks of wood to knock a grown man senseless, but until they check his lungs, I can't say."

"Has anyone come forward with any information? Who found him?"

"Morris Pratt. He was out takin' some pictures of the creek for the newspaper about a quarter mile from the bridge. Got more than he bargained for."

I shuddered. "And that's it? Did anyone else see him?"

He answered my first question. "That's all for now."

Meaning that there was more, but he wasn't going to tell me. "Would you give me that in a statement for the news?" I asked.

"Whenever you're ready."

The recorder was set up.

"I'll lead in with the basics," I said. "Just tell me whatever details you can.'' This was a routine we went through frequently, and Mac had no concerns about being recorded.

He cleared his throat and I punched the record button. He began speaking officially. ''Dr. Marchak's body was found not far from the bridge that runs over Cavalry Creek at Highway 16. He was pinned against a large tree. With the recent floods, Cavalry Creek is running fast, and a good four to five feet above normal.

''The sheriff's department would appreciate it if anyone with information about the accident...'' He paused a few seconds, then said, ''Jolie?''

I stopped the tape. ''I'm here.''

''Let me do that last line again.''

''Go right ahead.'' I punched the record button again.

''The sheriff's department would appreciate it if anyone with information on the incident would call us.''

''Thanks, Mac.''

We said our good-byes and I moved into the production room to edit the pause out of the tape and build my story around his statement. In the process I listened carefully to what Mac had said. He had replaced the word *accident* with *incident*.

SIX

I WAS OFF WORK at ten, still sitting at my desk, when I heard the back door of the station open. Jeremy came in, brushing off the rain. Even though he is only Matt's adopted son, and has been for only four years, he has taken on many of Matt's mannerisms. He stopped in the doorway and put his hand up to lean on it, Matt-like.

"Hey, Mom."

"Hi, honey." I got up and gave him a heartfelt hug. I was so grateful that he was here, that he was alive and well.

He hugged me back, hesitantly, as he has been doing since he hit his teens. He said, "Are you okay?"

"Fine. Fine. Have a seat. Do you want to go have some breakfast?" He was out loose on a Friday because the high school was closed—I'd read that in one of my announcements earlier.

"No, I don't have time. I just came by to get some money. I'm going to San Angelo."

"No! You ca—" I stopped myself before I even finished the word. I didn't want him on the highway in this terrible weather. I wanted him at home. I wanted everyone at home. I had a vision of our house, closed up tight with a ribbon around it, so that everyone would be inside, safe and warm where I could take care of them.

Jeremy was watching me with wary eyes. "What's the big deal?" he asked.

The big deal was that Dr. Bill was dead, and there was flooding and the world was awry.

Even so, I knew that you must trust that when people leave you they will come back safely. Especially teenagers. If you hold on too tightly they will fight until they break the boundaries you tried to place around them and that can break relationships, as well.

"I just—I don't like the weather," I said.

"Mom, it's clearing and we shouldn't have any more rain until this evening. You read that on the air."

"Oh. Right." I nodded; apparently I hadn't listened to myself. "So, why are you going to San Angelo?"

He came over and sat on the other side of the partner desk. "I'm taking Grams."

Grams being my mother and another of my concerns. "How is she doing?" I asked. "And where is she?"

"She's at the shelter—"

"The shelter? We have room for her, she doesn't—"

"She's just seeing if they can use her as a volunteer later. Don't start getting all protective now—you're the one who left her at the Marchaks' last night. You shouldn't have done that."

I don't know if there is a natural bond between all grandparents and their grandchildren, but there is certainly one between Jeremy and my mother. He and I lived with my parents for almost six months of Jeremy's first year, so Mom had the chance to rock him, walk him at night, and teach him to play while I went to work. It may have cemented the bond even more tightly.

I've also noticed that people become more patient with grandchildren than they ever were with their own offspring. One time in particular pointed that out for me. It was when my father was so ill, and Jeremy and I drove up to Dallas. Jeremy had complained most of the way, saying that he wanted to stay home. He was only ten at the time and his class was going to Moody Gardens in Galveston; he talked about the one-day trip as if it were a pilgrimage to Mecca rather than a visit to an amusement park.

He was still openly sulking when we reached my mom's

house. My dad was asleep in the back bedroom and she was at the front door waiting for us. Of course she'd gone straight for Jeremy to give him a hug and a kiss.

"What's the matter, Jeremy?" she'd asked. "You don't look like my happy boy."

He'd hauled his duffel bag out of the back seat and slammed the car door. "I'm not happy! I was supposed to go to Moody Gardens, but mom wouldn't let me." He didn't take it so far as to say that he didn't want to be in Dallas, but it was close.

"But your Grandpa's sick and he needs some hugs from you," she'd said. "I'll make you a deal. Next summer I'll take you to Moody Gardens with two of your friends and you can spend the whole day doing whatever you want. Does that make you feel better?"

Had that been me at age ten, my mother would have slapped me hard and told me I was lucky she didn't do worse.

It wasn't that she had been a bad mother, but times were different then and she was different, as well. Sometimes I envied their closeness.

"Jeremy," I said. "Last night your grandmother offered to stay with Gretchen; I didn't have anything to do with it."

"Mom, she was jet-lagged. She probably didn't realize how tired she was. Tonight she's staying at our house, in my room. I'll sleep on the couch."

Which had been my original suggestion, but it didn't matter because he was right, at least in part. I hadn't been conscious of my mother and her needs. I should have insisted, just like I should have insisted that Beverly not leave the party with Gretchen and Leigh. The world seemed layered with responsibilities I wasn't handling. "Great idea. Who is with Gretchen, now?"

"People from the hospital. There were probably ten people there when Grandma called me this morning."

Which is what happens in a small community, perhaps in any community. People flock around with food and caring.

I nodded in understanding. "I'll stop by later. So, why are you taking your grandmother to San Angelo?"

He gave me the look—the one that only teenagers can accomplish and only when they are responding to something a parent said or did. I waited him out.

"Because she doesn't have any warm clothes," he finally said. "She just came from Costa Rica, remember? Mom, she's wearing sandals! At least I found her a coat to put on."

She had been wearing some flimsy woven shoes last night, too, but it hadn't registered with me. I'd simply been too tired and too shocked to realize that she wasn't prepared for our rain and cold.

I pointed my finger at my head and fired an imaginary gun.

"I'm sorry," I said.

I did the only thing I could think of to assuage my guilt. I took out my purse and emptied it of every bit of cash that I had. "Here. This should cover gas and lunch with enough left over to buy Grams a warm sweater. Oh, take her to that Chinese restaurant—she loves that."

"I know."

"Actually, I could come along."

He paused before using his most diplomatic tone. "Mom, that's a great idea, but you have things to do, and there's really not room for three in the Beast."

He didn't say it, but I knew he was thinking that they would have a good time together while I would be in the way.

"Right. You're right, of course."

He came around the desk and gave me a quick hug, then pocketed the money. "Thanks." He started toward the door.

"You're welcome, honey," I said. It seemed the decision had been made without my ever giving consent. That was happening a lot lately. "Have fun. Drive—"

"Carefully," he finished with a wave.

I NEEDED COMPANY, perhaps even solace, and Matt is almost always my first choice in such situations. Unfortunately, when I called our house I got the answering machine, so I got in my car and headed for Diane's. I assumed Matt would be there, and if he wasn't, then I could spend some time with Diane who was my second choice.

The sun was actually showing itself through the haze of clouds and the unexpected lightness made Dr. Bill's death seem even more impossible. I wanted to believe it wasn't true, that perhaps this was still yesterday. Even with all its anxiety, yesterday had been a happier day.

I pulled into the empty drive at Diane's and from the front of the house everything looked normal. There was no water gushing across the porch or even standing on the portico. Unfortunately no one answered the door, so I walked around to the back.

Their beautiful brick patio with its garden area was the center of the work and now looked like downtown Kabul. There were gaping holes with trenches going off in several directions. Water filled one of the holes, and there were muddy tools, boots, and towels in a pile at the back door, along with two notes stuck to a board.

Di—
We had to get a pipe—be back later.
                    Trey

The one under it said,

Trey & Matt,
I'm taking a cake to Gretchen's house. Be back later.
                    Love
                    Diane.

I let out a heartfelt sigh and turned to go to my car. I was debating what kind of food I could make for Gretchen when I noticed Leigh Greer in her backyard. She was sitting on the steps of her deck, smoking a cigarette and staring sadly into space.

"Leigh?" I called.

She jumped, startled, and hid the cigarette behind her. "Oh, Jolie. Hi."

I moved toward the low brick fence that separates the properties. "You can smoke in front of me, I don't care. I used to smoke but I finally quit."

She brought her hand out and looked at the cigarette with great longing. Then she put it to her lips and inhaled deeply. "Tom hates for me to smoke," she said, letting out a stream of gray smoke. Beside her was a flowered apple-green bag, something like a tall knitting bag. Strips of calico cloth spewed out of the top like colorful spaghetti. "I'm not supposed to let anyone see me."

"Tell Tom he's behind the times. Smoking is all the rage again."

"Not in Purple Sage, and not at our house."

She put out the cigarette and pushed it between the deck boards. "I'm not supposed to do that, either, but Tom moved my ashtray when all the plants froze. Said it was out in plain view."

I didn't think smoking was a smart habit to acquire, however I also didn't think having a cigarette *polizia* for a husband would be much fun.

"Come on over," she said. "Do you want something to drink?" She held up her own mug.

"No thanks." But I still owed her a thank you. "I will join you for a minute," I said, walking to the iron gate at the back of the property and making my way through. Her grass was that wonderful emerald green that only comes in spring, and what I like to call the second spring. In Texas, that's fall when the heat is finally gone and the plants begin to thrive again. Not all of them, of course. We'd had two freezes and the potted tropicals that had graced Leigh and Tom's deck were brown and wilted, although the smaller pots of pansies and impatiens were bright.

"I need to thank you again for coming to our rescue last night," I said, as I got closer.

"Watch where you sit. The chairs are still wet." She moved

the green bag, then picked up an old towel and wiped a spot on the steps beside her. "Or, we can go in the house. I was just enjoying the sunshine."

"Me, too. This is fine," I said. "Anyway, thank you. I don't know what we would have done if you hadn't volunteered to take on the reception."

"It was fun. I like being the hostess and I didn't really have to do anything." She shrugged listlessly. Now that I was closer I realized that she wore no makeup and her pale skin was blotchy.

"Are you doing okay? Is anything wrong?"

"No. Yes," she said. "I'm just so bummed."

"What's wrong? What's happened? Can I help?"

"If I tell you, you have to promise not to hate me." She looked like a child. "Please."

I couldn't imagine what she'd done. "Of course I won't hate you."

"You say that now, but you might. Because, I was there, and I didn't..." Tears streamed out of her eyes and she reached for the ragged towel to blow her nose. "I saw him, and I just didn't get it."

I've known *of* Leigh for a very long time, but I never really noticed her until Tom decided she was the perfect woman for him. When that happened Leigh went from being the equivalent of an extra in a large movie to the evil seductress. It isn't often that I find someone I can look down on, but Leigh had been the perfect one. I didn't hate her; I felt superior to her.

Now, Leigh was turning into a real person looking to me for solace and forgiveness. I awkwardly patted her shoulder. "I don't understand."

"I saw him and it must have been right before..." She began to make a sound like two pieces of rubber squeaking together. "Right before..."

"It's okay," I said.

She took a couple of good breaths. "I'm sorry," she said, wiping her eyes with the back of her hand. "That's not like me, it's just that so much is going on. There's so much stress right now. You know.''

I had no idea why Leigh was stressed, but I said, ''Sure.''

She nodded and slid a cigarette from her pack, fondling it as if it were a friend. ''It happened during the search last night for Beverly's dad....''

She lit the cigarette and smoked it, telling me the story between puffs.

Leigh Greer's search area had contained a portion of Sage Lake at the spot where Cavalry Creek ran out of it. She checked the parking area at the dock first, then the few stores that were in the marina. After that she crossed the highway and did a slow drive through the trailer park north of the creek. When she didn't spot the dark green minivan, the object of our hunt, she had turned south on the highway.

''It was hardly raining at all when I started that way,'' she said. ''But after a while the sky opened up and it was pouring. I must have gone over ten miles by that time so I turned around and came back.'' Her shoulders were rigid. ''Anyway, I'm driving up to the bridge over Cavalry Creek and I see headlights down in the open area beside the creek. You know, where everyone parks? And so, I slow down, except now I'm on the bridge, and that doesn't seem very smart. I mean, it *was* raining and what if someone didn't see me? They could hit me, right? Would you stay there?''

''No, of course not,'' I assured her, wanting to reach for a cigarette. ''It would be foolish.''

''See, that's what I thought, even though I could see a man standing in the headlights.''

''A man? What man?''

''Well, that's just it. I thought it might be Mr. Kendall, Bev's dad, so I pulled past the bridge and looked back. That's when I noticed the car and realized it was white. It was pretty big, too. One of the SUVs. I kind of thought there might be a car parked on the other side of it, but finally I decided it was the shadow.'' She was puffing like mad. ''It wasn't Mr. Kendall, because the man didn't have a cane, so I didn't really think about it.''

"This man, what was he doing?"

"I thought he'd just finished looking at the creek because he was turned away from the water. You know, he was facing the car.''

I had to take a breath. "Okay. So you were past him, and up on the bridge—which means you could only see his back, is that right?"

"Uh-huh, and I couldn't see much because of his umbrella. Just his beige coat. You know, like a spy coat. And then Mac called me on my cell phone and wanted me to go farther around the lake, so I just drove on. Only…" She made the squeaking noise again. "I think it was Dr. Bill. I think I could have stopped him from committing suicide!"

"Suicide?" The word sucked the air out of me.

"And that's why I feel so bad."

I watched her, my emotions swinging from disbelief to anger. I couldn't believe Dr. Bill committed suicide. He had no reason, none at all, and in the fundamentalist town of Purple Sage, it would brand him as evil.

"Leigh," I said clearly. "Did you talk to the sheriff about this? Did you tell him what you saw?"

"Of course. Right after I heard that Dr. Bill was dead I drove to his office. Mac said not to feel bad, but I do.''

This is what Mac was hiding. "It was an accident—"

"No. Dr. Bill must have jumped in the creek."

"Dr. Bill did not kill himself!"

"Why are you yelling at me?" she asked, making that horrible squeaking sound again. "You weren't there. You didn't see—"

"I'm not yelling." Although I could hardly hold my voice down. "But you're guessing at what happened. You'll destroy Dr. Bill's reputation and kill Gretchen."

"I know that. People will say he can't go to heaven or be with God." Two tears rolled out of her eyes. "And it's my fault because I didn't stop him from committing suicide."

"He didn't!" Inside of me a living, breathing demon demanded I stand up and scream at Leigh. I stood, but kept my voice down. "Who else did you tell this story to?"

"No one." She swallowed.

"How many people did you tell? Who?"

"None. Well, except about an hour ago I told my friend Wanda. She works at the café."

More people get their news from the café than they did from KSGE. If the rumor about suicide was already going around this fundamental town, Gretchen would be shunned. They would talk about Dr. Bill as if he were the devil himself, and the funeral, which should be a celebration of a wonderful man's life, would not be attended.

"I have to go," I said.

"I knew you'd be mad."

I spun around. "I'm not mad that you didn't stop on the bridge, but I'm furious you started that rumor about suicide." I ran to my car.

SEVEN

I HAD BEEN propelled from Leigh's house on a stream of anger, a quote slamming my mind. "If it's to be done, you are the one." Assuming the rumor wasn't already flowing freely over the floodwaters of Purple Sage, it would be my chore to appeal to Wanda.

Wanda is not a friend, but someone I saw several times a week when I'd stop by the café for lunch or something to drink. We'd always visit for a minute or two, and I accepted her at face value as one does in a small town. She was divorced, had two kids in elementary school, Ramon in second grade and Anthony in fourth. She rented a little house on the north side and worked hard at taking care of her customers at the Sage Café, because that's how she was able to take care of her kids.

I hadn't known that she was a friend of Leigh's; on the surface the two had nothing in common. Leigh was slender and blond with an elegance to her face, while Wanda Esperanza was short and dark, with broad features. In a beauty contest Leigh would always be the winner, but Wanda would walk off with Miss Congeniality. She could, and did, talk with anyone and everyone. She always had a ready one-liner and a soupçon of gossip.

It was the gossip that concerned me.

The last of the breakfast crowd was lingering as I hurried in the front door of the Sage Café. The smells of bacon, biscuits, and pancakes filled the restaurant along with the soft scraping of silverware on plates.

Except on the busiest of occasions no one seats you at the café, so I took a look around for both Wanda and an empty table. Instead I spotted Diane, Trey, and Matt at a front booth. No Wanda.

"Hey," I said, sliding in next to Matt. In front of them were plates smeared with the remainder of their breakfasts. "I thought all of you were working."

"We were," Matt said, leaning over to give me a quick kiss before studiously appraising the check.

"Jolie, we didn't expect to see you," Diane added, suddenly fascinated with rearranging the red plastic flowers on the table.

Trey got busy scooting a last inch of toast around his plate to sop up nonexistent gravy.

"What's going on?" I asked.

"Nothing," Matt said, not looking up.

"Not a thing."

"Just breakfast."

"Really? You all look like you've been up to something."

Matt said, "We're just eating. Actually, we were just leaving. I'm sorry you didn't get here sooner."

But there was something. I looked from one familiar face to the other and realized that, once again, I'd interrupted an important discussion. This time I could guess what it was. Damn.

"You've heard about Dr. Bill supposedly killing himself," I said.

Diane let out a relieved breath. "You know."

Before I could respond, Maggie Mary, who owned the café, placed a glass of water in front of me. "Morning. You want some hot tea, Jolie?"

"Yes, please. And is Wanda around?" I asked.

"She left a little bit ago to take some soup to her kids. Anything I can do for you?" She looked more inquisitive than helpful.

"No, thanks."

"You going to have breakfast?"

I glanced at the empty plates she was gathering from our table. "No. Just the tea."

"Okay. And if you ask me it was pretty rude of them to eat without you." She whisked up the last of the dirty dishes, shot me one more curious glance, and said, "Be right back."

As soon as she was gone Diane turned to me. "Why did you want to talk to Wanda?"

"Isn't she the one who told you about Dr. Bill?"

"No, we heard it from Maggie not ten minutes ago. Everyone in the café was talking about it."

"Shit!"

"We knew it would upset you." Matt was watching me now, one arm gently around my shoulders as if to protect me.

"I was hoping the rumor wasn't circulating yet."

"Too late for that. It's well on its way," Matt said.

"Where did you hear it?" Diane asked, sipping from her coffee cup.

"From the twit herself. Leigh. She's the one who started it."

Diane put her cup down hard. The plates and cups are made of heavy plastic so no damage was done. "Why would Leigh do a stupid thing like that?"

Trey added, "What was the point?"

"I don't think she meant to—I just don't think she's got a brain in her head." I stopped myself. "Okay, she was upset and probably not thinking."

"You can say she's stupid if you want because that was a dumb thing to do," Diane said. "Maybe people won't believe it. I mean, unless someone comes up with a reason—"

"I still don't get it," Trey said. "Why would she say anything at all?"

And so I explained what Leigh had seen the night before.

They listened between asking questions and finally it was Trey who said, "Doesn't it make you wonder what she really saw?"

It was a tantalizing question and one I hadn't even considered. Our theorist Trey could spend hours on it, but Diane didn't give him the chance.

"I need out, honey, if I'm going to get on the road."

"And we need to get some work done or you'll never get your house back," Matt added, already pulling a twenty out of his wallet. While they paid their check, I found Maggie Mary and had her put my tea in a cup to go.

My mission had been halted, and I was feeling both relieved and bereft. My anger had shifted to sadness and my stomach had a homesick ache.

"You look sad," Diane said.

I nodded. "It doesn't seem fair. I mean, life is too short."

She knew exactly what I was talking about, which is one of the great things about Diane. She hugged me as we headed for the door.

"I know, that's why I'm going to see my parents." They lived in Menard, an hour and a half away.

We were outside by then, everyone going in their separate directions. Matt kissed me quickly. "I'll be home around five or six, I hope."

"Okay." I wanted to kiss him again, but he was already in the truck with Trey, giving me a final wave before shutting the door. Diane was in her silver Mercedes turning left out of the parking lot.

I stood there with my styrofoam cup thinking that everyone was going forward with their lives just as if this were a normal day. Didn't anyone realize how treacherous the world was, and that we needed to be together?

I got in my own car. There was no need to talk to Wanda now, and there was no need to go home, since no one was there. My mood was slipping down into that deep dark crevasse where no premenopausal woman wants it to go. Surely there was something useful I could do.

Maybe if I went by the hospital, and just saw the place where Dr. Bill did so much good, I might begin to understand.

I turned in that direction, thinking again of the curious question that Trey had offered. There had been no reason for Leigh to make it up, so she must have seen something.

The area near the bridge is on the highway, not heavily traveled, yet Dr. Bill had to have purpose for going there. It was not on his way home, the dark night was heavy with rain, and he'd left the party because he was tired.

Actually, he had left after most of the guests, and hadn't said anything except "good night' and "thank you."

The thin haze of gray sky above me began to turn darker as I drove up to Wilmot County Hospital. A tiny sign proclaimed, "Miracles happen here." I always look for it, and I always feel better for seeing it. There was another sign today, an illuminated message board. I was stunned to see the message, "Good-bye Dr. Bill. We'll miss you!"

I let out a long shaky sigh in lieu of tears. The message must have referred to Dr. Bill's retirement, but with his death... I took another long breath.

He'd always been so busy at the hospital, always on the go, but then hadn't we all? I had thought there was time.

Was that always the way when someone dies suddenly? You think of all the things you could have done, intended to do, and would have done if you had only realized that time was limited?

I was forty years old and just now realizing that I didn't understand even the basics of life and death.

Without thinking I turned the car up Pine and pushed on the gas pedal. I needed to check on Beverly. Having her reception at Leigh's house had been difficult for her, and I wanted to explain how sorry I was. It wasn't something I was willing to put off until later. Later was merely a probability, not a certainty.

Since her return to Purple Sage, Beverly had lived with her father—assisted living the old-fashioned way. Since it was Henry Kendall's home, he maintained a sense of independence, and yet still had someone to cook, clean, and generally care for him. It couldn't be easy. Mr. Kendall still tries to flex his nonexistent muscles, and the difficulties would be aggravated by the smallness of the house.

The neighborhood dates back to World War II, with quaint bungalows, and is not the place I would expect Henry Kendall to live. From what Bev had told me, he is attached to the house just as he was attached to her mother, who selected it before their wedding. The couple honeymooned there, and they had lived there when Bev was born.

Eight years later, when her mother died, her father remained in the house to be close to his wife's memory.

I imagine back when the neighborhood was new there were hopscotch squares on the concrete and roses in the flower beds, but now the area has aged along with its residents. The children are gone and the sidewalks cracked. Shrubs that started small have developed into monstrosities that have taken over complete flower beds, and in some cases, almost entire yards.

Still, I've always liked the neighborhood. I like the quiet dignity of the elderly residents, and while it's nice that a few of the homes have been sold to young families, I hope the changes they make are gentle ones.

The Kendalls' house has a hedge along the sidewalk, so I parked in front of a neighbor's—once a faded green, but now painted in two shades of gray with burgundy trim. The sky was only sending a drizzle of rain, allowing me to take my time getting to the front porch. It was Beverly who opened the door.

"Jolie! What a nice surprise. Come in." The words fit the genteelness of the house.

She gestured me into the small living room that still held the morning scent of toast. Dominating the room was an antique player piano, and a sofa with a brightly colored knit afghan over the back. The whole room had a dated look, but it was homey.

"Do you have a minute?" I asked.

"Of course. Come back to the kitchen and I'll get you some coffee." She led me into a small hall, and then into the equally diminutive kitchen, at least by today's standards.

The chipped ceramic tile on the counter was a soft shade of green-blue, with a narrow black accent. The cabinets were cherry, adorned only with chrome knobs, and had clearly been in use since the house was built.

I hadn't been inside since Bev had moved back, and she noticed me taking it all in. "You'll have to forgive the condition of this place. It's gone downhill in the last couple of years, and I couldn't keep up with it from Dallas."

"It looks wonderful."

"But if the spiders quit holding hands the walls will fall down." She gestured to the breakfast nook. "Don't sit in the chair with the pan—the roof is leaking."

Above that particular oak chair was an oval water stain on the ceiling. "And, of course, you can't get anyone to work on a roof in this weather," I said, sitting down in a vacant chair, and smoothing the green-checkered tablecloth.

"When the rain stops they will come," she said. "Actually, I shouldn't complain. At least we have a roof, and the leak is minor."

"So, where's your dad?"

"He's in his bedroom." She reached into a cupboard and pulled out a heavy white mug. "Oh, wait, you don't drink coffee. How about some tea? I think I have some blackberry."

"That would be great. How's he doing after last night? Is he okay?"

She put a copper-bottomed kettle on the stove and turned it on. "He's fine." She dropped her voice. "I think it scared him. He must have realized that he isn't capable of driving himself, or something, because he's been upset ever since they brought him home. He wandered around the house half the night. That's not too unusual for him, but this morning he seemed, I don't know, edgy." She sat down across from me. "It's got to be hard realizing that you're losing your independence. I think he's been pretending all along that I'm here so he can take care of me."

"I'm so sorry."

"Me, too." There was a great sadness on her face as she

filled a plate with homemade chocolate chip cookies and put them in front of me. "And it's not just him. Sometimes we go up to the senior citizens center, he's still a great pool player, and his friends there are disappearing one by one."

"How awful for him."

"But, that's our future, too, Jolie. Maybe even worse, what with all the advancements in medicine. They may be able to keep us around way past our usefulness. Not quite gone, but not quite here, either."

I had a vision of all of us, old and withered, propped up in bassinets like newborns; it wasn't something to dwell on. "So how is your dad doing physically?"

"Good some days, some days bad." She shook her head sadly. "They found a tumor on his kidney—that's on top of the other cancer. I don't think he feels too bad, except he gets so out of breath. At least he's not going to be driving my car for a while, since they had to have it towed last night." She reached for a cup that was sitting in front of her, took a sip, and made a face. "Cold." She put it in the microwave to warm. "But, you didn't come to hear me whine. Sorry." She began making my tea.

"You're not whining." And she hadn't. She'd never once said how hard this was on her. Had the situation been reversed, I certainly would have listed my personal complaints and talked about how it was affecting me. When my father had died a great deal of it had been about me.

"So. To what do I owe the pleasure of your company?" she asked.

"Well, first, I wanted to check on your dad, but then I wanted to apologize again. The more I think about having the reception at Tom and…at your old house, the more I think I must have been crazy. We should have postponed the damn party." Except, then perhaps Dr. Bill wouldn't have been alive to attend. Or maybe he would still be alive. I rubbed my forehead to ward off the *what ifs* and *if onlys*.

"Jolie, it's not a big deal. I was fine with it. It was much more difficult for Leigh than it was for me."

"Leigh?" I already had a cookie on its way to my mouth and my empty stomach. "Why in the world would you say that?"

"Because she's the second wife, and they always have it the hardest. Remember when Matt's first wife showed up for the centennial celebration? Remember how you felt?"

I did indeed. I had been a basket case, but then Matt's ex, the all-too-charming Cecily, with her even more charming British accent, hadn't arrived alone. Cecily flew from the UK to Florida so she could make the remainder of the trip to Purple Sage with Matt's parents. It had made her seem the favored daughter-in-law, even if she was the ex.

Cecily compounded her sins by staying with Matt's parents in our guest house and calling my mother-in-law *mums*. She called my husband *Mattie*.

"Yes, but Cecily," I said, "was an alcoholic and a bitch. You are neither one."

She fixed tea in an old-fashioned teapot with a twining-ivy pattern on it. Beverly grinned. "Oh, I can be a bitch, and with a little practice I'm sure I could be an alcoholic. After all, this is America, where all things are possible."

She placed the teapot in front of me, and pushed the plate of cookies forward.

"You shouldn't tempt me like this," I said, taking a bite of another one.

"Eat hearty, I made a triple batch. I'll even send some home with you." She took a hefty mug from the cupboard and set it beside the tea. "Let me check on my dad and see if he wants anything. Be right back."

I poured tea and thought about first and second wives. It was an interesting theory and probably valid. I didn't know what it felt like to be the first wife, although I'd had a first husband. That had been such a long time ago, or perhaps it wasn't the years so much as the experiences.

Steve and I had married when I was twenty-two years old, just out of school and far less mature than I chose to admit. The first year had been nonstop fun. We weren't making a lot of money, but what we had we spent on us. We ate in great restaurants, danced at all the hot clubs, and traded in both of our cars to get one terrific Camaro. It was life as it should be for the young and the frivolous. Then I got pregnant, and we began to change our values. At least I changed mine, and I thought Steve did, too.

After Jeremy was born I learned the hardest way that Steve had no intention of growing up and taking on the responsibility of a child, at least not then. He continued to stay out late, while I was home, cherishing my infant son.

I was happiest just rocking Jeremy and being the doting Madonna with child.

Then one night when Jeremy was three months old, Steve arrived home late only to say that he wasn't staying. Nor was he coming back—ever. Parenthood was not for him, and apparently, neither was I. He had a girlfriend named Candy, and she was fun.

He packed up his things and drove off with Candy and our new car, leaving behind a little boy without a father and a shattered young woman. I don't think he ever realized the damage he had done.

It had been the lowest time of my life. I'd been overweight from the pregnancy, without a job, and there wasn't enough money in the checking account to cover the rent. I remember holding Jeremy and telling him that everything was going to be just fine. His daddy was going to be back any minute, and we'd be a happy family, just like before. Except his daddy never came back, and when the month ended I had to call my parents to move me back to Dallas with them.

All during the packing, the moving, and even the months afterward when we'd lived in their house, my mother had maintained a slightly disapproving air, as if I was to blame for Steve's leaving. *If I had been a better person, if I had been nicer, prettier, a better wife...* She never said it aloud, but those *ifs* tormented me and I always wondered. Maybe if I *had* been a better wife,...

Steve never sent child support, didn't even show up for the

divorce. It took years to repair the damage to my ego, and sometimes I'm still insecure, but maybe that has nothing to do with Steve. Far worse is Jeremy's loss. That was Steve's greatest sin. Jeremy didn't have a father until I married Matt.

Henry Kendall's voice resounded clearly from his bedroom, pulling me back into the present. "I don't need a thing."

"If you change your mind, I have both tea and coffee made. And there are those homemade cookies..."

"Don't want to spoil my lunch."

"Okay, Daddy." Beverly left the door ajar.

I remembered all too clearly how my own father had physically dwindled during the last months of his life. "Has he heard about Dr. Bill's death?" I asked Bev.

"I don't know; he hasn't mentioned it, but I'm sure he has. He listens to the radio first thing every morning to get the news."

"Well, you haven't heard the latest." I poured more tea, then picked up my cup and blew on it. "Leigh is spreading the rumor that Dr. Bill committed suicide."

"Leigh? Leigh Greer? Why in the world would she do a thing like that?"

I put the mug to my lips. "Apparently she drove by the creek last night during the search and saw someone standing—"

A crash and a cry came from the bedroom.

EIGHT

HENRY KENDALL WAS on the floor wedged between the foot of the bed and the old-fashioned dresser. His walker was toppled behind him and blood ran down his face.

"Oh my God!" Beverly knelt beside him.

I crowded into the doorway. "Let me get a washcloth."

"A kitchen towel," Bev said.

I went back the way I'd come, while she turned to her father. "Daddy, where else are you hurt?"

I grabbed a fresh tea towel from the kitchen rack, wet one end, and brought it back. Mr. Kendall was still on the floor, sideways, his eyes open in what looked like shock.

Bev took the towel from me and gently began to wipe his face. "Does it hurt?"

"No." The word was more air than sound, yet still insistent. "Give me a minute."

"Sure." Bev continued to wipe blood, revealing a gash on his forehead. It had probably been caused by the edge of the dresser. "Well, it's not so bad, but you might need a stitch or two. How's the rest of your body?" She hadn't moved him, nor did he try to get up.

"Fine. It was that walker." He sounded a little stronger but his expression remained stunned.

"It's a tight squeeze in here."

He gave a faint kick with his foot. "God gave me two good legs—"

"It's only for balance." She continued to talk gently to her father and I stood by uselessly. When she finally looked up, I mouthed the word *ambulance,* trying to make it a question. Bev shook her head. "Daddy, does your back hurt? How about your neck? Should we get some help?"

"No!" His eyebrows shot upward. "I can get up."

And eventually he did, but it took the efforts of all three of us. When he was sitting on the edge of the bed, he saw his face in the dresser mirror. By that time his breathing was better and he seemed steadier. "It's not bad," he said. His forehead had almost stopped bleeding. "Beverly, just help me to the bathroom and I'll bandage it."

"I think you need stitches."

"I agree," I said.

His quick look of contempt clearly said, "women," but he didn't verbalize it. "A bandage will work fine."

My help wasn't needed. "I'll leave you to it," I said to Beverly. "Unless there's something you want me to do…?"

"Not a thing," Mr. Kendall said.

Bev smiled faintly. "I'll call you later."

"Okay."

"Oh, and take a couple dozen cookies with you. They're in a plastic bag in the second drawer."

I thanked her, found the cookies while Beverly moved her dad to the bathroom, and then let myself out.

I wondered how many times a week Henry Kendall took a fall, and how Bev continued to cope so graciously with her headstrong father. It made me think of my own dad. He had been a gentle soul, more so than my mother or me, but he could be stubborn, too, and toward the end he had been testy. He'd smoked up until a few months before he died of lung cancer. At least his death had been fairly quick, saving him the indignity of being an invalid for a long period of time. I wondered if on some level he'd wanted it that way.

I sighed. My dad had been so special to me, and only sixty-five when he died. Maybe the song is right and only the good die young. At least in my life it seemed the most caring left the soonest.

Which meant that since I could piss and moan with the best

of them, I would be around long enough to rival Methuselah's record. Just looking at the last twenty-four hours I realized that I had a houseful of guests and I hadn't done a thing to make them welcome.

Goodness and caring were a matter of choice. People like Dr. Bill and Beverly chose to take care of others, and decided to be happy about it.

I could do that.

Jeremy and my mom would be back from San Angelo in a few hours, probably a little tired, and I knew that Matt and Trey would have put in a long, cold day working to get the last of the water out of the Atwood's house. It made sense for them to come home to a warm fire and a nice meal that I had prepared.

I counted everyone who was staying with us and came up with seven, including me. Most of my adult life I have prepared meals for two, and the only large meals have been holiday dinners of turkey and dressing. That might be the tried-and-true menu, but I could hardly serve it tonight—it would make my ineptitude all too obvious—so I would try something else.

When in doubt I turn to the library or the Internet, and the library was closer. I could get some recipes and visit the grocery store all before driving back to the ranch.

"Hello there, Jolie." I was greeted as I entered the library by Mrs. Agnochi, the volunteer who sometimes covers the front desk. "How are you doin'? Staying dry?"

"I'm mostly dry," I said, shaking drizzle off my jacket. "How are you doing?"

She shrugged her shoulders. "Can't complain. Well, I could, but who would listen?" She turned somber. "Isn't that awful about Dr. Bill? I still can't believe it. A man like him."

The thought of his death caught in my throat. "He was wonderful."

"And then to hear that it was suicide." She made a disparaging sound.

Purple Sage was founded more than a hundred years ago by

a fundamentalist congregation moving westward. Some of those original nine families have grown large, while others have died out, but all have left their mark on the town. That upright, upstanding, and sometimes holier-than-thou attitude colors our community in ways that surprise me. Even Mrs. Agnochi, who has only been here for about two years, is concerned about suicide.

"I heard that rumor, too," I said, "but I don't think there's any truth in it. The sheriff doesn't know how Dr. Bill ended up in the creek, but it's doubtful he went in on purpose."

She looked thoughtful. "Sheriff said that?" I nodded. "Well, you know," she said, "I did think that was a pitiful way to kill yourself, especially for a doctor. I mean, there are quicker ways."

"You're absolutely right," I said.

"I'm glad you told me; I feel better. So, can I help you with anything?"

One more convert for the right side, and if I had told a small mistruth to accomplish it, I felt it was justified. "Cookbooks," I said. "I've got seven people staying with me, and I need to fix something warm, but not too tricky. And not too spicy. And I need to be able to get all the ingredients at Bellah's Market."

"Italian," she said. "And the secret is in the simmering and the herbs, so you can't miss. I'll give you my own recipe for lasagna."

Which she did, and which is why, as the gray sky outside shaded into night, my kitchen looked like the end of a bad Italian movie. Red sauce was dripped on the floor and sausage grease was spattered across the stove. Dirty pans were piled in the sink waiting for washing, and almost every spice I owned was on the counter. However, the house smelled heavenly and there were three large lasagnas in the oven. The makings for salad were in the refrigerator, and in the pantry I had two crusty loaves of bread from the Bakery. I would be feeding the multitudes in style.

Only periodically during the afternoon did I remember Dr.

Bill's death, and then it swept over me quickly, but disappeared as I concentrated on the task at hand. It appeared I couldn't multitask while I was cooking Italian. After checking the temperature in the oven, I reached for the phone and dialed Beverly. It was she who answered. "Hello?"

"Hi, it's me," I said. "I wanted to check and see how your dad is doing."

There was a half laugh. "I swear the man is more resilient than rubber. After you left I put a butterfly bandage on his forehead, and he napped for maybe half an hour. After that he was fine."

"That's wonderful. At least he must have good bones."

"And great stamina. You won't believe where he is now. The senior citizens center."

"You're kidding."

"No. Not only that, he took my car! The mechanic had just brought it back and Dad drove off in it."

"I thought it was damaged from last night."

"I did, too, but after they cleaned it up and got a good look at it, turns out there was nothing wrong. He must have flooded it." Her tone was half amazed, half exasperated. "Then his car wouldn't start this afternoon so I tried to get Dad to ride the senior citizen's van; they would have come and picked him up, but he wouldn't have it. He said that's for people who need it, and he doesn't. So he took my van again!"

"Amazing!"

"Jolie, can I call you back? I was just on my way out the door—"

"No need. I just wanted to check on your dad. Oh, and thanks again for the cookies."

"You're welcome."

We said our good-byes and I barely had the receiver in its cradle before the phone rang again. I answered, surprised to hear my sister's voice.

"Hi, Jolie. How are you doing?"

Elise is younger than me by four years, the baby of the family. There are three of us. The oldest is my brother, Winthrop, Win for short, which is a most appropriate nickname. Win takes after my dad's side of the family, which is Polish. He is tall and big boned, and very athletic. He excelled at baseball, football, and basketball, as well as any other game that required strength and coordination.

Elise, on the other hand, takes after my mother. She is tiny and fragile with big eyes and short hair and is musically inclined. She plays flute and piano and she sings. I spent most of my childhood on the sidelines watching Elise in recital or Win playing one of his interminable games. Still, Elise is precious to me, and I love her dearly.

I reached under the sink for dish soap to tackle the counters and the pans. "I'm fine. How about you? What have you been up to? How is Stewart? And the girls?" Elise has two beautiful little girls, Emma, nine, and Annabelle, seven.

"Everyone is fine. Annabelle has her violin recital next week, and Emma is clamoring for us to get a dog. All I can think of is Win and those monsters he has."

"His boys or the dogs?"

She laughed. "Oh, the boys are sweet, even if they are a little rowdy."

We talked about our families, just catching up, since we hadn't spoken in about a month. She told me about Win, and his latest adventure as a high school football coach; she keeps up with him better than I do. I countered with a story about Jeremy and the Blue Beast. Then she said, "So, is Mom there? Has she decided about dinner tonight?"

"Dinner? I just cooked dinner. Lasagna, no less. But she's not here; she and Jeremy went to San Angelo. How did you even know she was in Purple Sage?"

"Oh, she phoned me from the plane yesterday to tell me that she was going to visit you. Isn't that typical of her? Here she was, coming back from Costa Rica and during the stopover she just gets off the plane for good. She's amazing. I guess she really surprised you when she showed up on your doorstep?"

"Well, a lot was going on." I thought of the confusion of

the rain, the reception, and then my arrival home to find both my mother and Gretchen in my living room.

"Things must have been hard for you," Elise said, her voice soft with sympathy. "She told me about Dr. Bill. I'm really sorry; I know you thought a lot of him. We all did, but you knew him better than me."

"Thanks. It was just sad." I wasn't ready to say more—it might bring the pain to the forefront. "So, what's this about Mom and dinner?"

"She hasn't told you yet?" Elise asked, and I could picture her smiling like a little imp. It's what she does. "Then I'm not going to say anything. Mom can tell you."

"I don't get it? What can she tell me?"

"Mom may have a date tonight in Purple Sage, but I'm not going to say another word. It's her story. You're going to love it."

I felt like I'd walked into the last ten minutes of a soap opera. I had no idea when my mother had been asked out, who the man might be, and why the hell Elise knew when she was in San Antonio, more than a hundred and fifty miles away.

I propped the phone under my ear and reached for a scouring pad. "She called you yesterday and today?" I asked, scrubbing away.

"Yes. Does Jeremy have his own cell phone? I guess he does if she was using it."

Jeremy doesn't have full-time use of a cell phone, but he always takes either mine or Matt's when he goes out of town. Not that it mattered whether Mom had used a cell phone or crystals and a short wave set to reach Elise.

"So, what's this about a date? Someone in Purple Sage asked her out? She doesn't know anyone here."

"She does now," Elise said, with her tinkly little laugh. "Actually they met at your wedding. She wasn't sure that you'd approve. She should be back any time, and I'll let her tell you all about it."

The phone beeped to signal a second incoming call. Normally I do not like call waiting, and I refuse to say, "Hold on; let me get the other line." Like there might be someone more important phoning, however, Jeremy was on the road and Matt at the Atwoods, and besides, my sister had annoyed me.

"Just a minute, I need to get that." I couldn't believe that my mother had called Elise twice, and she'd hardly spoken to me since she got here. Last night was understandable, we were all operating on blind instinct, but this morning was another story. Mom could have come to the radio station to say hi. We could have had breakfast. Or she could have called *me* on the cell phone.

"Hello?" I said, attempting good cheer.

"Jolie, hi." It was Diane. "You sound weird, are you okay?"

"I'm fine. Just fine. How are you? How's the house? And where are you?" There was static in the background.

"That's what I'm calling about. We're on our way to San Angelo. We had the best luck. A friend of Trey's owns a couple of carpet stores, Lee Hooper, have you met him?"

"No."

"Well, anyway, the rain has caused slowdowns for the builders, so several of their jobs have been pushed back. That means Lee can send a crew out tomorrow if Trey and I pick out some carpet that's in stock. They've got to have something we like, wouldn't you think?"

"Of course."

"We're on our way right now." It would put them home around ten or eleven tonight. If they didn't eat in San Angelo, which of course, they would.

"Where is Randy?" Her son might at least make a dent in the lasagna.

"Oh, he's with us. Matt's here, too. He wants to talk to you."

Matt, too?

I heard the shuffling as she passed over the phone. "Hi, honey," Matt said. "How's it going?"

"Oh, fine."

"Are you having a nice visit with your mom?"

"Actually I haven't seen my mother. She and Jeremy aren't back yet."

"They aren't? They must be making a real day of it in San Angelo. I'll give them a call and see if they want to have dinner with us."

Mom could have her date join them, right there in San Angelo, meanwhile I would be at home baking lasagnas that no one was going to eat.

"Good idea," I said.

"Are you all right? You sound funny."

How do you explain that you're feeling left out, but it's really no one's fault? "I'm fine, but I have Elise on the other line."

"Tell her I said hi, and I'll call you when we're on our way home. Love you."

"Love you, too," I said. Then I pushed the flash button. "Elise?"

"Right here. Listen, I know you've got a lot going on, what with Mom staying, and Diane and Trey, so I won't keep you. I just wanted to find out if Mom was going on that date or not. She'll call and tell me tomorrow."

"I'm sure she will," I said.

"Don't let all your company overwhelm you; I know how you like your solitude."

I spent a moment listening to the solitude of my empty house. I didn't like it at all. "Okay. And I'll tell Mom you called."

"Give Jeremy and Matt a hug from me."

"Kiss the girls for me."

"Bye."

AN HOUR AND A HALF later the lasagnas were cooling and the kitchen was devoid of the remnants of all the work it had taken to make them. It was then I heard the front door open and Jeremy and my mother come in.

"We're home," my mother called as I entered the living room. "You've been cooking something and it smells heavenly! Here, Jeremy, would you take these upstairs to the guest bathroom? Oh, and do you have scissors so I can cut the tags off?"

"I'll put them all on the counter in there." He was carrying half a dozen large sacks. "Hi, Mom. Smells good—too bad I can't stay." He hurried past me.

"Where are you going?" I asked.

"I signed up to help serve dinner at the shelter," he said, starting up the stairs.

Obviously there were teenage girls either staying at the shelter or also volunteering. That left no one to have dinner with me, unless my mother was staying.

She was hanging a heavy coat in the closet. "That's beautiful," I said. I could hear Jeremy moving around upstairs, obviously putting the new clothes where Mom could get them.

"Oh, thank you; it was on sale. Well, I'm sorry you cooked, since I won't be here to eat, but I'm sure Matt and the Atwoods will enjoy it. You will save me some for tomorrow, won't you?" She was moving toward the stairs, almost sidling as if to avoid getting too close to me.

"Sure. So, you won't be here?" It was coy of me. "You're going someplace?"

"Well, actually, Jolie..." She stopped and took a determined breath. "I'm having dinner with a friend. A man. And, I know that in the past you haven't always approved of me dating—"

"Mom, it's none of my business."

"I'm glad you see that."

A flash of light from outside caught my eye and I turned to see headlights coming up our road. My mother saw them, too. "Oh no!" She checked her watch. "I've got to get ready. We'll talk later." She hurried for the stairs, then stopped halfway up them. "Jolie. Even if you don't approve, just be nice tonight, okay?"

"Mother! Of course."

"Of course." She hurried into the guest bathroom and closed the door.

I was stunned by my mother's comments. Who did she think I was? Even more frightening, had I done something to give her the wrong impression about me?

Growing up I had never been close to my mother or my sister. My sister had been too young, the one I always had to watch out for. I'd always called her spoiled, but thinking back I realized that pampered was a better word.

My mother always said that I was the problem, not Elise, but as a child I could never see my part in it. I still resisted seeing it, and all my most vivid memories supported my own position.

Like the time in fifth grade when I'd had a terrible cough, what was later diagnosed as pneumonia, and the three of us went to the grocery store. It was a wintry January day, and I'd barely been able to drag myself around the store. When we'd finally gotten home my mother had yelled at me for not helping Elise out of the back seat. When I did, Elise picked up an apple and went upstairs to play, while I had been required to carry groceries in and out of the cold.

Afterward I'd fallen asleep, wrapped in a blanket on my bed. When I woke up my father was home and asking where I was. My mother said I was upstairs sulking because she'd made me help.

She hadn't been intentionally unkind, I was sure of that, but somehow there was always a misconnection. With three children and all her church and volunteer work I assumed she was too busy to talk to me, but now we were adults, and obviously she was talking to Elise.

As for her dating, I had no opinions on that. Yes, my father had been a wonderful man, but life goes on when the grieving abates.

Then it came back to me.

About six months after my dad died, I had driven to Dallas to spend the weekend with my mother. She and Jeremy had gone someplace, probably the grocery store, and I had stayed home. It was fall, a beautiful, crystal blue afternoon with just a hint of the chill that would come with the evening. The doorbell rang and a man was there, an expectant smile on his face. That had changed to disappointment when he saw me.

"Hello. I was looking for Irene."

He was taller than my father, and he appeared younger, too. I don't know why that bothered me, but it did.

"She'll be back later. Do you want me to give her a message?"

I hadn't invited him in, although that would have been hospitable, nor did I introduce myself. He held out a sweater. I recognized it as one that my father had given my mother the Christmas before.

"Your mom left this in my car. Would you give it to her and tell her I'll call her Monday?"

"Sure." And then I had all but snatched the sweater away from him.

When I asked my mother about him later, she had been defensive, as if she'd done something wrong. It had never become an argument, just another of those times when we weren't on the same side.

Was it possible that the incident from five years before was still coloring her conversations with me today?

The doorbell rang and I started toward it, more concerned with past than present. I'd always thought that in time my relationship with my mother would change, but what time? As I'd recently realized, people didn't stay in this life forever. Sometimes they died suddenly, leaving us with nothing more than memories and a lot of *if onlys*. Nothing was going to happen to my mother, but that didn't mean I could wait. I needed to start talking to her before we let this visit end like all the others.

That was foremost in my mind when I opened the door to find the sheriff on the porch.

I jerked back to the moment, my heart stuttering. Sheriffs can bring bad news. "Mac. Is everything okay?"

He looked surprised. "Oh, sure. This isn't an official call."

I let out a relieved breath. I should have guessed. Rather than his usual khaki uniform he was wearing a red plaid shirt with a corduroy jacket and jeans. I didn't think I'd ever seen him dressed like that.

"That's good to know. Come on in."

"Thank you." He stepped inside almost shyly. "Is your mother ready?"

"My mother?" I stopped as the realization hit me.

Mac Donelly was my mother's date.

NINE

"CAN I GET YOU something to drink?" I asked the sheriff as he lowered himself into an aqua leather recliner that goes beautifully in our Southwestern living room. Mac has sat in that chair before, but he didn't look comfortable this time. I went on, "I've got soft drinks and—"

"No, thank you; I'm doing just fine. Sure does smell good in here. Spaghetti?"

"Lasagna."

"Maybe we ought to eat here."

"You're certainly welcome."

"No, thanks, I was just kidding."

I was glad. I can see Mac having dinner at my house, and of course I can see my mother doing the same, and I can even imagine the two of them going out on a date, but I couldn't imagine them having dinner, on a date, in my kitchen.

"So," I said, "how are things going?"

"I expect you're asking about Dr. Bill's death, and I can tell you truthfully, Jolie, it's the most puzzling thing I've run up against in a while. It just doesn't make sense." He shook his head. "You've heard that Leigh Greer saw him out at the creek."

"She told me this morning. That's what you didn't want to tell me last night."

"I didn't reckon it was something that Miz Marchak needed to know, at least not until I could confirm it."

"And can you?" I slid onto the wide stone hearth so I could face him.

He shook his head. "No, but I can't figure why she'd lie about it, either. And we know for sure he was there."

"What about her idea of suicide?" I asked. "Was there some reason he might do that? Maybe his health?"

"Off the record?"

"Way off."

"Okay. Well, I checked and he was in good shape for a man who didn't exercise and didn't eat very regular, and flat didn't take care of himself. A little creaky like all of us, but nothing more."

Before I could ask anything else, Jeremy came flying down the stairs, apparently intent on keeping Mac company while my mother changed clothes. "Hi," he said.

My son believes that Mac hung the moon, or at least lent a hand when it went up. Jeremy has many good reasons for thinking that. When a friend and hero of his was killed a few years back it was Mac Donelly who took Jeremy under his wing, teaching him that death is always a part of life, and you can't quit living because someone else has. Mac also showed Jeremy that although you may never be happy about one thing that happens, that doesn't mean you have to be an unhappy person. I think I learned those lessons along with Jeremy.

"Jeremy, how you doing?" Mac asked. "How's that new pickup of yours?"

"It Rocks." He sat on the love seat. "Drives like a champ."

"That's real good to hear. There's another one looks a lot like it around here, but I expect you knew that."

"Another one? No way."

"Must be one. One of my deputies came in, I think it was day before yesterday, and said he saw one looked just like it flyin' down the road at what he guessed was eighty miles an hour. He already had somebody stopped, or he'd've been after it."

Jeremy went pale, but he didn't volunteer a word.

Anger and fear hit me fast and my mouth was open, ready to start lecturing Jeremy, maybe even yelling, when Mac went on.

"Must've been some other person. Seems every year we get a new crop of teenagers goin' too fast for their own good, and then we get one or two who has a bad wreck. You remember Luke Simmons last year—I don't figure he'll ever walk the way he used to." He gave an unhappy shake of his head.

"That was bad," Jeremy said with a stiff nod.

"I'm making some changes in the enforcement practices to curtail that kind of thing. From now on my officers will ticket anyone under the age of twenty-one if they are more than three miles per hour over the limit. That's leaving some room for speedometer error, but none for speeding. I know it's stiff, but we want people safe. What do you think, Jeremy?" Mac was speaking comfortably, as if Jeremy had little investment in the conversation.

"Yeah. Uh, yeah. I can see that."

He had Jeremy mesmerized, like a cat tracking a moth. "I hate to be that tough, but it's not a problem if everyone drives responsibly. You might want to spread the word to your friends. I'd prefer not to be handing out any tickets."

"Okay. Right." Point taken, and Mac hadn't had to lecture nor had he lost any of his luster as a hero.

"Sheriff!" My mother made her way down the stairs and with her breezy entrance got Jeremy off the hook. "I'm so sorry I'm running a little late. Our drive back from San Angelo took longer than we expected."

"I don't mind a bit," Mac said, standing to greet her. "Jeremy and I were just talking about speeding, and how dangerous it is."

"Really?" My mother looked from one to the other, but didn't pursue the topic. "Let me get my coat. It's here in the closet." She was in a new, light gray wool suit, with an aqua turtleneck sweater that set off her eyes. She looked warm and happy.

Mac helped her on with her new coat, and she hardly acknowledged me until she was bundled up and ready for her date. Then she turned to Jeremy first. "Thanks again for being my chauffeur today. Oh, and have a good time at the shelter."

She winked at him, then turned to me. "I'll see you later tonight, honey. Don't wait up."

"Oh—okay. Have fun."

But they were already out the door.

A fairly subdued Jeremy watched them leave, then said, "I better get going, too, if I don't want to be late." He grabbed his own jacket. "Bye, Mom. And don't worry, I'll drive carefully. See you later."

THE MUD SQUISHED beneath my feet as I walked up the drive, through the dark and drizzly night to Gretchen Marchak's house. I kept thinking of the phrase, when life gives you lemons, make lemonade. I didn't have lemonade, I had lasagna, and I wondered if that counted. I was taking some to Gretchen. In the past I have avoided this particular ritual, not out of unkindness, but because I never know what to say or do. The few times I have gone to someone's home before or after a funeral, I am often the one who sheds the most tears. I don't cry for the person who died, but for those who are left behind.

My new resolution to be kinder meant I had no excuse to stay home, especially since I already had extra food.

As I approached the house, I could hear voices and see a woman standing alone near the gate. She was on a cellular phone.

"Tom, I can't. No, that's not fair and I don't think you should even ask. Please." It was Beverly, and I assumed the Tom she was talking to was her ex-husband, Tom Greer. Which made me wonder why, and what he was requesting.

"No," she repeated. "I can't."

Rather than eavesdrop any further I said loudly, "Bev? Is that you? I can't see a thing."

"It's me." Her next words were brief and too soft for me to catch, but she must have ended the call. I thought I heard relief in her voice as she said to me, "How are you doing?"

"Fine. There are more people here than expected. Dr. Bill was very popular."

"Or Gretchen."

I remembered her comment at the reception about keeping Gretchen away from her. Yet, Beverly was on hand, offering either food or solace.

"What's the story with you and Gretchen?" I asked. "After what you said last night, I didn't think you liked her." Bev moved closer, although in the darkness I still couldn't see her face.

"Oh, that. I shouldn't have said anything."

"But you did."

She took her time, her gaze falling to the ground. "It's not really about Gretchen, I realize that now."

"You had a problem with Dr. Bill? But he was your dad's doctor and from what I've seen, Dr. Bill always went over and above what was necessary for his patients."

"That isn't always a good thing." She turned to face me and said, "Two years ago when my father was first diagnosed with dementia, Dad signed a legal paper, a DNR. Do you know what that is? It's a do not resuscitate. If anything happened, my father didn't want anyone taking extraordinary measures to save him. In fact, he didn't want them taking any measure."

"Them?"

"Anyone. The DNR was on his medical chart with Dr. Bill, and it was on file at the hospital. I knew about it, everyone did. Then last year he had his heart attack and he died. Technically. He was dead for several minutes, but Dr. Bill insisted that they keep working on Dad, so they did all the magical things they can do. In the end he brought Dad back to life." Her voice was tight. "Dad was furious. He never wanted to age beyond his usefulness, and now he has. He blamed Dr. Bill for ignoring his requests."

"But, that's not Gretchen's fault."

Bev agreed. "But you see, Gretchen bragged about it all the time—how Dr. Bill had worked a miracle on Dad and what a saint Dr. Bill was. But he wasn't. He had no right."

I was stunned because this was such a reversal from all of our medical precepts, or maybe they were my own beliefs. "Is that how you really feel?" I asked.

She took a moment before answering. "At the time, I think I was grateful, because I wanted Dad to live. Selfishly, I wanted him with me. Can you understand that?" I nodded that I could; I knew that feeling all too well. She went on, "It wasn't until later that I realized the consequences of what Dr. Bill had done. My father hates his life right now. He's unhappy, and he knows it's hard on me. That part doesn't matter; I don't mind, but I see his point." She paused before saying clearly, "Dr. Bill shouldn't have done what he did. He was wrong, and what he did was wrong. He was playing God, and he had no right."

"But aren't you glad that you still have your father with you?"

She took her time before speaking slowly. "Jolie, he made the choice to have what he called a good death. Quick, almost painless, and one that happened before he was helpless. If we allow someone to take that away from him, then it can be taken from us, too." Her voice became soft. "Can you understand my feelings?"

"Yes," I said. "I think I can."

"So now you know." She gave me a quick hug, then said, "Sorry. I have to go." She turned away and disappeared along the lane.

I shivered as I made my way through the gate, trying to take in all she'd said. I would have given anything for Dr. Bill to save my father's life. Or would I? Quality of life played a big part, I knew that, but her father wasn't that bad off. Was he?

By that time I'd reached the porch, where several women were gathered, including one I didn't expect—Leigh Greer. She was talking earnestly with another woman and both were smoking.

As in chess, the pieces kept moving: Leigh was here, and her husband had been talking to Bev on the phone.

"Just take that on inside," Linda Beaman said to me, pointing toward the door with her heavy hand. Leigh lifted her blond head and nodded as I crossed the old wooden porch.

The front door was open, but the wooden screen was not, and it banged hard against the frame as I entered.

"Damn," I muttered, heads turning in my direction.

"Now, Jolie, isn't that nice of you to come by." It was Gretchen, moving as if through a mist. "You've brought food. How kind." She started to take the pan from me, but IdaMae Dorfman got to it first.

"I'll just put that on the table," she said. "Something Italian, and I'll bet it would go real good with some of my bread. Gretchen, why don't you come on over here and have some with me? I just hate eating alone."

"But I've eaten." She looked vague. "Haven't I? I thought I had." She turned to me. "I keep thinking that I have to fix something for Dr. Bill, but of course, he...he..." She gulped and swallowed.

"I brought lasagna, and it's Mrs. Agnochi's recipe, so you know it's fabulous."

IdaMae was sniffing the pan. "And I'll bet Jolie'd set and have some with us."

"I'd be happy to."

IdaMae nodded her approval at me, and then several women gathered around Gretchen, discussing the various dishes and urging her to eat something from the laden table. There was everything from Jell-O salad to barbecue brisket, and by the conversation it seemed that Gretchen hadn't tasted any of it.

IdaMae fixed the plates, and someone got glasses of iced tea, and I helped Gretchen into a chair. "Why do you all insist that I eat?" She sounded like a plaintive child. "I'm not hungry; I'm just not."

Everyone had some comment to make, but in truth, food is the universal panacea. It's what we know to do when someone is hurting.

Gretchen hardly listened. "I keep thinking that Dr. Bill is going to walk in that door, but he's not, is he?" She looked directly at me. "Is he, Jolie? Is that possible?"

"I'm afraid not," I said.

Before Gretchen could say anything else, IdaMae jumped

in. "But your sister ought to be here just any time," she said. "I know you're looking forward to seeing her."

"Oh, yes, of course. What time is it?" Gretchen asked. "What time is she flying in? Have I asked you this before?" She touched IdaMae's arm. "You know, I should wait and eat with her. Yes. I will." She was almost up when someone gently pushed her back down.

IdaMae countered. "No, no, she's eating on the plane."

By then there were three of us seated at the table, all with plates in front of us, and the other women had moved into the living room, probably with relief. Gretchen took a small bite, chewed it carefully, and swallowed quizzically. The second bite was still on her fork when she looked at me. "You know, Jolie, no one can tell me why Dr. Bill was at the creek. Do you know?"

I answered her question much as Mac had the night before, then spent the next twenty minutes coaxing Gretchen to eat. When I gave up, Gretchen had taken in only a few forkfuls of food.

We moved into the living area and she began her litany of questions again, directing them at newcomers. It was draining, so I cleaned up what little mess there was in the kitchen and slipped out the back door to take a few good breaths of air.

I know the place well, since we own it and I had done much of the work to make it ready for guests. In the spring the yard is filled with flowers. There is an arbor behind the house that is covered with brilliant red climbing roses all summer long. I slipped through it, thinking more of what it would be than what it was. When I came to the stone bench I wiped it with the napkin in my hand and sat down. By this time the rain had stopped completely, and only wisps of white cloud blocked the view of the stars and half moon. It wasn't so bad outside, and for some reason I didn't feel like crying. I was just sad.

I began wondering how I could get my purse and leave without being unsociable, when another small group came down the drive to the front door. I couldn't see them, but their voices were hollow with a forced cheerfulness, like nurses.

Then I realized that they *were* nurses, probably just getting off second shift.

By the time they were inside I heard more footsteps, these moving around the house toward me. I sat comfortably on the worn bench, tucked up under the vines, waiting to find out who it was.

"It isn't fair. It's never been fair. I mean, they cut me out without even speaking to me." It was Leigh. "I guess I can understand why Beverly didn't like me, but you know what? I'm tired of hearing what a saint she is."

Linda Beaman was walking with Leigh, directly toward the arbor. "She's got the reputation of being a real good woman."

"Big deal, all because she takes care of her dad. I was nice to him at the reception, but did anybody notice? No. I opened my house for a party for Beverly, but Diane Atwood and Jolie Wyatt hardly even said thank you to me."

I was about to stand up and let them know I was there, but the moment was awkward. And despite the confusion of yesterday I was almost positive that we'd been more verbal in our gratitude. I would go further, and first thing the following morning I would send flowers to Leigh.

"You know what Tom said?" Leigh went on. "He said it was because I was young and pretty. The women were jealous of me, and the men were jealous of him, because he was married to me. It does make sense."

"People can be like that," Linda said. "You take my Paige, she has to fight the same thing all the time. Sometimes it just breaks my heart to sit by and see the way people treat my baby girl—just because she's beautiful and smart. And when she made cheerleader at the university, lots of people were jealous."

I stayed in the shadows, hoping they would move on so that I could do the same.

"You know the worst?" Leigh asked. "They compare me to Beverly, who I don't even like. And then, Jolie got all mad at me this morning because I told the sheriff about seeing Dr. Bill at the creek."

"Well, you had to tell him; you can't keep that kind of thing to yourself. She ought to know that."

"Yes, but she was all huffy and she left right away."

"Now isn't that typical?"

I swallowed so hard it hurt my throat.

"You know what I think?" Leigh dropped her voice. "I think he must have had a reason for committing suicide, and I have an idea what it is."

"What?"

"I think someone was blackmailing him. What if he almost killed someone by giving them the wrong medicine? Or left a scalpel inside someone when he operated?"

My annoyance grew into anger.

Linda said, "I don't think he did surgery anymore, but you're right that there had to be some reason."

I was torn between remaining hidden and silent, and wanting to jump up and defend Dr. Bill.

Leigh Greer's whispered words were thick with satisfaction. "Or maybe—someone killed him to stop him from doing any more harm."

"Oh, wait, he was retiring," Linda whispered back. "He wasn't going to treat any more patients, so that doesn't make sense."

There was a pause before Leigh went on. "Okay, then," she said, "maybe…just maybe, he did something a long time ago, and someone wanted revenge. So, they arranged to meet him at the creek—"

"And then pushed him in."

Without another thought I flew out of the arbor. "That's the biggest crock I've ever heard!"

TEN

I MUST HAVE LOOKED like an avenging angel flying out of the
darkness because Leigh shrieked and fell back against the
house. Linda is more stalwart and only took in a noisy breath.
"Jolie Wyatt, what in the world do you think you're doing!
Scare a body half to death acting like that."

Leigh took her cue from Linda. "How long have you been
out here listening to us?"

"I wasn't—and what you were saying—"

"You sure as the world were," Linda snapped. "Sneaking
around in the dark, eavesdropping—"

"I was here first," I said. "And that's not important. You,"
I stared at Leigh, "are doing it again. Starting rumors about
Dr. Bill that have absolutely no basis in fact."

Linda sat up straight and snorted. "We were having a private conversation, which was, and is, none of your business."

"It's my business when you hurt Dr. Bill's memory—"

"You know what I think, Jolie?" Linda asked. "I think you
need to apologize. We were not gossiping, we were talking
and you butted in. And you know what else I think? I think
you need to see a doctor—and get your hormones checked
because you are acting downright odd."

I stared for probably a good thirty seconds, which can be a
very long time, especially when you are searching for the perfect comeback and nothing will come back. Finally I gathered
what little was left of my wits and my dignity and said, "I'm
sorry if you think I was rude. I didn't intend to be. I just
believe that in a small town like Purple Sage you have to be

careful of what you say because you can cause great damage by spreading supposition.''

It was as good an exit line as I was likely to get, so I turned and left.

THE FIRE SPLASHED warmth and color into the room helping to dissipate the chill. Diane was seated on the hearth, Trey was in the recliner, and I was curled up in Matt's arms on the love seat. Randy and Jeremy were upstairs doing something on the computer. The words I'd had with Linda Beaman and Leigh had been hours earlier, but they still remained in my memory, and not pleasantly.

"We should have taken you with us," Matt said, for the third time, holding me just a bit tighter. I agreed, but that was past. "I just assumed that your mother would be here, and you'd want to spend time with her. I know you don't get much of that.''

Matt noticed it while my mother never had, which made me happy and sad at the same time.

"You know what's really weird?" Trey said. "What you overheard at the Marchaks' house. That bit about Dr. Bill and how he took care of his patients.''

As I spoke I noticed headlights turning off the highway, heading toward the house. It was just past ten-thirty.

"What's up?" Matt asked as I leaned forward.

I pointed and all of us watched the lights stop at the gate, then shut off. Within seconds the sheriff and my mother came up the walk to the porch. They could see us as clearly as we could see them, which may be why their good nights were brisk. Mac said something, my mother nodded, touched his arm, and he said something more. Then the door was opening and I turned to the fire, pretending I hadn't seen them.

Matt stood up, "Come in and join us." My mother stepped inside, but the sheriff was already heading for his truck.

"I'll share the fire," Diane said, scooting to the side of the hearth.

"Would you like something to drink?" I asked, "We have coffee, tea, or hot chocolate. Do any of them sound good?"

My mom appeared dazed, looking from one of us to the other, and it was Matt who got up and helped her off with her coat. "Here, Irene, that's wet, let me hang it up in the laundry room. You don't want to wear a wet coat tomorrow." He took it with him as he left the room.

Mom nodded agreement, distractedly running her fingers through her damp hair. "Thank you."

"Are you okay?" I asked, moving toward her. "Is something wrong?"

"Oh, no, honey," she said. "Not wrong. It's just...the oddest thing." She went to the fire and warmed her hands. "And, I don't care for anything to drink. I'm really stuffed. We ate at that B & B—Shrimp Goldman, they called it. The dish, not the place."

"Red Roof Bed & Breakfast," Diane said.

"That's it."

"So, you had a nice time?" Diane asked. "And what was odd?"

My mother shook her head, as if still puzzling over whatever it was. "Neither of us could understand it. That's why Mac had to get back; apparently being sheriff is a twenty-four/seven job. He got a call on his mobile phone. Do you know a Leigh Greer?"

Diane kept all but a nuance of disfavor out of her voice. "We do."

I said, "You remember Beverly Kendall? She came over once when I was visiting you in Dallas."

"Oh, of course." Mom nodded.

"Leigh is married to Bev's ex-husband. What's she done this time?"

"Well, apparently, she's disappeared."

UNLESS THERE ARE unusual circumstances, I've been told the procedure with an adult missing person report is to do nothing for twenty-four hours. Mac assures me that there are valid reasons for the wait and usually such cases "sort themselves out." Often there has been an argument that law enforcement isn't told about, and within a reasonable time the missing person will return of his or her own accord.

In a small town, official action sometimes comes much faster than that, as it did in the case of Henry Kendall, but there are no hard and fast rules. With Leigh, Deputy Wiley Pierce took the first call and contacted Mac to make the final decision as to how to proceed.

I learned all this from Mac the following morning in his third-floor office in the old courthouse. The desk between us was a battered wooden relic of the forties and the matching side chairs were slatted wood and on rollers.

"So your deputies searched all night?" I asked. "And didn't see a thing?"

"Not a thing, but it was only Linc Draper on patrol last night, and there were two accidents and a boat loose at the marina, so he was pretty busy.

"I kept hoping she'd show up at home." Mac shook his head. "Do you know enough about her marriage to guess whether she might have taken off on her own?"

"Not really." I thought about what little I knew on that subject. Initially Tom had talked as if his marriage to Leigh was a miraculous event like the Immaculate Conception or the Assumption into Heaven, although that had to have changed, but I hadn't any idea whether or not the Greers were actually having problems. Tom's view on cigarettes was enough to cause a ripple in the relationship. "I know he didn't like her to smoke."

"Long time to be gone if she just went out for a cigarette."

I smiled at his attempt at humor. "Guess it doesn't matter."

Mac was holding an eight-by-five studio portrait of Leigh, and he gazed down at it, as he had periodically while we'd talked. "She's a real pretty gal. Real pretty."

"What does that have to do with anything?"

"It can cause trouble." But he didn't volunteer what that trouble might be.

Tom Greer is a CPA, and the day Leigh disappeared he had been in Fredericksburg helping with an audit. From what Mac had already told me, Tom had called Leigh around 4:30 to say that he wouldn't be home for at least a couple of hours, probably more like three, so she should go ahead and have dinner without him. Instead Leigh had bought a cake from the Bakery and had delivered it to Gretchen's.

All of that was in line with what I knew of Leigh's visit at the Marchaks', although I had left before she did. It was Linda Beaman who had seen Leigh head off in her turquoise Tracker around 6:30. A neighbor had noticed Leigh's car in her own driveway about twenty minutes after that. When Tom got home at a little before eight, Leigh was gone, as was her car.

Tom had waited several hours before calling the sheriff's office and at that time he had been calm. Concerned but calm.

After we heard about Leigh's disappearance from my mother, Matt phoned Tom and volunteered to drive over to keep him company. Tom had been gracious, but said it wasn't necessary. He'd been so convincing that Matt had stayed home, for which I was grateful. I needed to spend some time with Matt. Which we did. We had talked some, or rather I had talked and he had listened, but I would have settled for just breathing the same air.

His presence is especially comforting because he loves me unconditionally. Even when I've said something idiotic, or when I've done something I'm not proud of, Matt is there for me. By then I wasn't very proud of my attitude toward Leigh Greer.

I even had a particle of fear that I might be the reason Leigh was gone. Perhaps I had upset her more than I'd realized and she had decided to go somewhere to blow off steam, or run and hide, or whatever Leigh did in such an instance.

Then this morning even Mac Donelly looked worried, when usually his demeanor is official and stolid.

"Will there be a full-scale search?" I asked.

"Not now. If she did just up and run off, then it will make it real embarrassing when she comes back and finds everyone out hunting for her. I expect we'll hear something pretty soon. In the meantime, we'll all be on the lookout for her.''

"You don't want to make an official statement?''

"It's a question of jurisdiction.''

Mac was referring to the fact that several law enforcement entities function in Wilmot County. The police department handles everything within the city limits of Purple Sage, whereas the sheriff's office covers from the city limits out to the county line. In theory the sheriff has jurisdiction over the whole county, but Mac prefers not to push the theory.

There are two other law enforcement agencies, as well. The Department of Public Safety works the highways, and the Texas Rangers step in when there is a call for additional manpower, if a crime covers several counties or involves law enforcement personnel. I don't know who handles a missing person case.

"Didn't Tom contact you?'' I asked. "Wouldn't that mean you take care of it?''

"Not necessarily. Call me just before your noon newscast; I'll let you know then.''

He knew the KSGE schedule as well as I did, which wasn't surprising. There were other news stories. "I know you've been busy—'' I stopped short and rephrased my question, because I didn't want Mac to think I was talking about his date with my mother. "Busy with Leigh's disappearance and all,'' I amended, "but I was wondering if you knew anything else about Dr. Bill's death.'' He gave me the oddest look, just staring at me for a moment. "On Dr. Bill's death. Do you have anything more?''

"Oh. No. No word from Austin's autopsy team yet, nothing beyond that.''

There was something on his mind, something that I had set off with my question, but before I could ask we were interrupted by the dispatcher, Relda, who stepped inside the door. It's Relda's version of an intercom.

"Sheriff, Tom Greer is on the phone.'' I could read in her voice that this wasn't his first call of the day.

"Did his wife come home?" Mac asked.

"No, sir, and he wants to know what you're doing about it."

Had I been sheriff I might have tried to duck that one, but Mac nodded. "I'll take it."

She left and I stood, ready to follow her out.

"Uh, Jolie," Mac said.

I turned back. "Yes?" There was a quirky twist to his mouth. "Something else?" I asked.

"I just wanted to, uh, well, I was hoping that you, um, didn't mind." It seemed a tough speech for him to make but he valiantly persevered. "I hope you didn't mind that I had dinner with your mother. She's a real fine lady, and she says you object to her going out with men. I wouldn't want you upset with her. Or me."

"What?" I was stunned. It was bad enough that my mother didn't understand me, but far worse that she'd discussed our personal miscommunications with Mac. "No. Of course not." This was my town; these were my friends and my professional contacts. Why had she said anything? I swallowed, realizing the *why* was irrelevant, because she had. Damn.

"Good," Mac said.

I wanted him to know how wrong my mother was. "It's not…"

I was about to explain, but he was already reaching for the phone, leaving me no choice but to make my exit. I suppose it was the best thing, since I didn't want to hear his conversation with Tom. I was still nursing guilt regarding Leigh. Maybe I had been overzealous with her, but I had only been attempting to protect Dr. Bill's memory.

I took some satisfaction in the clatter of my feet on the wooden staircase as I descended to the ground floor of the old courthouse.

At the bottom, I looked at my watch. Seven thirty-five a.m. This was Saturday, and our first full newscast began at eight, late for a farming and ranching community like Purple Sage, but the owner of the station can't get anyone to come in early enough to do it sooner. At least we had a news director these days; we go through one about every seven months. A small town like Purple Sage is not high on most people's career path. Having a news director meant that I could leave as soon as I got off the air.

It wasn't raining and I had walked from KSGE, so now I exited north toward the police station.

The courthouse is a beautiful old limestone structure in the center of the town square. Sixteen stately pecan trees encircle it. Usually the grass surrounding it is a lush green carpet, and the Beautify Purple Sage committee keeps the flowerbeds filled with whatever is most abundant and appropriate to the season.

Because of all the rain, the sea of grass was a moat, and the purple-and-yellow pansies were facedown in the mud. I kept to the sidewalk, feeling a little like the pansies, with my head drooping. Maybe Linda Beaman was right and my hormones were out of whack—I certainly wasn't my normal proactive self. As Jeremy says, I don't ride waves, I make them.

"Miz Wyatt?"

I looked up to find Bill Tieman lumbering toward me. He is the chief of police for Purple Sage, and not a tall man, but large. At first glance he is the perfect mix of country cowboy and today's business world. He wears starched white shirts, pressed jeans, and a sports coat. A little over a year ago he ran for mayor against Trey Atwood, and since I had been Trey's campaign manager, it put me on the opposing side. We won, but not by outmaneuvering Bill. I simply think that Trey is more popular in the community and has more leadership qualities. Besides, Bill had a bad habit of wearing shirts that gape at the belly, revealing dark hair that no one wants to see.

I moved toward him, noticing that his coat was new and buttoned firmly. "Chief, good morning."

"How you doing today?" He always acts as if he's pleased to see me.

"I'm doing fine," I said.

"Did the sheriff give you a statement on the Greer disappearance?"

Greer disappearance. For a moment the words didn't mean anything. Then I realized that he was talking about Leigh and she was gone. Really and truly gone. I took it in for the first time.

"No. No," I repeated. "He didn't."

"Well, it might be a tad early on that one. How about the Marchak suicide? Need anything on that?"

Marchak suicide?

It hit like a punch and almost felled me. As the chief of police, Bill Tieman was an official source, and people listened to him. If he was saying Dr. Bill's death was suicide, then the myth would become truth in Purple Sage.

My words came out slowly, with great effort. "But, wait. I didn't think that—"

"Oh, you may be right. That may be Mac's jurisdiction more than mine. But, don't you worry none, I'll keep you posted on the Greer thing."

With surprising alacrity he went bounding up the steps of the courthouse and through the heavy doors. He seemed cheerful. Happy that…what? That he was going to be quoted on the news? That people were dead and missing? That all of these horrible happenings were neatly filed in their proper categories? Missing. Suicide.

I became more and more angry as I skirted the courthouse on the slick sidewalks. Bill Tieman didn't know that Dr. Bill had committed suicide. Mac wasn't even sure of that and he was the sheriff—he had jurisdiction. Unfortunately that wouldn't stop the story, which would move from rumor to historical fact in the swiftness of a lightning strike.

A small branch fell from one of the pecan trees and hit my arm. I grabbed it as I crossed the street and threw it toward the ground. Damn it—no one knew what happened that night at the creek.

A horn honked. The Blue Beast was in front of me, the grill less than a foot away, and I was moving toward it. I hadn't even seen it.

"Mom? Are you okay?" Jeremy asked, as he opened his door.

The passenger window rolled down and my mother put her head out. "Jolie, you almost walked right into us."

"I'm sorry; I was thinking."

"Get in," Jeremy said. "We'll give you a ride."

"No thanks." Then I had another thought. "But come by the station after the newscast. I'm going to need some help."

I was going to need a lot of help to find out the truth of what happened at Cavalry Creek.

ELEVEN

I HAD HOPED FOR some time with both my mother and my son, perhaps even to engage them in a conversation with me, but that was like trying to hold the attention of butterflies during migration.

"But, Jolie, we can't go out to breakfast," my mother explained. The two had arrived as I finished my newscast and now we were all in the news office. "We just had breakfast."

Jeremy frowned. "Well, you had to go on the air, and it's been almost an hour since we saw you. We had to do something."

"That's fine," I said. "We don't have to eat anything—I'm not that hungry, anyway." I was, but it wasn't as great as my other need. "I have an idea and I want some help. I was hoping you could do that."

They looked from me to each other. I was trying to read their expressions, and came up with frustration or annoyance.

"Honey," my mother said, "you know that I'll do anything I can for you, but we're scheduled to be at the Flood Relief Center."

"We could stay a few minutes," Jeremy said as if to placate me.

I felt like a homeless person looking for a meal, and instead I'd been handed a penny.

"Fine. A few minutes is enough for me to explain and we can go from there." I pulled out chairs from the large partner desk. "Here, you can both sit down. Mom, do you want some coffee? Hot tea? Jeremy, what about you?"

They sat down, my mother on the edge of the chair as if not willing to commit enough to lean back. "We really don't need anything, since we just ate," she said, watching me picking up the clutter that was scattered across the desk. "You know, since we're in a hurry, you could just sit down and talk with us. You're making me very nervous."

"I'm sorry. It's just that this place is such a mess." I sat in a side chair. "Anyway, here's what I'm thinking. Our chief of police stopped me this morning and asked if I needed any information on the Marchak suicide. He's going around town openly saying that Dr. Bill killed himself. And he's official enough to convince people of that."

My mother straightened. "So?"

"Mother, he's saying suicide! I can't believe he'd say such a thing. People in this town will condemn Dr. Bill to some horrible fundamentalist hell. There won't be anyone at his memorial service."

"Jolie," she said, her voice kind but with obvious patience, "Dr. Bill is dead. No one can hurt him anymore. Besides, I can't see what it has to do with us."

She wasn't getting it at all. "Mom, Dr. Bill was brilliant, and he was a wonderful man. Think of everything he did for us."

"I can't agree more—he was wonderful, but it's too late to repay that kindness now; we have to pass it along. It's just as our parents did for us; we can only give back by providing for our own children. It's the way of the world."

Another of her favorite soapboxes and I had all but asked her to stand on it. "You're right, of course, but look at it another way. He was a doctor. A brilliant man—"

"You're saying that he was too smart to jump into a raging creek, is that the point?"

"Yes."

"I see. So, what do you want from us?"

It was an opening, albeit a small one. "No one is investigating Dr. Bill's death. Not the chief of police, and not the sheriff. It will be ruled some kind of accident or maybe suicide.

Someone needs to find out what really happened when he went in the creek, someone who is not biased, and will get to the truth.''

"Jolie, I'm sure your heart is in the right place, however, this is not something for us to get involved in.''

"Why not? No one is investigating, and someone should. We can make a difference.''

"Jeremy and I *are* making a difference. He put in several hours at the shelter yesterday working on distribution of the household items; he'll be doing a lot more of that today. And I'll be helping people apply for government loans to rebuild. Those are differences you can see and touch.''

My mother and her charity work. I thought of the year she spent my birthday at some hospital because they were short-handed. I had been seven, and she had been busy elsewhere when I wanted a mom. Even at that age I had recognized that complaints would only beget lectures on selfishness and the virtue of doing for others.

I could remember those seven-year-old's feelings clearly, because I was gripped by them again.

"Fine.''

She raised one eyebrow. "I don't appreciate that tone of voice.''

"Fine.'' I used the exact same tone.

She stood up. "Jeremy, are you ready to drive me to the relief center? I don't want to be late.''

"Sure, Grams.'' He stood reluctantly, torn between us. "Mom, uh, maybe later I could call you.''

"Don't bother. I can do this myself.''

"Do what?'' my mother asked. "Just what do you think you can possibly do?''

"I can find out what happened and—''

"How? You're not a trained investigator and you're talking foolishly.''

I stared, my chest heaving, afraid to speak. The rift between us had deepened and more words would only make it more treacherous. It was a rift that had widened for years, and here we were again, looking at each other across the abyss.

She picked up her purse and started for the door. When she was in the hall she turned back. "You cannot do a damn thing for Dr. Bill, and I'm sorry you're not able to see that. It's time you realized how you've behaved all your life."

It was a final insult from my mother.

Jeremy looked stricken, as I suppose I would have in such a circumstance. I took in a couple of deep breaths before I spoke to him. "You'd better go, honey. They need you at the center, and it's important that you don't let them down."

He bent to give me an awkward hug. "It's okay, Mom," he said as he left. I didn't know if he was absolving me for my part in the argument, or saying it was okay that he was leaving.

"Right."

He was halfway down the hall, and I was still by the desk when I heard the back door open.

"Hey, Jeremy." It was Matt.

"Hey, Matt. Mom's in the news office." His tone was filled with relief. He had passed off his obstreperous parent to a steadier hand and could leave without guilt.

Instead, I felt guilty. And angry. And sad.

"Hello, my sweet." Matt swept me up in a hug, but it lost its exuberance when he felt my stiff body. "Something's wrong."

"My mother."

He sat down on the side chair and pulled me into his lap. "Want to tell me about it?"

"What's to tell?"

Years ago I read a book on fair fighting, and one of the rules that has remained with me is that you cannot bring up the past during an argument, because then you refight the same battles over and over. According to the author there has to be a time when you let go and move into a clearer, cleaner arena. My mother should have read the book.

But she was gone, and I was here, and I wanted to talk

about how awful she was so I could be okay and on the side of right. I did. I told Matt much more than what had just taken place that morning.

I started slowly, picking my way around the emotions, and then speeding up until it all seemed to spew out of me with volcanic pressure. I related the disagreement we'd just had, as well as the time when I was nine and had not wanted to attend another of my brother's baseball games. My mother had all but thrown me in the car, calling me an insensitive brat.

I told Matt about Mac Donelly relating that she'd said I didn't like her dating, which was nonsense. I paced while I brought up another old argument about her charity work. Through it all Matt listened.

"And do you know the worst?" I asked, finally settling. "She said that I shouldn't try to find out what really happened to Dr. Bill. Only she made it sound like I couldn't because I'm too stupid or incompetent."

"I'm sure she didn't mean it that way."

"Why not? She's meant it before. I even asked her to help, but she said no. Or maybe she didn't want to because it is an unworthy task. She wants to help the living, my mother of the Holy Order of Charity." I took a painful gulp of air. "Someone should tell her that charity starts at home."

Matt's expressive face held sadness. "She only sees your strength, not what you need."

"I don't need shit from her." But I did, and I always had. It made me miss my father even more, because he was the one I had gone to for comfort and love. It also made me miss Dr. Bill, because he was capable of that same warmth and giving. He had been there for me when no one else had been. At least not my mother.

A disconcerting thought surfaced. "I'm not like her, am I? I mean, I do give a lot to you and Jeremy, don't I?"

He took his time, thinking over his response until I was almost afraid to listen. Finally he said, "You are the sun of our universe and without you, Jeremy and I would die for lack of heat and love."

It was so flowery, and so unlike Matt, that at first I could only stare. Then a few tears escaped, but they came with an undercoating of laughter.

I wiped my eyes. "Have I ever told you how wonderful you are?" I asked.

"It bears repeating."

I laughed again and hugged him.

In truth, Matt is the core of our family universe. He is the strongest one, the kindest one, and the most solid. Jeremy and I rotate out like planets, sometimes straying far from center, but rarely for very long.

Matt slid both arms around me, and said, "I'm sorry that you're hurt by all this." His kiss tasted salty and held the warmth that eases sadness.

"I'm okay," I muttered, kissing him again. My body pressed into his arms, the tension receding, as did thoughts of my mother and son.

The next kiss was even more interesting, and Matt's hands began to caress my back. I was entertaining ideas of closing the office door when I heard the control room door down the hall open. It was followed by footsteps coming in our direction.

We broke apart, and my breathing was less steady than it ought to have been. "Damn," I said.

"A disappointing interruption." He was smiling, but a sadness still lingered. I wondered if his expression mirrored my moods.

"Very disappointing." I let out a breath as Marylyn, the deejay that morning, hurried past, intent on getting to the restroom or the coffee. I sat on the edge of the desk. I said to Matt, "You didn't come by just to hear me whine. Or to kiss me. Did you?"

"Maybe to kiss you."

We smiled at each other. "Right. And afterward you were…?"

The smile slipped off his face. "Going over to Tom's. Leigh

still hasn't shown up, and he has to be devastated." He reached out and touched my cheek. "I know I would be."

I held his hand for just a moment. "Thanks."

"No charge. So, what are you doing today?"

"I don't know. Do you think I should go with you? I'm not sure what I could do, but—"

"I don't think that's necessary. You and Leigh weren't close."

The guilt cut through me again. "No. No, we weren't. In fact…"

"What?"

I let out a long breath. "I have this awful feeling that it might be my fault Leigh took off." I felt no relief in saying it, and Matt didn't offer the exact right thing to make me feel better, either.

Instead he said, "If you're concerned, then you need to talk to someone about it."

"A counselor?" Matt had done some therapy years ago and he was far more mentally healthy than I will ever be, but I wasn't ready to check into a treatment center.

"I was thinking of Linda Beaman," he said. "If she was with Leigh, and if they were friends, then maybe she'll know if you upset Leigh or not."

"I don't much care for Linda Beaman."

"And, she is also someone who might know where Leigh is."

I thought about that, but there was something else that seemed more vital. "Matt, remember I told you that Linda and Leigh were talking as if someone might have pushed Dr. Bill into the creek? What do you think about that? Does it seem possible?"

He paused. "I don't know. What does Mac say?"

"There's no investigation going on." And then it struck me that Linda might also know more about what Leigh saw at Cavalry Creek.

There was little chance that Linda would absolve me of

guilt, but curiosity overcame distaste, hope overcame good sense. "Okay," I said. "I'll go."

"Then we can walk out together."

I phoned the front desk to tell the receptionist I was leaving for the day, then picked up my purse. "Sure you don't want to stay here and do some more kissing?" I asked Matt. "I really liked that part."

He stopped halfway to the door and gave me a bad-boy grin. "Tonight. Count on it."

THE RAIN WAS OVER for a while. The tropical storm had spun back to the coast and was making its way into the Gulf of Mexico. It was good news for Texas, although if it continued its northeasterly movement it could be bad for Louisiana. If it moved quickly, then it would bring nothing more than a welcome rain, however it could continue to dawdle, and dump the kind of water it had here.

I glanced up to see a distant blue sky beneath the gray. It was both promising and lovely. I hoped it was a good omen, since I was on my way to the Beamans'. I had thought about calling before driving all that way, but chickened out. The youngest Beaman child was in his teens and still living at home; when you have teenagers, drop-ins are expected. Besides, any excuse would have kept me from driving out there.

The Beaman ranch is a good ten miles beyond our house on a side road that is usually a dusty white ribbon of caliche winding between fence rows. In the summer it's hot and dry, and now with the recent rain, the road was slick and the trees bare so that the farm looked interesting in the way that an Ansel Adams photograph might be.

Once I was through the wire gate I slowed because of the mud. The house was at the far end of a circular drive. It was an old square box of a house, craftsman in style with cement pillars on the front porch. The clapboard siding had once been white, but was now spattered with mud, although the porch was both inviting and attractive. It was painted a dark green and had planter boxes filled with bright pink cyclamen in full bloom. They radiated joy. I hadn't expected that.

Two dogs, loud and rambunctious, came racing toward the car. One was a low, slinky-looking border collie with black spots near its flank, and the other looked to be a mix of breeds topped with a heavy rottweiler face. They stopped just before they got to the car and flung themselves into the air next to my window so they could better see in. I was in jeans and tennis shoes, but I didn't want to be covered with mud. I also didn't want to get bitten.

I rolled down the window an inch. "Hey, guys, back off." They jumped higher and one slammed against the car door. "Nice going," I said. In a firmer tone, I added, "Back. Get back! Now." Both halted, and one even lowered himself to the ground.

"Good dogs," I said, opening the door a crack. The rottweiler rose up and lunged toward me at the same time I heard a shout from the porch.

"Killer, you get your butt down!"

The young man heading toward me was young Travis as Linda called him. He was the one who had been on Jeremy's baseball team, and a nice enough kid.

"Hey, Trav," I said from the safety of my car. "Think it's okay for me to come out?"

"They won't hurt you, Miz Wyatt," he said. He had Killer by the collar and was holding him up on two legs. "You don't want them jumping on you—especially Killer. He's just a big pup and he'll knock you over."

"Right." I slipped out of the car, my eyes on the dogs. Killer was making some dramatic choking sounds. "Is he okay? Doesn't that hurt him?"

"No, ma'am. But if I let him down before you get in the house he'll drag me all the way to the front door and my mom will have my hide for getting that muddy." He grinned down at me. "We'd all be a muddy mess." Killer lunged but with less enthusiasm and Trav pulled him back in line. "Calm down!" The freckled border collie was yelping excitedly, still mostly on the ground, although he seemed to be leapfrogging toward me.

"You're sure they don't bite?" I asked, moving sideways toward the house.

"No, ma'am. I mean, yes, ma'am, I'm sure."

I got to the porch and saw that there were delicately patterned lace curtains over the windows and through them I could see a Tiffany-style stained-glass lamp with a lovely hyacinth pattern. For a moment I wasn't sure I was in the right place. I turned back to Trav.

"Are your parents home?"

"My dad's in San Angelo and won't be home 'til tonight, but mom's here."

The door opened. Linda Beaman blocked the light with her body. "Well, Jolie Wyatt, to what do I owe the pleasure?" There was no pleasure in her voice.

TWELVE

IN THE COUNTRY, when a friend comes to call they are taken into the kitchen, where everyone sits around the table, talking and drinking iced tea. I, however, was shown to the front room, what would have been called the parlor fifty years before. In those days it was where one visited with clergy and in-laws, and now I suspect it's where one visits with door-to-door salespeople.

It didn't bother me, since I hadn't expected to be greeted with hugs and flowers, and the front room was the one I had seen through the window.

The walls were painted a deep blue-green with beautiful dark wood trim. The furniture was mission style and several of the pieces were truly exquisite, including a library desk in quarter-sawn oak, and a rocker that I would have sworn was a Stickley.

On the floor was a handmade rug woven in a style I've never seen before. The weaving was so tightly done it might have been sisal, except I could see the various patterns of the cloth used for the weaving. In the center was a multidimensional square the same color as the walls and it was set into an intricate geometric design.

I stopped at the settee, carefully avoiding any contact between my shoes and the exquisite rug.

Linda took the rocker. Once she was settled she said, "Miz Wyatt." Statement, question, and challenge all in one.

I looked away from the rug. "Linda, I'm sorry to come by without calling first, but I wanted to talk with you." I sat up straighter, as if it might cut my verbal prevarication as well. "It's about last night…" I paused, hoping for some help from her, but her solid face was empty. She wasn't going to make this any easier.

"Last night," I went on, "I may have been more emphatic than I should have. About Dr. Bill. You were right, it was a private conversation, and while I didn't intend to eavesdrop, it amounts to the same thing."

"Are you apologizing?"

I actually thought about that and decided the answer was both yes and no. Eventually I said, "I'm not sorry that I defended Dr. Bill, but I am sorry that I upset you and Leigh. Really sorry."

She weighed my words and tone, then nodded. "That's fair."

One down, more to go. "I'm not clear why you think Dr. Bill wasn't a good doctor—"

"We were conjecturing. He was a pretty good doctor, but he was bound to make mistakes, being human like the rest of us. He was forgetful, sometimes, too."

"Senior moments."

"I suppose we all have some of them," she said. "Look, Jolie, we weren't saying Dr. Bill deserved to die, or anything like it, we were just saying that there was something funny. I know you don't believe he'd commit suicide, and I don't think I do, either, especially now. Oh Lordy, something is bad wrong, what with Leigh disappeared."

I hadn't expected that. "I'm not sure what that has to do with it. She probably just ran away, don't you think?"

Linda shook her head no just one time. "Not possible."

"What do you mean? Maybe she just got mad, maybe because of me, and—"

"You weren't that important to her."

"Okay. There were other reasons. She said that life was stressful right now. She told me that. Maybe it got to be too much."

"Leigh's life was always stressful, and running away would have made it worse."

"Why was Leigh's life stressful?"

Another shake of her head. "I don't believe it's my place to say." There was so much I didn't know, and so much Linda did.

I took a breath. "Then how can you be so sure that Leigh didn't just go away for a while?"

"Because she was supposed to be here today." Linda looked around the room, her eyes taking in the rug, a mosaic vase, the walls, and then coming back to rest on me. She was no longer the heavy, hard woman who was standing between me and what I needed to know—she looked weary and concerned in a way that a mother can be.

"You were friends," I said.

There was a real sadness on Linda's face, as once again her eyes scanned the room. "Yes, we were. We did lots of things together; we did all this. We painted the walls, and went to estate sales." She swallowed. "We made this rug. She was real talented."

Past tense. I remembered Leigh on her deck, just yesterday morning, crying. My stomach tightened, as if to steel itself from the sorrow in the room.

I started to say something, but a tear slid out of Linda's eye. Her emotion seemed to catch at my throat.

She wiped the tear away with the back of her hand. "I think that rug is my favorite thing in this room."

"It's beautiful," I said. "I noticed it first thing."

"I saw you didn't step on it."

"It looks delicate." The not-so-subtle change of subject gave her a chance to sniff hard and get herself back under control.

She said, "It's not so fragile as it looks, but I do love it."

"I can't figure out the technique." I leaned down and turned over the corner of the piece. The hemming around the border was done with such careful stitches as to be almost invisible. "It's not regular weaving, is it?"

"It's called locker hooking. You've never seen that before? It's real easy, and much faster than regular weaving. We'd work away, and start talking and pretty soon, we were almost done." A couple more tears slid out, and she stood up. "Would you like something to drink? A soda pop? Tea? Coffee?"

I let out a long held breath. "That would be very nice, thank you. Tea."

"I got hot water on the stove, if you want to come on back."

"Okay." I stood up, carefully avoiding the rug again, but Linda cut right across it.

As we passed through the hall I glimpsed other rooms, and I would have enjoyed living in any one of them. The furniture was primarily the simple and straight mission style, with wonderful colors and plenty of wood. I had a peek at what must have been her son Travis's bedroom, and it was a masculine haven in hunter green, beiges, and plaids. Old rodeo prints in shades of sepia were triple matted in dark wood frames, and a collection of western hats topped one wall.

Until that moment I had seen Linda as a pushy hausfrau. She'd never displayed any style, and I don't think I ever wanted, or tried, to talk to her. No wonder the woman hadn't liked me. I had written her off based solely on her appearance, and yet, she obviously had exquisite taste, and was handy as well.

"Your home is lovely," I said, following her into the kitchen. It was an old country-style room with golden wood on the countertop, and cupboards of that same wood with inset glass fronts. A hunter green stove with gleaming chrome stood against one wall, and tucked away in the breakfast nook was a rectangular table with a seating bench on one side and three simple chairs on the other.

"Have a seat," Linda said, gesturing to the table.

While I slid down on the bench, Linda went about making tea. She poured hot water from a copper kettle into a delicate porcelain pot, swished it around, then emptied it into the sink.

Next she opened a cupboard to get a box of Typhoo tea and measured loose leaves into the pot, along with more hot water. While that was steeping she laid the table with cups and saucers that matched the pot, and a plate of Cadbury's shortbread biscuits.

I watched fascinated, as if at a stage performance.

A silver sugar bowl and creamer came next, as well as two silver teaspoons.

Linda saw me watching her. "Those are real pretty, aren't they?"

"Gorgeous."

"They were my great grandmother's, and they keep getting passed down, so someday I hope I'll be having tea at my grandkid's house using that same silverware. They're silver, too, which was real important back a hundred years ago."

"Oh? Why was that?"

"Silver kills bacteria. Before refrigerators, people left milk in a silver pitcher so that it would stay good longer without spoiling. You didn't know that? Pioneers used to throw silver dollars into their wells to keep the water drinkable, too."

"No kidding. I had no idea."

She added some tongs to the tray, I assumed for sugar cubes. "Back when they had plagues in Europe, rich people would give their children silver spoons to suck on, so the children stayed healthy. That's where the saying, 'Born with a silver spoon in his mouth' came from." She turned away in what appeared to be embarrassment. "I shouldn't be going on so much. It's not bragging, or anything, I just like finding things out. Like about the silver. Travis says I'm like a dog with a bone, and I just don't give up when I want to know something. I got real interested in antiques when Leigh and me were going to auctions."

And this was a woman I had ignored for years—"I think it's fascinating. I never knew why silver was so coveted. I thought just because it was pretty."

"I'm sure that was part of it, too." She placed an ornate

silver strainer on each cup and began to pour the steaming tea. "This is real English tea. Ordered it off the Internet."

I am a tea drinker and had been a tea drinker even before it was popular, yet I have never been served any more elegantly than Linda was doing. My pleasure was tempered with humility. I pride myself on being a sensitive, even caring, person but it was clear that while I have no prejudices when it comes to race or religion, I am as guilty of prejudging as the next bigot. I just use different standards, which doesn't make them, or me, any better.

"I didn't know you were a tea drinker," I said.

"Always have been. Don't like the taste of coffee."

We both played with our drinks, stirring in cream, savoring the aroma, then sipping gently. We were using ritual to avoid speaking to each other.

"Look, Linda, I feel really rotten about last night and—"

"And I feel bad 'cuz I've been pretty rude to you ever since you came to Purple Sage. I had no call to be that way."

At least it hadn't been one-sided.

"I didn't make any effort, either. I just assumed that because you lived out in the country…that…" The hole I had dug was deep and treacherous. "That we wouldn't have anything in common. I was wrong. I'm sorry."

I was holding up my teacup and Linda raised hers, touching it gently against mine. "Apology accepted."

"Yours, too," I said.

The tension in the room lessened some.

"These look wonderful," I said, lifting a cookie.

Linda nodded. "I get them special for Leigh. They're her favorite." She swallowed hard. "I'm sorry. I'm having a bad time with this."

"Linda, are you sure, absolutely positive, that Leigh couldn't have just gone off somewhere? Maybe because of something that Tom did?"

She was adamant. "She had no reason. Oh, she had issues with Tom, that's what she called them, 'issues,' but they were the kind that running away would only make worse. Besides, she didn't even see him yesterday after he left for work.''

"Maybe they argued on the phone. We've all done that.''

"I told you, she was supposed to come out here today. She was coming right after lunch and we were going to work on another rug.''

"Maybe she forgot,'' I said, stubborn for the sake of offering hope to us both. "Maybe she was so mad she just drove off without thinking.''

"She wouldn't do that. Besides, she'd be thinking by now, and even if she didn't call Tom, she'd've called me.'' She heaved a sigh. "She loved coming out here—she said it was like a vacation just getting to decorate, or paint, or whatever we were doing.'' Linda's shoulders slumped. "She couldn't do those things at her house.''

"She couldn't?'' I asked. "Why didn't Leigh redecorate the place? It needed it.''

"I'll say it did, but Tom wouldn't allow it. I swear, you'd've thought Beverly died the way he insisted that house stay just like she had it. Like some kind of shrine, only he expected Leigh to be happy with it. It was just awful.''

I was stunned. Tom was the one who wouldn't let the house be changed? "Wait, that can't be right. Tom divorced Bev. He's the one who walked out. He's the one who fell so madly in love with Leigh. Didn't he?''

"Oh, he was like a lovesick schoolboy at first. The way Leigh told it, he swooped in like some Prince Charming and swept her right off her feet. She hardly even knew him and he was proposing marriage!'' Linda frowned. "This is going to sound crazy, but marriages *are* crazy sometimes. I think there was as much father-daughter as anything.'' I must have looked as surprised as I felt because Linda went on, "Well, Leigh lost her father back when she was twelve, and she liked having someone older and wiser to lean on. And she thought he was rich, too, which didn't hurt. I suppose he was rich compared to her.''

I was reeling. "He didn't *treat* her like a daughter. Did he?''

"You mean sex?"

"I think I do."

"Oh, that was pretty regular according to what Leigh said. He just didn't trust her judgment and he wouldn't let her change anything in the house." Linda let out a long sigh. "I never wanted to believe it, but I don't think Tom ever stopped loving Beverly. Leigh thought that."

I sat back in the chair trying to absorb the idea. It made a bizarre kind of sense. Tom and Beverly's younger daughter had just gone off to college when Tom suddenly fell in love with Leigh. She could have been a substitute for his own girls. Leigh stepped into the place of youth and beauty that they held. Something like that.

As for Tom still loving Bev…that was harder to assimilate. And yet it did explain a number of things. For one, why the house hadn't changed, and also why Tom insisted on hosting the party for Beverly. Maybe it even explained Leigh's interest in Bev's dad.

Poor Leigh. It's impossible to live like another person, or had she tried to be another person?

This accounted for Leigh's recent stresses, too. I had worried so much about Beverly's feelings and how she was coping with coming back to Purple Sage and seeing Tom that it had never occurred to me Leigh might find it difficult to deal with. Even when Bev had suggested it, I had dismissed it.

The last several weeks must have been terrible for Leigh.

And then I remembered Bev's phone conversation with Tom last night. Something about him asking too much. How could he ask Bev for anything after divorcing her? And why would he? And what about Leigh?

"You know," I said, rubbing my forehead. "If I were Leigh, I would have run away long before this."

Linda agreed. "Except you and I have a lot more self-confidence than Leigh ever had. Makes a difference. She didn't have anyplace to run to, either. No family, and no friends outside of Purple Sage. She was determined to stay and fight it out, or whatever it took to keep her marriage."

The things we don't know about other people.

"Look," Linda said, suddenly intense. "I wasn't supposed to tell you any of this. You've got to promise me that you won't spread it around. It would just kill Leigh if other people knew."

"I won't say anything."

"Thank you. I shouldn't have repeated those things, but I'm just so worried, and Leigh needs some people on her side."

I nodded. "For whatever it's worth, I'm on her side."

"You aren't still mad at her for saying that about Dr. Bill's death?"

"No," I said. "I'm not mad."

"She was telling the truth, you know. There's something not right about him dying like that, and I just can't believe it was an accident. You see that, don't you?"

I had seen that all along. "Yes."

"He was walking away from the creek when she saw him. Away from the creek."

"But it couldn't have been suicide, either."

"So somebody pushed Dr. Bill into the water." Her heavy body shuddered as the phone rang.

THIRTEEN

"I SEE," LINDA SAID into the telephone. Had some coldness slipped into her voice? Was it anger or self-protection? "I could do that. You tell the sheriff I'll be there real soon. Tom, too. Did you want to talk to your wife? She's settin' right here."

Apparently it was Matt. Her eyes on me, Linda nodded twice, as if in response to his words, then said into the receiver, "I'll pass that on." After she hung up she said to me, "Matt and the sheriff would like us to join them at Leigh's."

"Is she…? Have they…?"

"No one's heard from her so they want us to look through her things and see if anything is missing, like she might have taken it with her."

A foul taste rose in my throat. Of all the things I didn't want to do, and places I didn't want to go…

"Of course," I said. "Right now?"

ON THE DRIVE into town I tried to think of things that a woman might take with her if she ran away from husband and home. Drawing on my own past, my strongest visions were of running *to* places—to my parent's house when my father had his first heart attack, and to my sister Elise's when she had been in a bad accident.

I have little memory of the packing or the trip to my father's bedside. The mind apparently blots out what is too frightening to remember.

With my sister's accident I'd felt more in control, still frightened, but able to cope. I had packed rationally as I recall, although on the drive to her house I do remember looking down to see what I was wearing. I was relieved to find that I was not in my pajamas.

If Leigh had left of her own accord, as I wanted to believe, then she had been running away. I'd only done that once in my life, running from Matt. Actually, Matt had little to do with it—he'd been out of town at the time. It was early in our marriage and after years of being the sole support for Jeremy and myself, I'd been running from commitment and dependence on Matt, which is something quite different.

In that instance I hadn't been packing clothes, but rather the possessions that gave me strength and separation. I'd put all my computer equipment and disks in the car first because those offered me some sense of identity and future. I'd taken picture albums and mementos that represented my past, and I'd been worried about Jeremy's belongings. Jeremy was furious with me for leaving Matt, and I knew that any little thing left behind at the ranch would merely feed his anger.

Eventually, of course, I had gotten around to all the mundane baggage that is part of our existence, but not initially. And shortly after that, Matt and I had gotten back together.

Surely if Leigh had been leaving for good she would have taken enough that Tom could tell. It brought me full circle, to Linda's insistence that Leigh wouldn't have left. So where was the woman? Driving around thinking? Staying in some motel in Austin or Llano?

Matt opened the door before I touched the bell. His handsome face was strained, even the cords on his neck looking tight.

"Hi," he said, before pulling me in and holding me close for a moment, as if in relief that I was there. He kissed the top of my head, my forehead, then my lips. He still held me as he said, "Are you okay?"

"I'm fine. How about you?"

"Much better now. I couldn't reach you at home, and then you didn't answer your cell phone."

"Oh…I'm sorry." Normally Matt doesn't worry about me, but under the circumstances, today was the exception. "I didn't even think about the cell. I went to Linda's."

"I remembered, eventually. How did that go?"

Before I could respond Linda pulled into the driveway, and came marching toward us, head lowered and fists clenched.

"Matt," she said with a nod.

He ushered her into the house, and Tom appeared from the kitchen. His eyes skimmed over us, then to the door that Matt was shutting, as if Leigh might have been with us.

"I'm sure this is nothing," Tom said first thing. He seemed tired, a stubble of a beard on his face, his hair greasy looking as he ran his fingers through it. "I know there's some logical explanation and Leigh will show up any time, but the sheriff seems to think…that it might be better if—"

Mac interrupted him from the staircase. "We're just covering all the bases," he said in that easy tone I admire so much. "Linda, why don't you and Jolie come on up here with me and see if you notice anything unusual? From a woman's point of view."

"Okay," I said, and Linda grunted, leading me upward, her footsteps heavy on the wooden risers. I followed her with the dread a child feels following a teacher to the principal's office. The master bedroom was down the hall on the right, and Mac stopped at the doorway.

"Y'all just go ahead, but call me if you find anything that doesn't look right."

I stepped into the room with a sense that I didn't belong. As I looked around the feeling became even stronger. The room was arranged exactly as it had been when Tom and Beverly had slept in it. And while the antique quilt on the bed wasn't the same one that Beverly had used, it was very similar. A reproduction antique trunk served as a night table, and lace curtains graced the windows. I was in very familiar, yet oddly unfamiliar, territory.

Linda's expression was sad.

"Are you doing okay?" I asked, stepping close to her.

She bobbed her head resolutely. "I am." With determination she went to the closet and looked at the clothes on the hangers. The first was a red striped T-shirt with odd bulges caused by a pair of jeans hung underneath. Next was the black dress Leigh had worn at the reception; fresh and sophisticated, it was ready for the next party.

I went into the luxurious master bath, flicking on the light to reveal a shiny world of sand-colored marble and sparkling mirrors. It was accessorized with thick towels, some deep mauve and others in navy blue. A navy one lay crumpled on the marble floor.

There were two sinks, and one of them had cosmetics on a mirrored tray, obviously Leigh's, so I opened the drawer nearest it. There were hair accessories in every style, size, and color, along with a couple of hairbrushes and several cans of hair wax, a tube of hair gel, and a curling iron.

The next drawer down was compartmentalized with plastic trays. In them I found makeup and facial products ranging from cleansing foam to glittering body gel. The drawer below held nail polish and remover, some expensive bath salts, and a set of travel cosmetic bags, brand-new with the tags still on them. They were empty.

I wasn't being efficient. I knew I should be looking for the basics that everyone packs for a trip. I looked around with purpose. In a gold cup on the counter were two toothbrushes, one navy blue and the other white and burgundy. The medicine cabinet on Leigh's side held toothpaste, her antiperspirant, dental floss, and some inexpensive lotion that was well used and small enough to travel. There was a prescription allergy medication, almost full. I looked at the label and saw that it had been refilled two days before the reception.

No sign that cosmetics or personal toiletries were missing, which made it appear that Leigh hadn't planned on being gone.

I closed everything and caught sight of myself in the mirror. My hair was damp and stringy, and my eyes looked lost—I felt that way, too. I ran my fingers through my hair and wiped a smear of mascara from under my eye. Despite my appearance, I wouldn't have used any of Leigh's combs or brushes for anything in the world. Under the circumstances this elegant marble bath felt like a tomb, and Leigh's things held distance and maybe death.

I washed the fingers that had touched the drawer knobs, then turned off the light and stepped into the other room.

Again there was the off-kilter sense of déjà vu, being in Beverly and Tom's room, when it wasn't Bev and Tom's room. I hadn't spent much time there in the past, but once or twice after a shopping trip we would sit there while Beverly unpacked her finds. Back then it had made me feel young and silly, whereas now I felt old and sad.

Linda was going through drawers, her nose wrinkled as if the clothes weren't clean.

"Any luck?" I asked, trying to bring a lightness to our dark task.

She shook her head and closed a drawer resolutely. "Nothing obviously missing. Anything in there?"

"Nothing."

The sheriff must have heard our voices because he stepped in from the hallway. "Linda, you think Leigh went on a trip?"

"No, sir, I don't. As far as I can tell, she didn't take any suitcases, or any clothes."

I added, "Or cosmetics. Although, I did have one other idea." I looked from Linda to the sheriff. "Did Leigh have anything that she liked to do a lot? Maybe she worked on a computer, or a favorite book—"

"Locker hooking," Linda said. "She kidded about being addicted to it. She'd be cooking dinner and working on some piece at the same time."

"Where did she keep her materials? Was there something portable?"

"A bag, kind of like a carpetbag, but taller and softer material. A green calico print." Linda added, "She hid her cigarettes in it, too. Sheriff, have you seen it?"

"No, ma'am, I don't believe I have. We'll need to ask Tom."

We followed him down the stairs to where Tom stood in the kitchen. He was holding a cup of coffee, watching the rain drizzle down the window. He looked up expectantly. "Did you find anything?"

"Linda," Mac began, "would you explain what you were asking about?"

She mentioned the green bag, and Tom started nodding, a dim hope appearing on his face. "Of course. She was always working on something. Placemats or hot pads, even rugs. I don't know why I didn't think of that." A brief smile slid across his haggard face. "We kidded about her being the Purple Sage Hooker. If that bag is missing then it would mean she intended to be gone a while. Wouldn't it?"

"Might," the sheriff said. "Let's give the house a look-see."

Matt appeared from outside and we fanned out through the rooms. It was the second time in a week that I had searched this house. This time there was a frantic hope, as if finding the bag was actually important. Like it might tell us something, but at some point I came to the realization that it wouldn't and we were simply filling time.

We didn't find the bag and Tom was clearly pleased. "That's a good sign. It means she took it with her. She meant to be gone, so at least we know she's all right."

I didn't know that at all. Leigh could have slid off the road into a ditch somewhere or been abducted. I could think of a dozen not-all-right things that could have happened to Leigh, with or without the bag, but I nodded at Tom, anyway. If this illusion made him feel better, then it wouldn't be me who shattered it.

"Sheriff," Tom continued, "I'm going to run upstairs and take a shower and put on some clean clothes while you do whatever official things you do." He turned to Matt, his hand outstretched. "Matt, thanks for visiting with me. I'm fine now. As Bev's dad says, 'I don't need no baby-sitter.' But I really appreciate the company." He shook hands with Matt and even smiled.

"Not a problem," Matt said.

Tom shook hands with the sheriff. "Mac, I appreciate your help, but I think it's going to be okay." He was looking toward the stairs, a man on a mission, which I guessed was to prepare for the return of his errant wife.

But why just because of a craft bag?

Mac slowed him down. "It's been almost twenty-four hours and I figure it's time to put out a missing person report. Make it official. Get some people looking for her."

"Why?" Tom appeared surprised. "We know she left on purpose and she'll be back. Probably in an hour or so."

I departed, not wanting to be there when Mac pointed out oh so gently that Tom was living in Wonderland.

FOURTEEN

THE LASAGNAS WERE finally on the table along with two loaves of warm bread, a salad, and a rich merlot. In the refrigerator was dessert, a lemon meringue pie from the Bakery. All of my guests were actually seated around the table, talking, eating, and having a wonderful time. Beverly and her father were joining us after dinner.

"What do they call that restaurant? PF Flyers?" my mother asked.

"Those are tennis shoes!" Jeremy said, and everyone laughed. "PK Wangs."

"That's the place," Diane agreed. "That's where we had dinner last night. I can't believe you had lunch there."

"I'll never go back," my mother said. "That waiter! 'And I'll mix your sauces so that they are both delicious and authentic.' Authentic from where? I asked him. I mean the kid was from the Midwest and we were sitting in the middle of San Angelo! When I was in China I took several cooking classes. Nothing on that menu was authentic. He was really snippy when I told him that."

"Let me tell you what he said to us," Diane countered. Diane has never been to China but she never loses at Trivial Pursuit. If they ever got her on "Who Wants to Be a Millionaire?" she'd walk out with the money and all three of her lifelines still intact. "He told us that all Chinese food is low fat. And he meant it! I read that in China they deep-fry fat."

My mother agreed. "It's a delicacy, but the first time they

put it in front of me I was trying to say 'thank you' in Chinese and not throw up, all at the same time!''

More laughter. Everyone was so jovial it looked like a TV commercial.

I managed a smile, but I felt like I was watching it from the outside.

I'm not sure why that happened, but the more fun they seemed to be having, the more detached I felt. Even the weather was on their side, with blue skies and fluffy white clouds that looked like mountains and ships, but my mood remained dark.

I kept thinking about Dr. Bill and Gretchen. His sudden death still hurt me and I knew how much worse it must be for Gretchen. At least she had some company; several of her old friends from Dallas had arrived, along with her sister. Friends were important but they couldn't fill that horrible void left by the death of her husband. He had been by her side for more than forty years, her best friend through her adult life. And what did she know about his death? Had she heard the suicide story? I didn't think she'd believe it, and just the thought of a rumor about her Dr. Bill would make her angry. That might not be such a bad thing; it wouldn't stop the grief, but it might allow her to put pieces of it aside while she fought back.

I couldn't even blame Leigh for starting the rumor because she was gone. G-O-N-E, gone, as she had said of Mr. Kendall at the reception. The sheriff had organized the search from the Greers' house, using only law enforcement officers, not civilians.

Matt nudged my arm. ''Are you all right?'' The others were busily chatting along, paying no attention, until Matt spoke.

''Just thinking,'' I said with a smile.

My mother gave a half laugh. ''Jolie had some cockamamie idea about Dr. Bill's death and it came to naught. She's sulking.''

''I'm not.''

Trey and Jeremy weren't sure how to react, and Randy gave a small snort.

Matt said, "Jolie gave up sulking for Lent years ago and hasn't done it since. And when she wants to find out something, she's usually successful."

"Really?" my mother said.

"Absolutely," Diane agreed. "She's the best newsperson we've had on KSGE since…well, since I moved here. She uses those same investigative skills in her writing. Have you read the book she sold? I know it isn't out yet, but—"

Diane was over the top on this one, and I was relieved when the phone cut her short. Even with two teenagers in the house I got there first. "Hello?"

"Jolie? It's Tom Greer. Is Matt around?" He sounded out of breath.

"Is Leigh back?"

"Not quite, but close. They found her car out by the lake. It's a long story. Can I talk to Matt?"

My husband was already beside me, as if he'd known that it was going to be for him.

"It's Tom," I said.

Matt braced himself, or maybe I imagined that momentary muscle stiffening, as he reached for the phone. "What's the news?" he asked.

I stayed by his side, listening as he nodded and asked questions that gave me little information.

"Where? On the north end?… They did?… What does Mac think?… Uh-huh… But…" Then he listened for a long time without speaking.

At last he hung up and I discovered that I wasn't the only one waiting for Matt to tell the story. There was silence in the dining room.

Matt touched my elbow and together we walked back to the table.

"They haven't found her?" Trey asked.

"No."

"You aren't going over there?" I asked.

"Not tonight. Tom thinks it will all be over in a few hours."

"He does?" I pulled out my chair and sat.

Matt said, "They found Leigh's car somewhere out on the northwest end of the lake, beyond Sage Lake Estates. It must have been one of those small roads that doesn't pass any houses, but winds through the trees, directly down to the water. Obviously she wasn't in the car, but then neither was her purse, or that bag with her craft things."

"What craft things?" my mother asked.

"Leigh was into locker hooking," I said.

Diane explained further. "They take strips of calico material and weave them through rug backing. It's really beautiful and Leigh loved doing it. I'd see her out on her deck just working away."

Mom nodded. "Yes, I've seen some. It's very pretty."

"Leigh always had her bag of materials close by," I said. "Tom was thrilled that we didn't find it at the house. Now they haven't found it in her car."

"So, what does that mean?" my mother asked.

"I don't know." I was envisioning a number of scenarios that weren't encouraging.

Matt was the one who explained. "Tom thinks Leigh left because she wanted to. She planned to be gone long enough to do some weaving, but not so long that she'd need an overnight bag. He didn't let her smoke in the house, so he thought maybe she'd gone somewhere to sit inside and work on some mats that she was making."

"So that was her plan?" Mom asked. "She intended to sit in her car and watch the water and weave. She could smoke in her car, couldn't she?"

"I assume so," Matt said.

"She could," Diane said. "I had to get a ride with her one day, and the inside of the windshield was gray with smoke."

Matt told us the whole story. Apparently Leigh's car got stuck in the mud on the side of the road but she didn't walk out to the main road looking for help. Instead it appeared like she waited until someone came along to rescue her. The sheriff's office could tell by the tire tracks that a second car had been there, and it appeared that Leigh had gotten into it and they had driven off.

Even though it hadn't rained since yesterday evening it had drizzled enough that it was impossible to tell how fresh the tracks were, so the sheriff couldn't say when Leigh had left the lake. It could have been last night, it could have been half an hour ago.

"Cell phone!" Randy said, joining the conversation for the first time. At sixteen he and Jeremy believed in all the finest electronics. "Did she have a cell phone with her?"

Matt looked surprised, either at the question or at the realization that both Jeremy and Randy were still in the room. So did Trey.

"Didn't you two rent a movie for tonight?" he asked.

"They did," I said. "Go watch someone blow up the world, okay? We'll bring your pie later."

"In other words," Jeremy said, "you don't want us to hear what you're going to say. Nice and subtle, Mom."

Randy untangled himself from the chair legs, saying, "They're probably going to talk about sex."

Diane raised an eyebrow. "This is Purple Sage, a shallow and fundamentalist community. People do not have sex in Purple Sage."

"And," I said, "I want to know why you thought of that? What have you two been watching?"

"The news," Jeremy said.

My mother patted Jeremy's arm as he went by her chair. "Don't worry, honey, if we say anything really interesting, I'll be sure and tell you."

"Thanks, Gram. Bring pie, too."

As they climbed up the stairs Trey looked around at us. "You know, that question about a cell phone was a good one. Did she have one?"

"She had one," Matt said. "But it was either turned off or not charged. Tom said that was pretty standard with Leigh."

Diane had gotten up to pour more coffee. "There's a little glitch in the scenario about Leigh getting stuck in the mud and then being rescued by a good Samaritan."

"Who could have been a very bad person," I added.

"Yes, since she hasn't shown up, but there's something else. That area of the lake is pretty remote. Trey, remember when we were looking at property out there? You couldn't see the water from the lake road anywhere in that area; in fact, you had to drive for at least a quarter to a half mile to get to the lake. If Leigh was parked near the water, weaving or whatever, a car on the Lake Road couldn't see her. It makes me suspect that Leigh was meeting someone out there."

Trey said, "Then there is sex in Purple Sage."

My mother was frowning. "Couldn't there have been another reason to meet someone out at the lake? It's not much more than, what? ten miles from town?"

"Fifteen to that area," I said. "And it was remote, secluded, and very muddy."

"I agree," Diane said. "It was also still drizzling, and it was cold. If you're going to meet someone innocently, then why not at the Sage Café?"

We were silent for a while, thinking that one through. Finally it was my mother who said, "I understand that she was young and very pretty, and that her husband was older."

Trey said. "Our age. That isn't a *lot* older."

"What I was wondering about," Mom went on, "is whether she might have had a boyfriend? Any gossip about that?"

We talked it through and concurred that none of us had heard even a wisp of a rumor. It left me as puzzled as ever, but my mother had other thoughts.

"If this were Dallas or Houston it would be a forgone conclusion that someone had come along and either kidnapped Leigh Greer or killed her. Probably raped her in the process. And just because this is Purple Sage doesn't mean it didn't happen. Criminals don't respect county lines."

Which brought us back to the question of where Leigh was now and what was happening to her. Or what had happened to her.

I WENT TO BED in a dismal mood and even Trey's good night to all of us, "See you in the morning. And remember, this is

Purple Sage. People don't have sex in Purple Sage," hadn't gotten much more than a wan smile out of any of us.

The phone hadn't rung, and none of us were willing to call Tom's house on the off chance that he was actually sleeping. Nor was I willing to call the sheriff's office for information. So we slept fitfully, and I woke with a feeling of urgency.

Dr. Bill's funeral was to be held on Monday, just one day away, and if the rumors continued there would be few to honor him. I had to do something about that, and I intended to; I just wasn't sure what.

Breakfast was a big noisy meal, with Trey, Matt, and my mother all cooking. My mother made blueberry pancakes, something I had no idea she could do, particularly since I would have sworn there were no blueberries in the house, or in Purple Sage. Still Mom worked some magic and church was skipped so that everyone could partake.

After effusive thanks to the chefs, Diane and I foisted the cleanup on Jeremy and Randy, saying it was only fair, since they had eaten the most. Then Matt went to help feed the cattle, my mother left for the shelter, while Diane and Trey drove home to see about the arrival of their new carpet.

Left in an empty house, I went into town. I'm not sure what I planned to accomplish. My excuse was to pick up milk and a few groceries, but my first stop was the radio station. It was quiet—a taped program was on the air, and I merely waved at the announcer as I headed straight for the news basket. But there was nothing. The story on Leigh Greer mentioned the finding of the car "near the lake." That was all. I had hoped that overnight something new had been released, but it doesn't always happen that way. I was frowning about it when the phone rang and I picked it up automatically.

"Jolie, it's Ute," she said in her soft German accent. "I'm at the newspaper office and I saw you drive by. I hope you don't mind that I called."

"No, no, I don't mind. What's up?"

"When I got back from church I had a message from Rhonda. She needs pictures of the drawdown tube for tomorrow's paper. The problem is that I don't know what a drawdown tube is, or where it is! Have you heard of this?"

"Sure. It's like an overflow tube at the lake. When the water gets too high it runs down the tube into Cavalry Creek. That's part of what makes the creek so high."

"Can you give me directions? I'm sorry to be so slow, but I'm not familiar with the lake."

Ute and her family had only been in Purple Sage for about five winter months, so there had been no reason for visiting Sage Lake.

"Look," I said. "Why don't I ride with you? I'd like to see it, anyway."

"I have to photograph the road where Leigh Greer's car was found, as well."

A shiver ran up my arms. "I'll go there with you, too."

"Really? You would do that for me?"

"Actually," I said honestly, "I'm doing it for both of us."

"I will be there in two minutes before you change your mind."

"Meet you at the back door."

I reached for my purse, and on the way out I stopped to check the weather computer. The news was not what I had hoped:

Tropical storm Regan has picked up intensity over the gulf and is now making her way landward at approximately twenty miles an hour.

   It is expected to make landfall tomorrow near Galveston, moving inland to Friendswood and Houston.

   If this storm follows its previous pattern, heavy rains could occur, causing flooding at low water crossings and in low-lying areas.

   The potential for flooding is particularly dangerous where the ground is already saturated.

FIFTEEN

"IT'S AROUND THIS CURVE," I said as Ute piloted her minivan along the Lake Road.

Except for the very elegant Sage Lake Estates, and a rather rustic public dock and marina, most of the land around Sage Lake is undeveloped. There are oak and mesquite trees, mingled with juniper and algarita bushes. Scrub, they call it. In the spring, which I hoped would be soon, there would be wildflowers in colors from white to scarlet, and the purple-blue of the bluebonnet.

Today, with the sky still deep and clear and the trees freshly green, the lake wasn't a bad place to be. Except for our mission.

"Up on the top of the bridge would be the best place to view the drawdown tube," I offered.

"Why don't we go first to the road where they found the car? We can get the worst over right away."

"Fine."

"Look, we can see the creek." She pointed to our right. We were on the bridge now, and in the distance was the highway, where the creek ran under it; through the trees beyond I could just make out the level spot where Dr. Bill's car had been parked the night he died. A sadness washed through me, warm, yet painful, like a slowly bleeding wound.

Ute's face went cold as she must have spotted the place, too.

"That was so tragic about Dr. Bill," she said. "He was

such a nice man. I have a wonderful picture of the two of you at the reception. I must send it to you.''

"I'd love that, although, I don't know if I can look at it yet.''

"I am just the same way. I cannot bring myself to look at the video I made. I want to take a copy to Gretchen, but it might be very painful for her right now.'' Her eyes were back on the road, and she seemed softer, more her normal self. ''It is not possible that he jumped into the creek to kill himself. Do you believe that?''

"No.''

"And do you know what really makes me upset?'' Her voice thickened with anger and accent. ''That people would say such a thing, and then condemn Dr. Bill. It was Leigh who started it, wasn't it? And then it went on and on through the town, so that everyone is talking. If he killed himself, which I don't believe, then whose business is it? Why do they think they have the right to comment?'' There was no answer and none was expected. ''It's especially terrible after everything Dr. Bill did for this community, and for that church.''

"The Lakeside Fundamentalist Church of God,'' I said.

"Do you know I almost went to this church when we first came to Purple Sage? The children were invited to Sunday school and I thought, well yes, why not? But then, one of the little girls told Jessika, my daughter in ninth grade, that the minister at the church preached about evil, and do you know who he said was evil? First he said Islamics because of the World Trade Center.''

"How awful.''

"Yes, but then he talked about more people who were evil. Germans. Because we were Nazis! That is like saying Americans are immoral because of what Bill Clinton did. Or all Muslims are bad because of Osama Bin Laden.'' She stopped and said, ''How can anyone blame all Germans?''

"You can't. It's like blaming me for slavery—I wasn't even born,'' I said. ''It's ridiculous to hold a grudge against a whole country or race or even a religion.''

"That is right, and my children are certainly not responsible for what some madman did almost seventy years ago. To blame *them* is evil."

"Speak of the devil," I said, "there's his church."

I had seen it before, but that was during the building stage. Back then I had not realized the new minister, Brother Binder, was using his pulpit to segregate the congregation from the rest of the community.

Ute slowed the van and I had time to stare at the building. It was ugly, with tin siding in beige and brown, and with a tall white spire reaching up from the roof. The combination was odd, but no more so than the grounds. A white picket fence went across the front of the church yard with flower beds both in front of it and behind. Lawn surrounded the building, ending at sidewalks that ran next to the gravel parking areas.

It looked cheap, like a stage set viewed too closely.

The car was barely crawling along now.

Ute said, "I think he has told the people not to attend Dr. Bill's funeral. Did you notice that no one from the church had gone to Gretchen's house?"

"I noticed," I said. We were the only car on the road, so Ute took advantage of the emptiness to stop completely.

"I wonder what he preached this morning?" she asked.

"People gawking at his church?"

Which was exactly what we were doing when the doors opened and the congregation came pouring out.

Ute sped up and we went over a hill putting the church out of sight. "Yesterday he said that Dr. Bill was in hell, and they should not mention his name."

"Are you serious? That's horrible. How do you know?"

"Franzi is working part-time at the Bakery," she said. Franzi was Ute's oldest daughter. "You know how busy they are on Saturdays. A customer came in to buy bread and she said it was for Gretchen. When the woman left, one of the other girls told Franzi she shouldn't speak about Dr. Bill, because he was burning in hell."

"You read about things like that," I said "but I didn't think it happened in real life."

"I did not know that Purple Sage was this way, or we would not have moved our family here."

"It's not this way," I said. "At least not *all* this way." I explained about the nine founding families, all from one religious congregation, and how their influence could still be felt. "But it's never been this bad before. It's Brother Binder. Before he came there was a portion of the town that didn't drink or dance, but it wasn't a big deal. Now it's getting worse."

Ute braked at the stop sign marking the beginning of Sage Lake Estates. It didn't take long to drive through the small community with its forty or so immaculate homes, then Ute started counting roads off to our left.

"It's the third road," she said, slowing at a break in the trees. "The next one."

We turned and were back in the wilds. No phone lines, no mailboxes, no sign that anyone else had ever been here except for the one-lane, deeply rutted road in front of us.

"I hope we don't get stuck," I said, after a few minutes of driving through the heavy mud.

"If you are feeling brave," she said, "we could walk."

"Fine with me."

She parked off to the side, where there was some ground cover that would give our tires something to grasp, and we climbed out. From here we could no longer see the road behind us, or the lake in front of us. It was quiet except for the sounds we were making as we walked along, trying to stay as far off the muddy road as possible. That wasn't much more than a few feet because of the dense brush.

Just a few minutes' walk and we came to the place where Leigh's car had been. It was easy to spot; the multiple tire marks, apparently from official vehicles, ended almost in a solid row. Beyond them was a large empty area that overlooked the water. There was no beach, and the lake was so high that below us trees were half submerged.

"What could she have been doing here?" Ute asked, taking it all in.

I told her what little I knew, and some of what we had surmised the night before. Ute nodded. "Yes, this would be a very peaceful place to spend some time alone, but of course, she couldn't have been by herself.'' She pointed to the tire marks. Many feet had walked around the tread marks, probably deputies and such, but still it was clear that two vehicles had been parked side by side.

''So sad,'' she said, with a shake of her head.

I agreed but in the sunshine there was no feeling of Leigh's presence, and the land held no sorrow at her absence.

Ute began to shoot pictures, and I moved out of range, to the edge of the lake. It was dark and murky, silt rising with the warmer bottom water. Almost fifteen feet out a bird was perched on the top of a tree.

I wondered if Leigh had seen that same treetop; if it was the last thing she had ever seen.

No, ridiculous. Leigh had left this remote place with her purse and her apple-green craft bag. A kidnapper wouldn't take those things. Oh, perhaps he would want the purse if it had money or credit cards, but certainly not the locker hooking bag. To me it meant Leigh left with someone she knew.

Someone she met here by a fortuitous accident? Or on purpose?

It didn't matter. What was important was where they had gone, and I didn't have a single idea.

''Do you think the sheriff searched for her body?'' Ute asked.

''That's an ugly thought.'' I went to stand where she was peering into the brush. I saw what I thought were signs that people had gone through this way—weeds flattened by heavy boots, twigs that had been broken, and narrow paths that were too tall to be created by animals.

The wind was picking up, and I realized that I had my arms wrapped tightly around my body. I might have been imagining all those telltale clues to the investigation, but Mac could tell me when I called the sheriff's office later.

Ute slung her camera over her shoulder. ''You look cold; I'm sorry. I am finished now. Are you ready?''

''More than ready.''

The walk back to the car was brisk, and as we were slamming the doors, Ute said, "I know I should not feel this way, but I am still so angry at Brother Binder. It is like a cancer growing in me; do you ever feel that way?"

"Unfortunately, yes."

"And I am mad at the whole Lakeside church, too. All of them, hypocrites. Is that the word? Where they preach about doing one thing and then do another?"

"That's the word," I said.

She was backing and turning to get out of the tiny lane. "I am especially angry at the minister. Brother Binder preaches that they are so good and so holy. Above the rest of us in Purple Sage, yes?"

"I've never actually heard him, but yes, I've been told that he says most of us are sinners."

"You see! Wolfgang and I were in San Angelo, and we stopped at the liquor store because I wanted to get some Kahlua. I love Kahlua, and I would be fat if I drank as much as I wanted! When we were walking into the store I saw the owner in the alley putting a whole case of vodka, a case, into the back of a green minivan. It was almost exactly like this one and Wolfgang teased me that I had a doppelgänger who drank a lot. When the car drove off it went right past us, and guess who was driving?"

"Brother Binder?"

"Exactly."

"He could have been getting empty boxes. For a move, or something."

"No. You can tell when a box is heavy by the way it is carried. This one was heavy." We were on the Lake Road now, headed back the way we had come. "Besides, I said to the owner when he came inside, 'That was Brother Binder from Purple Sage.' And do you know what he said? He said, 'Please pretend you didn't see him. He is one of my best customers.' A best customer! I have never told anyone that I saw him until now, but now I am mad. He can drink all he wants but if someone else does, then they will go to hell. And if someone dies in a creek, then they suffer in hell. I don't believe in hell. I should have been Jewish—they don't believe in hell, either.''

"It makes me angry, too. Especially because people won't attend Dr. Bill's funeral because Brother Binder told them not to.''

"Then we must talk to him now. Right now while we are angry. We will tackle the lion in his den.''

I turned to stare at her very determined profile. I had always thought Ute was quiet and sweet; little did I know what a powerful will lay under the gentle exterior. "I don't know that we should—''

"Of course we should not, but he *should* hear a piece of our mind. For once he should know the consequences of what he has done.''

"What would we say?''

"Whatever comes out of our mouths.''

"Oh, Lord. Literally!'' She reminded me of a forties movie heroine who suddenly turns into what the hero calls a hellion. The speed of the minivan even matched her anger. "Wait, slow down a little and let's think about this. Just for a minute, okay?''

Ute looked at the speedometer, and immediately took her foot off the gas pedal. "I am sorry, I do not mean to kill us. Even if there is not a hell we don't want to be dead.''

"Okay,'' I said, "we'll tackle Brother Binder, but do you know the saying that you catch more flies with honey than with vinegar?''

"No.'' She frowned. "But I see what you mean. You think we should be kind when we approach him. That we might get him to agree.''

"Absolutely. If people get defensive then they won't change their position. We have to appeal to his sense of goodness; then we'll have a chance.''

She spent more time considering it, then slowly nodded as the church spire came into view. "Yes, we will do this. Although I would like to yell at him. For Dr. Bill's sake and for the satisfaction.''

"So, if you're still mad after we talk with Brother Binder, then we can slash his tires."

THE TWO GREEN minivans were side by side, the only two vehicles on the right side of the church. In the other lot was an older white Chevy.

"So, we know he is here," Ute said as we made our way to the small metal building marked "Office."

Inside, behind the cheap metal desk, was a thin middle-aged woman who gave us a bright smile.

"How can I help you?"

"We are looking for Brother Binder," I said. "But if this isn't a good time…"

"Oh, I'm so sorry. He is having dinner with the Ozdorfs." Dinner in the country being at noon. "I don't expect him back for another hour or two."

"His car is here," Ute said.

"Yes, I know. He rode over with some other folks. Is it urgent, or can I help you?"

"No," I said. "We can catch him another time."

Again the bright smile. "Thank you for stopping by. I hope we'll see you both later."

I suspected that she was talking about during church service, but Ute had her own take on it.

"Yes," she said, "I'm sure we will see you at Dr. Bill's funeral service tomorrow. You will be there, won't you?"

The woman stiffened, her eyes suddenly wide and tight. "No, no, you won't see me."

"You didn't know Dr. Bill?" Ute pushed.

"I knew him, of course." She looked around to make sure that no one else was nearby. "Right now I'm so mad at him that I could spit. Suffering in hell for eternity, for no good reason! He was a smart man—he should have known better than to commit suicide."

"You don't have any proof that he killed himself," Ute said, her eyes blazing right back. "It could have been an accident."

"That's not what we were told."

"Well, maybe the person who told you was wrong. Or a liar. Or just a bad person."

The woman was surprised and words failed her. "No. Uh, no."

"Why? Wasn't it a human being? People have faults, you know. All people."

I slid my arm through Ute's, saying to the woman, "We'll talk to Brother Binder when it's more convenient."

Ute balked, but the woman was over her moment of speechlessness. "Talking about someone in hell is a sin, and 'the wages of sin shall be death.' That's what Brother Binder says."

"That is a lie," Ute snapped. "Do you make up your own Bible—"

"We do not. We read the Good Book, and we have a minister who is versed at the interpretation. Evil shall be damned, and I hope you know that."

"Thank you," I said. "Thank you so much for your time."

Ute was with me now, and we hurried out the door to the waiting minivan. I almost got into the wrong one. I was reaching for the door handle when Ute called to me.

"Jolie. This one. That's Brother Binder's."

"Sorry." I was in a hurry to get away, but I still peered in the windows as I passed. There was nothing to see; why would there be? The green van was parked in full view of his congregation.

"Witch," Ute mumbled as I climbed in the car and she started it. "I think she cursed us."

"A death threat? It was just a quote. A misquote. Who says you can't talk about someone in hell?" I paused as she pulled out on the highway. "It's insane."

We were silent as we sped along. I was grateful that we were away from the church and even more grateful that we hadn't found Brother Binder, although I did think there was a great deal to be said to the man. He needed to know that despite the fundamental leanings of the community there had never been a rift in the population until he'd arrived. He needed to understand that we were a small town that pulled together, because that's the way of life in the country. If we wanted schools that had anything to offer our children, and amenities for the rest of us, then we had to unite to provide them. As the African fable says, it takes a village to raise a child. It also takes a village to deal with disaster, care for the elderly, and create a warm and loving space for all of those things to occur.

Brother Binder needed to understand that when a leader pulls one group aside and says we are different, special, and better, then that leader is feeding separatism. It creates bigotry and hate between people who have fewer differences than they have things in common.

Ute was right, someone ought to have a long talk with Brother Binder, but I wasn't the one to do it, at least not today.

"Right here?" Ute asked. In front of us was the bridge, and I had been so absorbed that I had almost let her drive past it.

"Yes. You can park on either side."

She pulled into a grassy area next to the bridge and took her camera from its case before we got out. The air was heavy with humidity as we walked along the sidewalk that crossed the bridge. The sound of the moving water was loud here. I looked down. The lake was dark, filled with mud from the bottom, as it surged down into the drawdown tube.

"It is quite something," Ute said. She was almost yelling to be heard. "I can't believe how loud it is, and how fast the water is moving."

We reached the center of the bridge and looked right down into the tube. It was like peering down a tub drain as the bathwater rushed out. Amazing to think that usually the tube stood well out of the water and only the excessive rain had made it useful. By channeling the overflow across to the creek it saved the lake residents from flooding.

As the water went into the tube it was thin and almost transparent. I saw a fish go over and wondered if it would survive.

"I wish I had a basketball," Ute said. "To throw in, and see it come out over there."

"I'll bet we're not the first ones to think of it," I said, as she began to snap pictures.

The water continued its furious flow down the tube. I crossed the bridge to watch the water emerge, frothing as it poured onto the surface of the creek. It was just as loud here, and even more powerful looking.

"We have a parade," Ute called.

I went back to see what she was talking about. Apparently debris had broken loose from some nearby spot. There were chunks of a Styrofoam cooler matted with broken fishing line, a few branches, and something that I couldn't quite make out. It was green, but so knotted it was impossible to tell what it was. One small area billowed up as it filled with air, and I realized it was a piece of cloth. Probably a bathing suit that someone had laid out on a rock to dry.

As the clog of things drew closer I realized that the material was calico. It must have been a child's swimsuit. That gave me a shiver, but there was no sign of a child attached and there hadn't been any report of a child missing.

"I'll get a picture and we'll caption it, 'Anyone missing a cooler?'" Ute said.

I nodded but didn't take my eyes off the material. I had seen it somewhere before—recently.

The jetsam was pulled along by the force of the current, swirled, then paused almost underneath us when it caught in some mysterious current. I could see the apple-green calico material clearly. The mass surged forward and slid almost gracefully toward the tube. One of the tangled branches caught and hung on the edge, giving me one more long look at the calico. There was some light wood on it as well. A handle. It seemed to pause one tantalizing moment, then the whole tangle and all the pieces rushed away.

I watched the material go, and suddenly I knew what it was. My stomach roiled and my knees went weak.

It was Leigh Greer's craft bag.

SIXTEEN

THE BAG AND all it might tell us had slipped away.

I stood watching in desperation as the water gushed down and away. And then I remembered that it wasn't gone. We had one last chance to capture what we'd seen, and that, too, was brief.

"Ute, we need a picture. Quick!" I pointed across the road and she turned. Without thinking, or looking, I grabbed her arm and made a dash for the other side of the bridge. In my haste I almost got us hit by a car.

"Dear God!" she said, running with me.

Once we were out of harm's way, I said, "I'm sorry. Quick. Down there."

"What?" She peered over the side, her camera already up to her face.

"That cooler is going to come out. And the green cloth. It was Leigh Greer's craft bag, I'm almost sure of it. There! There it is!"

Ute was focusing and snapping the shutter with amazing speed. I think she had gotten five shots before the bag, now no longer recognizable as anything but a color, disappeared under the water.

"That's the end," she said, taking her first breath since we'd torn across the road.

"I'm sorry; I didn't intend to make that so dangerous." I was also sucking in air, in part from the urgency of our moves, but also to soothe my churning stomach. "Someone needs to know about this. I think the sheriff is the right person, because this makes a big difference to what might have happened to Leigh.''

That was the crux of the matter—if Leigh's things were in the lake, it was less likely that she had disappeared of her own volition, and far more probable that something terrible had happened to her. It was that knowledge that made my stomach hurt.

We started toward the car and I took another look at the drawdown tube, wishing I had imagined what I'd seen.

Another possibility caught me. I clutched Ute's arm as I said, "What if Leigh was on the edge of the lake—on one of those rocks and she fell in and drowned?"

"Oh my God. Of course that could have happened! The water is so dangerous when it is rising fast, you don't even realize that it is moving swiftly. She could have been carried away without anyone knowing."

As soon as we were in the van, I said, "I kept believing that someone else had to be involved. You know, a kidnapper or another man."

"Yes. I thought, 'Now here is a beautiful young woman with an older husband. If she is missing there must be a boyfriend, someone young and handsome.' But that could be all wrong. It could be an accident."

I pictured the swiftly moving water near the drawdown tube and shivered. "Will it take you long to get the film developed?" I asked.

We were entering the city limits of Purple Sage and Ute was taking her own back route toward downtown. "The camera is digital—the pictures are on a disk, so all you have to do is put them in the computer and you can see them."

"Can you do that at the sheriff's office?"

"Their computer is so old it still has a green screen. No, I will have to print them at the *Tribune,* but it won't take more than fifteen minutes."

I looked at my watch. "I'll bet the sheriff is at the courthouse. Can you drop me off there? Maybe we can catch him before lunch; it's almost noon."

"Oh, no! Is it that late? I was supposed to pick up Jessika fifteen minutes ago. She's at the library. Jolie, do you mind...?"

"Of course not."

"It will only take a moment. If I know Jessika, she will be standing out front waiting."

When we pulled up in front of the library I had expected to see one very annoyed Jessika, but she was sitting on the edge of the flower bed, reading.

Ute stopped the van, her window already down. "Jessika, I am sorry we are late."

Jessi looked up, the expression in her big brown eyes surprised, as if she had been far away in the pages of the book she held. "Oh, that's okay," she said, hoisting up her backpack and climbing into the back seat. "Hi, Mrs. Wyatt."

Jessika is a year or two younger than Jeremy, but in Purple Sage we don't have a middle school, only elementary and high school, so the two of them had worked together on a school library project, which is how I knew her.

Jeremy called her "the kid," although I noticed that they spent a great deal of time on that project. There was never a date, Jessika was too young for that, and Jeremy didn't date much, but they had gone horseback riding a couple of times at the ranch.

The project they tackled was the progress of a book from inception to print, and Purple Sage's resident author, June Ingram, had contributed most of the materials. I am also a writer, although my career is in the early stages. My first book was accepted for publication just a few months back, and besides a small advance check, I don't have much to show just yet.

Still, Jessika used some of my manuscript pages for the display, and had the great good taste to enjoy those few pages so much she asked to read the whole manuscript. Which, of course, I let her do. And she loved the book.

I concluded she is a young woman who is wise beyond her years and brilliant besides.

"Hi, Jessi," I said. "It's my fault we're late. We were out

at the lake." I didn't say more. I wasn't sure how much she knew about Leigh's disappearance, or how much Ute wanted her to know.

Jessika was far ahead of me. "Mom said she was going to take pictures of the place where they found Leigh Greer's car."

"Then you know all about that."

"As a parent, you cannot stop it," Ute said. "It is the real world, and they have to live in it. So, we talk about these things as a family." Her accent seemed even more pronounced when compared to the perfect English of her all-American daughter.

"Besides, everyone at school is talking about it." Jessi rolled her eyes. "One girl even said she saw Mrs. Greer the night she disappeared."

"She did? Who was it? Did she tell the sheriff?" I asked.

Jessika shrugged. "No. It doesn't matter though, because I don't think she was telling the truth. You know that kind of person?"

"Not so many anymore," I said. "Who is she?"

"Well…" Jessika looked uncomfortable. We had just hit the teen code of silence. "I'm sure it wasn't true."

Ute said, "It is all right, you can tell Mrs. Wyatt. It is more important that Leigh Greer is found, don't you think?"

"Sure. It's just that she, the girl, wasn't supposed to be at the lake, and if her parents find out, she'll be in big trouble. You know."

"We are not going to her parents," Ute said.

Jessika took a breath and said, "It was Faith Melman."

Of course she wasn't supposed to be at the lake, or anywhere else that was fun, but Faith had her own way of dealing with her parent's strict rules.

I had experienced it firsthand one evening when Jeremy and a friend were taking dates to San Angelo for a concert. Since the ranch is on the way, the other three picked up Jeremy. Faith Melman had come in the door a plain, mousy young woman in a nondescript dress. She carried a large brown paper bag with her.

"May I borrow your bathroom, Mrs. Wyatt?" she had asked as soon as the introductions were over.

I wanted to ask her where she was planning to take the bathroom, and wouldn't she prefer simply to go in it, but I merely said, "Of course," and showed her the way.

She stayed in the bathroom for more than ten minutes, and while I was getting concerned the three teens seemed not to notice her absence or the passing of time. Just when I was ready to say something, Faith Melman emerged, but as a totally different person. Her hair was fluffed and pouffed, her makeup was expertly, although a little too generously, applied, and she wore a Lycra dress that was about the same length as a T-shirt, only much tighter.

We all ogled her, especially her date. When he moved in to put his arm around her, she smiled up at him seductively, then noticed that I was in the room and dropped her head in a gesture that was probably intended to look shy and proper. It was too late for that.

Jeremy had spotted my expression and immediately herded the others toward the door. I barely had time to throw out the obligatory, "Have fun" and "Drive carefully" before they were gone.

The next day Jeremy and I had a discussion about the whole thing. Admittedly she hadn't been Jeremy's date, but I'd still felt used and told him flat out that I would not be a part of that kind of deception again. While he argued that Faith was really a nice girl and it was all her parents' fault, which may have been true, I think he realized that Faith was a huge problem just waiting to happen to someone.

I also understood why Jessika didn't believe Faith's story but any grain of truth might help in the search.

"Jessi," I said. "Were there other people who heard Faith say she saw Leigh?"

"Uh-huh. She was bragging about it."

"Who is this Faith Melman?" Ute asked. She was driving now, but slowly.

Jessika said, "Faith is in Jeremy's class."

"The family has a farm south of town," I added. "They don't socialize a lot. Jeremy was in 4H for a while, and the Melmans were big supporters, which is the reason I know them. I've only seen Faith to talk to a few times since then. Once she stopped by our house to pick up Jeremy for a date."

Jessika's eyes popped open. "Jeremy went out with her?"

"No, no. She was with someone else. A double date. They all stopped to get Jeremy."

"Oh." She looked relieved. "Faith doesn't have a very good reputation."

We were nearing the courthouse with traffic picking up a bit, at least by Purple Sage standards, and Ute said, "I wish I could place her. I'm sure I have seen her."

"Well," Jessi said, "you could see her now. She's working at the Bakery part-time."

"Of course," Ute said. "She works with Franzi. And she goes to the Lakeside church."

Faith had no doubt been at the lake with someone she wasn't supposed to be, doing things her parents would be upset about, which is why she couldn't say anything. It's why she'd had to dress at my house for a date. But if she really had seen Leigh Greer, it could be important to the search, and I couldn't ignore it or forget to mention it to Mac.

Orange and white striped barricades blocked off a portion of the street, and stacks of sandbags protected the south side of the square. Ute drove carefully around the courthouse and finally pulled into a parking space in front of Henshaw's Hardware. Wispy clouds were beginning to gather, and already the sun was blocked out.

Before I got out of the van I turned to Jessika. "I don't want to get anyone in trouble, but there is a chance that Faith could help the sheriff in his investigation." She watched me, waiting for whatever I said next. "Someone needs to tell him about Faith and it would be best coming from you, since you were the one who was there.''

"Me?" She looked at her mother, then back at me. "But he can't tell Faith that I told him. He wouldn't have to do that, would he?"

"I'm not sure this is a good idea," Ute said.

"No one has to know," I said. "Jessi, you said a lot of people heard Faith. Ute, I think it could be important. I'd really appreciate it if you'd let Jessika come with me and talk to Mac."

She hesitated, apparently trying to choose the correct response. Her eyes shifted to her daughter, and her expression slowly softened. Jessika saved her from further deliberation.

"I'll go," Jessi said, her big brown eyes without a flicker of visible fear. "You're always telling us to act on what we believe, and I believe in helping people. And in Sheriff Donelly."

As I said, she is wise beyond her years.

Her mother still looked undecided, but she could hardly talk Jessi out of going. "Okay. You go with Mrs. Wyatt. Or do you want me to come, too?"

"No, I'll be okay."

Jessika climbed out of the car as Ute said, "Then I'll bring the pictures just as soon as I get them printed." She added something in German to Jessika. "It's our family good luck saying," she explained to me.

We closed the doors and she backed the van out quickly and was gone.

I touched Jessi on the shoulder. "Don't worry, Sheriff Donelly is very discreet, and very nice. Besides, if you do this well, you just might end up a character in my next book."

"That would be fun," she said, but her smile was weak. "Just don't make me the murderer, unless I kill Faith Melman."

As we waited for the traffic to clear, another minivan pulled into the space vacated by Ute. It was Beverly Kendall, for once alone, her face pale and drawn as if she were cold.

"Jolie," she said, getting out of her car. "How are you doing?"

"Fine. I see your car is all clean."

"Better than it was before."

"How's your dad?"

"My dad?" Bev's expression went from distracted to bleak. "I can't really tell."

"No bad effects from his fall?"

"Oh, no. Physically, he's fine. Mentally, who knows? Sometimes he seems lost, and at other times he's consumed with things that aren't real. He seems to be on some mission that only he can understand. Like yesterday afternoon, he was working on drawings; I couldn't make out what they were and he finally told me he was building a playhouse for his little girl. Me." She shook her head with the same distress I could imagine in her father. "He gets distraught because he says he's behind on his plans. And he makes lists, too."

"I'm so sorry. It's got to be hard on you."

She took a hearty breath. "It's okay. The house seems pretty cramped at times but I'm grateful we're together. And dad is functioning and he isn't in pain. That's the most I can ask for right now." She paused then said, "Have you heard anything new on Leigh?"

My hand was still on Jessi's shoulder, and I squeezed it lightly, hoping she would recognize it as a request for silence. I trusted Bev completely, but it was inappropriate to tell her any news before we gave it to the sheriff. "I left the radio station an hour ago, so I haven't heard anything that hasn't been on the air. Have you?"

"No. And poor Tom is so upset. I think it's the not knowing that's making it worse. And of course, he's had people in and out of the house so he can't even find a private minute to stop and think. I know everyone wants to help, but it's too much, you know?"

"Of course." There was a pang of guilt as I remembered that I was one of those people who had taken up space in his house, but I had been there at the request of the sheriff and

Tom. Or had it just been the sheriff? "Oh," I said, "I haven't introduced you. Do you know Jessika Roesner? Ute's daughter?"

"Hi," Jessi said.

Bev smiled, her eyes not quite focused on Jessi. "I've met your mom. She took pictures at the reception. I have to remember to get copies."

"When things settle down," I said. "Ute will hold on to them for you."

"Good." She looked at the sky, which was gray with clouds. "It's going to rain again; I'd better get moving. I don't like leaving Dad alone too long. Sometimes he disappears when I do that."

"Have you thought about disabling his car?"

Bev actually smiled. "I took the distributor cap off his engine and when he tried to drive it, he came in the house swearing like crazy. 'Some damn fool stole my distributor cap. Call the damn sheriff and see if we can get it back.' I tried to convince him it was just kids, but he was so insistent I had to pretend to find the stupid thing! Can you believe that?"

I had to laugh. "I don't know why that seems logical for your dad, but it does."

"I guess he's crazy like a fox." She turned to Jessika. "It was nice meeting you. Say hi to your mom." Then she gave me a quick hug and a final good-bye before she started toward the drugstore.

Jessika and I waited for traffic to clear, then ran across the street and up the sidewalk to the front doors of the majestic courthouse. She slowed as we entered the doorway and started for the wooden stairs that lead to the second floor and the sheriff's office.

"Are you sure he'll believe me?" she asked. "I mean, I'm just a kid."

"Well, he's always believed me, and you're much more credible than I am."

She didn't smile. "You're just being nice."

"Yes, and as Jeremy will tell you, it's a rarity, so enjoy it."

This time one corner of her mouth twitched. "Besides," I went on, "do you know what quid pro quo means?"

"Kind of."

"Well, after we tell the sheriff what you know, and what your mom and I found at the lake, maybe we'll learn something new from him."

I had no idea how true that would prove to be.

SEVENTEEN

SHERIFF MAC DONELLY reached over and picked up a phone, pushing a button before he put the receiver to his ear. "I want you to call Deputy Draper and ask him to go on over to the Bakery. There's a young woman there by the name of Faith Melman and she apparently has some information on our missing person's case. Ask him to bring her over here if she is willing."

Jessika and I sat across the desk from him in his antique looking office. It hasn't been carefully decorated to appear that way, it just never changed from years back.

The door to Mac's office was open so I could hear Relda Iley, the dispatcher, responding. "And what if Faith Melman is not willing to come in?"

"Not a problem. Have Linc tell her that we'll be happy to contact her parents and go through the formal channels."

Very clever of Mac. He knew quite well that Faith didn't want her parents notified, and while there were protocols in dealing with minors, his suggestion would certainly put Faith in her most cooperative mood.

Linc was also the right person to talk with Faith. He had a daughter of his own who was not that much older and he spoke the language, as it were.

"I'll do it," Relda said, as cheerful as if he'd told her to pick up her lottery winnings.

Mac hung up the phone and jumped up from his old wooden chair, rubbing his hands together. "Well, that takes care of that. Jessika, I appreciate the way you came up here and all—

could make a big difference. And don't you worry, we'll be real discreet about how we found out about Faith.'' He held out his hand to shake hers, which she did. ''I won't hold you up any longer.''

He was about to shake my hand when I said, ''Wait. Mac, I have more to tell you.'' He glanced at his watch, and I added, ''Do you have to be somewhere? Are you late?''

''Oh, no, nothing like that. I just have an appointment.''

''I'll be quick, it's just that we have to wait for Ute, who has the pictures.''

He sat back down. ''And those would be of…?''

I leaned across the desk. ''I think I should explain.'' I told him where Ute and I had been and why, Jessika listening quietly. Finally I said, ''Ute was taking pictures of the drawdown tube. There were pieces of a Styrofoam cooler all tangled with fishing line and some material.'' I paused to think how best to phrase this next part. ''The material was apple green, a calico, and it looked familiar.''

''Did you say green?''

''Yes. Apple green—''

I was interrupted by the sound of feet pounding up the wooden staircase. Then Ute's voice came. ''Hello,'' she said to Relda. ''I am looking for Jolie Wyatt and my daughter Jessika. I have some pictures for the sheriff.''

''In his office,'' came the reply.

I was in the doorway by the time Ute got past the counter. ''How did they turn out?'' I asked.

''Very good, even if I do brag on myself. I blew up the one picture so you can see the material clearly.'' Inside the door she stopped. ''Sheriff. Hello. Did Jolie tell you about these?''

She held out the pictures and Mac took them, gesturing toward chairs at the same time. Ute remained on her feet. ''I am sorry, but I have to run again. Kevin is at soccer practice and I cannot be late to pick him up.'' Kevin was her youngest, only nine.

''I understand,'' Mac said. ''And I appreciate your help.''

''You're quite welcome. It was very little to do.'' She

started toward the door. Jessi gave me a last wave and a faint smile before following her mother out.

"So let's see what we've got," Mac said, resting his hip on the desk.

I was at his elbow, curious to see the photos, too.

Ute had done some digital magic, and now each picture was eight by five. She had also made the first a very tight shot, the water white and swirling, yet without the perspective of size it could have been beer being poured into a glass. Except for the cloth. She had caught only a fragment of it, but the color was true. In the next three shots the craft bag became progressively more pronounced, until in the last shot it was almost gone.

Mac looked up. "Is that the bag of Leigh Greer's?"

"That's what I think, but I only saw it once a couple of days ago and I wasn't paying close attention. Linda Beaman could say for sure. Or Tom."

"I hate to show these to Tom until we're positive." He reached for the phone. "I reckon I'll call Linda Beaman and see if she'll come back into town."

"You don't have a deputy who could run them out there?"

"Not at the moment. Wiley is driving the lake roads, John is catchin' up on some sleep, and Linc is talking with Faith Melman at the Bakery."

The front door of the courthouse had opened and closed a dozen times while I had been in the sheriff's office, but always the footsteps had gone for the elevator to the third floor, or had turned into the offices on the bottom level. This time I was only dimly aware of the door opening until the steps sounded on the wooden stairs.

"Think that's Linc?" I asked.

Mac's eyes widened and he looked at the clock, then at me. "I surely do hope so."

"Are you okay? Is something wrong?"

He didn't answer, and we stood in silence until the footsteps made their way into the outer offices.

I heard Relda say brightly, "He's expecting you, and he told me to send you right in."

And so my mother swept into the office carrying a picnic basket and wearing an expectant smile.

"Mom," I said without meaning to.

Her expression was not nearly so happy when she saw me. "Jolie."

"We were just going to have a bite to eat," Mac said. "Things have been so busy around here—"

"I decided to make sure he had a decent meal," my mother concluded, gesturing with the basket.

I thought my mother played bridge and went on cruises and stayed in nice hotels with chocolates on the pillow and a concierge. She didn't deliver picnic baskets in Purple Sage.

I studied her. She was about my height, around five-four, with hazel green-blue eyes like mine. She was plump with pretty little plump hands, and short hair that was now mostly silver. The style was sleek, yet casual, and it framed her face perfectly. A stylist on the *QE2* had created the look for her a few years ago.

Her clothes are usually lovely. Lots of soft colors, aquas and peaches in natural silks. She didn't wear a lot of jewelry, but it was always in excellent taste, and always a compliment to her clothes.

The woman in front of me could not be my mother. She was wearing jeans and a flannel shirt. Her hair was mussed. She didn't look a bit sophisticated, in fact if I hadn't known her better, I'd say she was blushing.

I looked at Mac. His expression was more that of a teenager caught parking than a mature adult engaged in a perfectly normal activity.

Unfortunately, my response was off key, too. "Oh, right, of course. I mean, I understand. How nice of you, Mom." She raised one eyebrow, and I went on speaking as I inched toward the door. "Well, I'm finished with everything I needed to tell you, Mac, so I'll just run on."

"You could join us," my mother said. "There's plenty of food. I didn't know who else might be here and be hungry."

"That'd be real nice, Jolie," Mac said.

"Oh, no, I couldn't. Really." I sounded like a boorish guest refusing a second helping of something she was craving. Only in this case, I wasn't sure I wanted to stay.

"Have you eaten?" Mom asked.

"No."

"Then I insist," she said, plopping the basket on the desk. "Relda can join us, too."

Relda can join us, too. My mother actually knew the dispatcher's name. Obviously my mom had spent more time at the sheriff's office than I had lately.

She had also spent time in somebody's kitchen, because after she pulled out the barbecue purchased from Ronnie's Green Mesquite, she pulled out a plastic bowl of her famous potato salad. I checked out the bowl, under the pretense of helping, and saw that it was mine, so it had been made in my kitchen. That made me feel better, although I couldn't say why.

Mom stepped out into the front office. "Relda, come and fix yourself a plate; we can't let good barbecue go to waste."

"Yes, ma'am, I'll be right there."

"I was hoping," Mom said, "that we could eat under the trees, but it's starting to sprinkle again."

Interlopers had ruined their tête-à-tête, and even the weather was uncooperative. While we put out paper plates and plastic silverware, Mac appeared to be trying not to look disappointed. He is old stock Texan, a man with Southern gentility and pioneer ways bred into him. His credo is, if someone needs help, then it's your place to help them; if you have shelter and they don't, you give them a place to sleep, and if someone is hungry and you have food, you feed them. All the qualities that made him an excellent sheriff and a wonderful person. Of course, he didn't have to be happy about doing those things…at least not at this moment.

"That's the last thing we need is more rain," Mac said.

My mother handed him a well-filled plate, along with several napkins, and gestured to his chair. "Go ahead and sit down; you need to take advantage of the calm before the storm. Literally." He sat and my mom went on, "Anything new on the Greer investigation?" She began fixing her own plate.

"Actually, could be something new," he said. "Jolie, why don't you hand your mom those pictures you and Ute took."

I did as requested. Then, while Mom studied the photos I put dabs of food on my plate and arranged myself in a chair next to her.

"I'm not sure what I'm looking at," she said.

"Leigh Greer's craft bag," Mac explained. "Leastwise, that's what Jolie thinks it is and I tend to agree with her."

"I see. The infamous craft bag."

Had I told her about that? Or had Mac? Perhaps they had discussed it when they arranged lunch.

Relda popped in. "Oh, Irene this all looks wonderful. You shouldn't have."

Irene? Relda had only been with the sheriff's department for two months and I barely knew her, but she was on a first name basis with my mother.

"Help yourself; I brought enough food to feed half the people at the shelter."

Mac sipped tea before saying, "How are things going over there?"

"Actually pretty well. There are only four families left. Everyone else has either found temporary housing, you know, taken in by friends or relatives, or they've been able to get back into their own homes. I'm all but out of a job."

"Well, that's good news."

The conversation was homey, the "how was your day?" kind of exchange. Their relationship had gone far beyond the first date, but when had that happened, and where had I been? And why hadn't anyone told me?

My mother had never confided in me, so it was unrealistic of me to expect her to start now. Still I wanted to know more about her and I could never make that happen. I was always out of step with her life, and in her presence I felt out of step with my own.

I was guessing that my sister, Elise, knew all about my mother's relationship with Mac. I won't say that I was jealous of their easy closeness, but I wanted to understand how they came to it. I'd wondered if my distance with my mother went all the way back to when I was born. She'd been used to my rowdy older brother, Win, so perhaps she hadn't been able to stretch her mothering far enough to include me. Maybe she didn't know how to raise a girl, and she'd only achieved the skill by the time Elise came along. There was no doubt that she was better with Elise.

Or maybe it was Elise who was better.

Watching my mother, so at home in the sheriff's office, it was made evident, once again, that she and I were out of touch. Rather than focus on my sorrow over it, I did what I always do—I turned my attention to other things. I looked outside and saw Ute's dark green minivan pulling around the square. Or was it hers? Hard to tell from this distance. Then there were people coming up the stairs, more than one person by the sounds of the footsteps, and it didn't take long before they appeared in the doorway.

Linc Draper, a muscular man in his late forties with salt-and-pepper hair, stopped to let someone come through the door first. It was Faith Melman. She was in mouse mode, her hair pulled back from her face, her clothes loose and dull, and her face without even lip gloss to relieve the pallor. The situation might have added to the whiteness of her face. It can't have been easy for her to leave work and come to the sheriff's office without worrying that her parents would hear of it.

Linc said, "Sheriff, this is Faith Melman."

Mac put aside his almost empty plate and rose, then stepped around Linc to offer his outstretched hand to Faith. "How do you do?" They shook hands, although Faith never quite met his eyes. Mac went on. "I understand you have some important information for us regarding Leigh Greer's disappearance. I sure appreciate your help.''

His summation of the situation was very gracious and Faith lifted her chin as if to live up to it. ''Thank you, Sheriff. I do have a little to tell you, but not much.'' She glanced around at all of us. ''And it needs to be confidential.'' When no one responded she added, ''I mean, if you can. You know. I don't want my mom and dad to find out...''

''Not a problem,'' Mac said. ''If y'all will excuse us.'' He nodded in our general direction and led Faith to the deputy's office next door.

My mother gestured to Mac's desk, which was littered with food. ''Deputy, I'm Irene Berenski, Jolie's mother. We have plenty of food here, please help yourself.''

He stepped forward saying, ''If you're sure there's enough.''

''Plenty. I'll make you a plate.''

''Then I don't mind if I do. Smells great.''

''We have Ronnie's Mesquite Barbecue and my famous potato salad, plus all the fixin's.''

Somehow my mother had slipped into a down-home mode that made her look every bit the countrywoman. The jeans and turquoise flannel shirt didn't hurt, but there was also a softness to her language that was pure Texas. She seemed gentle and warm.

It made me miss her, even with her standing right in front of me. I missed all the time I hadn't spent with her, and all the conversations we'd never had. She was busy with Linc now, helping him fill his plate, but perhaps this afternoon I could have her all to myself. We could bake Tollhouse cookies together like we'd done once when I was twelve and had pneumonia. We'd leave out most of the chocolate and put in a double dose of pecans, just the way we both liked them.

I've heard it said that it's never too late to have a happy childhood, so maybe it's never too late to have a happy relationship with your mother, either. I could certainly try.

Relda was telling my mother about the ''sights'' around Purple Sage. There aren't that many, nothing commercial like theme parks or shopping malls, but we had our own historic spots. Right off the top of my head I could think of the old POW camp and Bowie Oak out at the park. There were others, too, and if the weather held, perhaps I could drive her around and show them to her.

I would have suggested it, but I didn't want to interrupt their animated conversation. It was nice that Mom was having a good time. I stepped back to watch, and it was like seeing an almost-forgotten play.

After a moment or two I realized I was hearing another conversation, as well. From my new spot I could make out what was going on in the next room, the deputy's office where Mac was interviewing Faith Melman.

"...I see no reason why we'd have to tell your parents," Mac was saying, "unless you have to testify in court and that could be two to three years away. A sworn statement might be sufficient."

"Then I'll swear to it—"

"Jolie," my mother interrupted, "there's peach cobbler."

"Oh, no thanks, Mom, I'm full. Everything was wonderful."

I tuned back in to the conversation next door and Faith was speaking. "...so we pulled into this little road. See, we were just going to see how high the lake was, I mean, we weren't going to do anything. We just wanted to look at the water. And the level."

"I understand," Mac assured her. "And what did you see?"

"Nothing at first. The road is kind of long and it's winding so you don't see anything at all until you go around the last bend. Then I saw two parked cars. Well, not really two cars. One was a car, it was Mrs. Greer's little turquoise car. I recognized it right off. She comes to the Bakery a couple of times a week, and we talk to her a little, so that's how I know her. I've helped her carry things to her car, too."

"Then you'd certainly recognize it. What about the other vehicle—you said it wasn't a car?"

"I didn't really look at it much. I was embarrassed because I thought she was there with someone. I didn't want her to see us or think that we were spying on her, you know?" She waited for something from Mac, and must have gotten it because she went on. "So I told, uh, my friend to turn off his lights and back up, quick!"

"Did you see Mrs. Greer? Or anyone?"

"Well, not really. I just sort of saw the back of her head. In her car. I think she just had pulled up. My, uh, you know, friend said he thought he saw her parking lights go off, but I was so freaked I just wanted out of there."

"And the other vehicle? Tell me anything you can remember."

"It was green. Darkish green, and big. Like a minivan or an SUV or something. I didn't really look at it because I was so freaked, you know?"

A dark green minivan or SUV? How many of those were in town, and who owned them? First in my mind was Ute, since I'd just been riding with her, but to suspect her of hurting Leigh Greer was beyond far-fetched. Ute was the mother of three and a charming woman. But charm or no, I didn't think a woman had anything to do with Leigh's disappearance. Perhaps it was prejudice or some subconscious profiling, but I would have bet money that it was a man who made Leigh disappear.

"I'm going to need the name of your friend," Mac said. "Just because he might remember a whole lot more about that other vehicle than you do."

"But I can't tell you! He wasn't supposed to be out there, either."

"Jolie," my mother said.

I looked up to find my mother, Linc, and Relda staring at me. "I'm sorry. What?"

"Did I catch you eavesdropping?"

EIGHTEEN

MOM'S COMMENT about eavesdropping jerked me back into the room. I could feel myself flushing as Linc looked at me sternly and Relda stared purposefully at her empty plate.

If I'd had days to think up a response I'm sure I could have come up with something witty and urbane that would have made the situation amusing. I didn't have the luxury of time to think, so I mumbled, "Sorry, I was off in space. Shall we clean up the remains of lunch?" It was delivered without looking anyone in the eye.

I decided that I would not be making cookies with my mother that afternoon, nor would I be driving her to the hot spots around Purple Sage. It was obvious why we didn't have a close relationship—the woman simply didn't like me. And it didn't matter. I had made it through forty years of life without having a doting mother, or one who supported my endeavors, so it was a little late to worry about what I was missing. And it was even later to think that I could curry her favor.

"So, Jolie," she said as I carefully sealed the last of the potato salad, "what are you doing this afternoon?"

Something slipped out that was totally unplanned. "I'm going to the funeral home for Dr. Bill's visitation. I'm afraid there won't be many people there." It was the right response; I could see it in her face. As they say, hope springs eternal, so, I added, "Would you like to come with me?"

She smiled. "I would love to, but I still have some things to do at the shelter," she said. "Thank you for asking, though."

"Oh. You're welcome." That was logical, and perhaps there was still a chance that we'd do something together. "Maybe we could spend some time this evening. You know, bake something or..." Her expression stopped me. "No, probably not."

"I'm sorry; I already have plans."

Relda was watching, her cheeks pink with embarrassment for me. "Well," she said. "I'd better get back to work, but lunch was just wonderful. Thank you so much, Irene."

"You're quite welcome, Relda. It was fun—we'll do it again sometime."

"Great," Relda said, slipping into the outer office.

Silently I helped my mother repack the picnic basket, wondering why I could never get it right with her.

I was still trying to understand the painful puzzle, when Mac returned with Faith Melman.

Faith remained in the doorway, her expression not quite happy, but calmer, as if the fears of exposure and the guilt of her prolonged silence had been set aside. Mac appeared frustrated and annoyed, but his voice was cordial.

"Linc," Mac said. "Would you run Miss Melman back to the Bakery?"

"Oh, no," she said, suddenly animated. "I can walk. Really."

"It's not a problem."

"That's all right. I'd prefer to walk. I don't want to put you out—"

Linc stopped her persistent assurances, by saying, "Don't mind a bit, but I believe we'll just take my truck instead of the sheriff's car, if that'd be all right with you."

Faith let out a breath. "That would be great."

Then her friends wouldn't suspect that she'd been talking to the sheriff. Mac nodded his approval and they left, with a few more thanks.

Mac sank into his chair, saying, "Damnedest girl I've ever met. I hope she's not a friend of Jeremy's."

"Not much of one," I said. "They've double-dated once or

twice, but I convinced him that she wasn't a good person to hang around with."

My mother made a noise, then said, "They only double-dated once, and Jeremy didn't want to do that, but he was stuck. He'd said yes to his friend Jared before he knew who Jared was going out with." To Mac she added, "He has his faults, but Jeremy is one bright young man."

"Spoken like a true grandmother," Mac said with a hint of a smile.

Once more I was put back in my place, somewhere in the outer edges of the family circle. I let out a long sigh before I'd realized it, but no one noticed.

My mother was saying to Mac, "You seem to have quite a bit on your plate right now, and I'm not talking about food."

"Some days I could use an army to do this job. At least a platoon."

"Why were you frustrated with Faith?" I asked. "Couldn't she help you?"

"She should be able to help; she *was* out at the lake, and it appears she did see Leigh Greer. She actually saw a vehicle parked next to Leigh's—exact spot we found the car in, but Faith can't tell a model T from a two-ton truck." He turned in his chair, which groaned loudly. "Said it was dark green. Might have been a minivan or an SUV. 'Or a big kind of truck.' I'm quoting her."

"What about her date?" I asked. "Surely he knows cars better than that."

"Wouldn't tell me who it was. No amount of coercion would budge her, even when I suggested that I might ask her parents."

"Jeremy!" my mother said. "I'll bet he could tell you who Faith is dating."

"Or Jessika," I responded. "She might know, too."

Mac rubbed his jaw. "That might be the way to go."

"It is," I said. "I'd bet Jeremy's allowance on it, and I'd be happy to talk with Jessi. I'm pretty sure I can track her down."

"And I know where Jeremy is," my mother added.

"I'd appreciate that," he said, his face as solemn as I've ever seen it. "That would give me a chance to tend to the underwater search."

My enthusiasm petered out. This was not a game, and I doubted that there would be a winner.

"Then you think she's in the lake," my mother said.

Mac nodded. Speaking slowly and solemnly he gave us his thoughts on what I'd seen that morning. Hearing it in his words and in his voice gave the information weight and authority, whereas before I had held it as supposition.

"Then you think it was murder," Mom said.

"I can't see two drowning suicides in Purple Sage within two days of each other."

"I can't see even one," I said.

His only response was a long look, which made me wonder if he agreed with me.

Finally I asked, "What can I put on the air?"

He rubbed his face, thinking about that. "Just say we have a witness that places Leigh Greer at the lake around seven Friday night, but don't mention any names. Say we're following up that lead, and if anyone else has additional information they need to contact us. Don't mention the underwater search just yet. Might not get that going until tomorrow and I want to tell Tom myself. No need to hear it on the radio."

"Of course."

My mother said, "A story about a witness could make someone very nervous."

"I certainly hope so. Someone who drives a dark green minivan or SUV," he said. "Jolie, you know anyone like that?"

"Only three or four. Ute Roesner drives a green Ford Windstar. And so does Brother Binder."

"I think I'll have Relda do a search on the computer. I figure we'll pull up a whole list of folks who drive such a vehicle."

"So, why not say it on the air?"

"A little pressure can go a long way. We're talking about somebody who, more'n likely, already killed once. I'd like to believe that wasn't true, but the odds are not in our favor." He shook his head. "Damn, sometimes I just hate this job."

Before I could say anything, my mother leaned over and patted his hand. "Mac, there's nobody on earth who could do it better. And just think of all the good you've done over the years."

He looked up and their eyes met with a spark of electricity that charged the room.

I had to remind myself to take in air, and then I stood. "I've got to get going."

They both looked at me, as if surprised by my continued presence. Mac said, "Thanks again, Jolie."

"You're welcome. And thanks for lunch, Mom."

I went out the door and waved good-bye, but nobody noticed, not even Relda when I went through the outer office. Once outside I realized that my car was at the station and I was going to have to walk, so I pulled my jacket tighter and started off, accompanied only by my thoughts.

Someone in a green minivan or SUV had probably killed Leigh Greer, and my mother was in love with Sheriff Mac Donelly. As if that wasn't enough to send shock waves through my mind, Dr. Bill was being accused of committing suicide, which was insane, and the sky was spitting down on Purple Sage again.

I cut around some orange and white striped barriers, then climbed over a two-foot wall of sandbags. The world was topsy-turvy and there was only one thing I could think of that might help me get through it—a conversation with my dad.

It would have been so nice to talk with him and have his undivided attention. He wouldn't actually help while I baked cookies, but he'd sit in the kitchen and talk with me, and somehow seem just as involved as I was. He'd tell me how great the cookies smelled, and how wonderful it was that he had a daughter with so many talents.

My shoulders slumped even further as the sprinkles turned

to big drops. No one was ever going to say that to me again. Every time that realization hit me I felt my father's death all over again. It was haunting me of late, pulling at my heart to create pain.

I was feeling sorry for myself, and I knew it, but sometimes it's okay. Walking alone in the rain, it seemed fine.

God in his wisdom gave us two parents, I suppose in case we lost one, but in my case, my parents weren't interchangeable. I was sure that my mother loved me, but I didn't think she really liked me. It occurred to me that if she married Mac I wouldn't be losing a mother, I'd be losing a sheriff and a friend.

There was a crack of thunder as it started to pour down rain. I took off running. By the time I got to the station I was sniffling, and wet. Diane was waiting for me in my office.

"Where in the world have you been?" she asked "And why didn't you take your car?"

"Long story," I said. "Bad day."

"I guess so. Why don't I make you some hot tea? Or, here, take mine. I haven't even tasted it yet." She handed me a cup of ginger-peach tea that she had no doubt made in the break room. "I didn't really want it, anyway. I just made it to fill some time until you showed up."

"Thanks. I'd love it." I took a sip and sank into my chair with gratitude. I might not have a doting mother, but I have some wonderful friends. "What are you doing here? And how's your house?"

Diane waved away my final question. "Don't ask. I thought I ought to go to the visitation for Dr. Bill and I couldn't face going alone."

"I'd go with you, but I promised Mac I'd talk to Jessika Roesner. And I have to write a quick news story. There should be time after that, if you can wait."

"I'll wait all day."

"I've got a lot to tell you. A lot." My fingers were already on the keyboard as I said, "And you might think about who drives a green minivan or SUV in Purple Sage."

"Because…?"

"Because Leigh Greer was parked next to one at the lake the night she disappeared."

"I LOVE THE IDEA of your mother and Mac dating. They're so different—they're perfect for each other."

"Don't start, okay? I have other things I'd rather worry about," I said as I climbed out of Diane's car and started up the walkway to the Roesners' home. It's one of the newer homes on the south side of town, two stories of soft blue-gray siding with white trim. A darker gray outlined the window boxes, which held draping ivy. There was a beautifully manicured yard, but no flowers, anywhere. I suppose I shouldn't have been surprised; with the weather we'd been having lately it would have been easier to grow rice than flowers.

"Does it bother you that someone might replace your father?"

"No one, and I mean no one, could ever replace my father. At least they couldn't fill the role he played in my life. As for someone taking his spot in my mom's life, no, it doesn't bother me a bit. I think she should date and marry some wonderful man who will travel with her and make her happy."

"So, why not Mac?"

"He has a job and he can't travel. He can't live in Dallas, either. If he does move, then we lose the best sheriff we could ever have. And I'd lose a friend."

"Your mother could move here."

"Thank you," I said. "That really brightens my day."

Our conversation ended as we reached the door. I rang the bell and waited, but there was no answer. "You don't think they'd still be at the soccer field?"

"Not with the rain." Diane reached around me and rang the bell, again.

I was about to give up when the door suddenly opened. It was Ute. Her hair was wet and sticking to the sides of her head, and her mascara was streaked down her tight face. Before I could ask her if everything was all right, she spoke.

"Jolie, hello. And Diane. Won't you come in?" She stepped aside, although she didn't look pleased about our visit.

I shook my head. "We only have a minute," I said. "I was hoping to talk with Jessi. Is she around?"

"Jessika? She's not here right now; I just dropped her off at the shelter. She was going to visit a friend there. Is it important?"

I explained that I was representing the sheriff and had an additional question for her daughter.

Something about Ute's face changed. "Why don't you ask me," she said. "Possibly I can help."

"Oh, well, sure. Faith Melman talked to Mac, but she wouldn't say who she was with Friday night. Do you know? Or do you know who she's dating?"

Ute's teeth were on her bottom lip, clenched as if holding something in. Finally she said, "No, I'm afraid I don't know the answers to either of those questions. I will go get Jessika, and ask her—"

"No, no. We'll just run up there. It won't take a second," I said.

Ute nodded. "I would appreciate that. I'm just going to the airport in San Antonio in half an hour and I wanted to get changed."

"We won't keep you then," Diane said, with a smile. "Thanks for your help."

We turned toward the car and the door closed behind us. Not sharply, but certainly quickly.

"Did she seem strange to you?" I asked.

"Not her normal self, that's for sure. I always thought Ute was pure sunshine and flowers."

"No flowers today."

While Diane drove I tried to puzzle out why Ute was no longer cheerful. She seemed concerned, as if there was something she didn't want me to find out. Or was she just in a hurry?

"She drives a green minivan," Diane said. "And she knew Leigh Greer, although I don't think she liked her very much."

"What are you talking about? How did she know Leigh?"

Diane carefully maneuvered around the barricades that remained on Winchester and said, "I was in the Bakery about two weeks ago and Ute was there to pick up Franzi from work. I didn't mean to eavesdrop, but I heard some things."

"Like…?"

"Apparently Franzi had been invited to Leigh Greer's house, and from the little I heard I gathered that Ute was not pleased with Franzi's choice of role model."

"Did she say anything specific?"

Diane thought hard. "I inferred most of the disapproval. What I primarily heard was Ute telling Franzi that she, Franzi, couldn't go to Leigh's. Something about schoolwork, and her room to clean. You know, all the excuses we make when we aren't going to let our kids do something."

"What was Franzi's reaction?"

"She said that Leigh was lonely with Tom out of town all the time, and Leigh didn't have a lot of friends. Ute said that Leigh needed friends her own age. I got the impression that it wasn't the first time they'd had the discussion, and that there were things that Franzi wasn't saying."

We were just pulling up to the shelter, which in drier times was the high school gymnasium. A large van from Anderson Distributing in Abilene stood out front, and a Red Cross truck was beside it. I had done a story a few days before about the donations that were coming in from businesses all around central Texas and it was nice to see that the help continued, even though the stories about Purple Sage probably weren't making headlines in the metro areas anymore.

It was drizzling and the sidewalks were wet but several kids were riding skateboards or scooters around, bike helmets securely on their heads, playing some kind of tag on wheels. There were some others sitting on the raised flower bed in front of the school. Only two, actually, deep in serious conversation. They were older than the other kids, and as we continued walking I realized it was my son, Jeremy, with none other than Jessika. Before I got to them he reached over and brushed something off her shoulder. Gently.

"My, my," Diane said quietly. "Did you know about that?"

"No, but it explains his total dedication to the shelter. Apparently it didn't have much to do with the flooding." I raised my voice and called, "Hey, Jeremy. Jessika. Just the two I was looking for."

They both jumped guiltily and spun around to face us, looking much the way Mac and my mother had.

"Mom," Jeremy said. "Uh, hi."

"Mrs. Wyatt," Jessika added.

They were standing two feet apart, stiff and straight, their eyes locked on Diane and me—all but at attention.

"At ease," I said. Diane smiled but she was the only one. "I'm sorry I startled you," I said, pretending I didn't notice that they were watching me with way too much focus. "I've just come from Mac's office, and he thought maybe one of you could give him some information."

"Grams already asked us," Jeremy said. "She left just a few minutes ago."

While we were at Jessika's house talking with her mother.

"So, who was it?" Diane asked. "And please, don't say it was Randy," she said, thinking of her son. "If you do I'll have to kill him, and that would really add to the problems in Purple Sage."

"It wasn't," Jeremy offered. He moved his body enough to adopt a more normal stance. "Tad Ohlman was the main guy, but he wasn't the only one she was seeing."

Lloyd Longmeyer, the principal of the high school came striding out of the gymnasium door. Like his name, he is long and thin, with legs that remind me of a stork's. He was wearing light brown dress pants that clearly showed his knees as he walked. A dress shirt, tie, sweater, and a red windbreaker topped the pants.

"Ladies," he said by way of a greeting, as he turned toward the staff parking lot.

"Lloyd," Diane responded with a nod.

I watched him walk to his vehicle—a dark green Toyota minivan. I had never before noticed how many green cars there were. They were ubiquitous. Or maybe sprouting up from all the rain.

When I turned back to the conversation, Jeremy was saying, "They weren't really going together or anything."

Jessika was twisting her mouth as if there was something more she'd like to add but was trying not to say it.

Diane asked, "Who else was Faith seeing?"

Again Jeremy and Jessika turned to each other, their faces mirroring looks of indecision. Finally Jeremy said, "Oh, I don't know. I mean, well, uh, you know."

There was obviously more to this story than they were telling.

NINETEEN

DIANE MOVED US "inside out of the rain" and finagled Jeremy to the other side of the gym, ostensibly to help her get coffee and tea for us. There were only about twenty adults scattered about the cavernous gymnasium, which was divided into sections. There was a dining area at the far end near the kitchen, with cafeteria tables in the center, but off to one side was sleeping space with rollaway beds and cots, while closest to the front doors there was an area with a desk, three tables, and several chairs, apparently the office and "living room." A five-hundred-piece puzzle of Russian mosques was partially complete in the center of one table, and another table held an assortment of board games. There were two television sets, although no one was watching them. Not surprising when I realized they wouldn't get many channels without cable.

It was in the living area, where Jessi and I sat on scratched metal chairs.

"I can't thank you enough for telling me about Faith," I said. "I think it's going to make a big difference."

"Really? I didn't do anything."

"Sure you did. No one else told that story. Now Mac might actually have a way to find out the truth about Leigh's disappearance. That's important."

Jessika nodded, looking pleased. "Good. I'm glad I helped."

I paused before asking, "Is there anything else you can tell me about Faith Melman?"

Jessi's glance moved up to the metal encased lights on the

ceiling. "Well..." She looked like a half-grown-up cherub with a problem on her mind. "I don't know..."

"I promise I won't spread it around town. I won't even tell Mac if I don't think it can help."

She nodded, still debating. After a fleeting look to the other end of the gym where Jeremy stood with Diane, purposely being detained, she took a big breath. "Faith went out with a lot of boys. A lot."

"She doesn't strike me as the type to be popular."

"She isn't with girls. The boys just like her for one reason."

"Sex?"

Jessika nodded, relieved that I had said it first. "That's it. It's sad, too, because at school, they hardly talk to her." She looked as if it mattered to her, and I touched her arm.

"There have been girls like that forever. There were some girls like that when I was in high school, and probably when your parents were teenagers, too. It's something that doesn't change." What I didn't say was that in a big city that sort of morality might be accepted or ignored, but we were small town, where the rules were different.

"But in Purple Sage, everyone knows about Faith—everyone in high school, at least. What's she going to do when she grows up?" Jessi's dark eyes were genuinely troubled.

"With any luck she'll move away and figure out that she has more to offer than she thought. It's about self-confidence, and I guess she doesn't have much. It's not good, but it's not the worst thing a person can do. At least she hasn't gotten pregnant and made an innocent baby suffer." I waited while Jessi took that in, then I added, "It would help if you could name the boys that she's gone out with lately."

Jessika gave a slow thoughtful bob of her head, before saying, "She could have been lying. You know, just to look more important."

"The sheriff can sort that out."

"I guess." Still not happy, but at least willing, Jessika said, "There was Brant Longmeyer."

My reaction was a visceral revulsion. Brant was a clone of

his father with the addition of pimples. He was tall, thin, and pedantic, although he was good on the basketball court, which redeemed him in the eyes of most of the high school girls.

"Does his father know?" I asked.

"I don't think so."

"Who else?"

"Trav Beaman."

I was surprised. I wouldn't have suspected that any son of Linda Beaman would have more on his mind than staying out of trouble with his mother, baseball, and his 4-H projects. Which was a large Charolais calf, if I remembered correctly.

"Is Trav popular?" I asked.

Jessi smiled. "All the girls like him. He's kind of goofy, but he's cute, too."

Live and learn. "Anyone else?"

"Not in the last couple of weeks."

THE FIRST HALLWAY at Jackson's Funeral Home was crowded with people, all talking and telling stories as if at a party. Someone had set up trays of food and brought more chairs than were usually present. I looked at the small black sign that said, "Rose Campbell." I knew of her, a descendant of one of the founding families and a charming woman who supported the library.

"This way," Diane said, leading me through the crowd.

We went to the second hallway to find it quiet and solemn; it was also empty except for about ten people, including Gretchen. I felt sick—it was worse than I had feared.

"Go right on in," we were told in a whispered voice. The woman looked a lot like Gretchen.

Once inside the viewing room, Diane moved close to the casket and I hung back near the door so that she could have a private moment to say her good-byes. I spent the time looking at the flowers; trying not to think about the hundreds of people who weren't here.

Nearest me was a vase of long-stemmed red roses from the nurses of Wilmot County Hospital. Next to that was a wreath with yellow gladioli and blue stock interspersed with greens and baby's breath. The card said it was from the other doctors in Purple Sage, and their massive gift was probably intended to stand over the grave in the days after the funeral.

Another container held lilies with both white and magenta stock, almost startling in their brilliant colors. The pungent scent was heavy with memories for me. I used to love stock, but now it is the funeral flower, inexorably linked with sorrow. The card said the arrangement was from a local pharmacy.

Diane turned away from the casket and nodded to me as she slipped out of the room. I moved forward with trepidation.

I drew closer to see the tufted beige satin, and finally I saw Dr. Bill, lying in his coffin. It brought back the image of my father and the way he had looked the last time I had ever seen him—pale and without the vigor of life. I sucked in air and closed my eyes to shut out the picture.

I needed to pray, but what was I supposed to say?

On most nights when I pray I simply thank God for the protection, gifts, and health He's given us. Especially to the people I love. And then on other nights, when I'm overly tired or alone, or maybe when my hormones are off or the moon is in the wrong position, I lay in bed and think of all the terrible things that could happen to my family and friends. Of car wrecks, of cancer, of plane crashes, and other life-shattering events. Then I pray with intensity, begging God to keep everyone safe and well.

But here, now, none of that was appropriate, so what did I say? Thank you for taking my friend away? Or should I say, "If there is a heaven, please make sure that he's in it?"

I wanted to cry, but inside of me there was only blackness instead of tears. Even breathing was a burden, because it kept me alive in the here and now. I wanted to be in the past, the long-ago little girl who was safe and warm, away from all the hurt that life and death bring. I wanted to be with my dad.

When my father died, everyone agreed that he was too young, but there were also those who said that his death was a blessing. He had been in pain both from the disease and from the cure. He had lost his hair, his muscle, and his strength. His feet had swollen so badly that he had no shoes to fit, and food was distasteful to him. He told me often that what he really wanted was a tall glass of cool water, but even water tasted vile and made him sick.

None of those things had mattered to me, because I wanted my father with me. I thought of Beverly, angry that Dr. Bill had brought her father back to life. None of it made sense to me, not death and not even life. My father had always made it seem so simple.

I opened my eyes and let air out, thinking what it would be like to have him beside me now. I could almost hear his words, because I'd heard them said so often and so gently in the past.

"It's okay to hurt sometimes," he would tell me, and then he would put his arm around me so that his warmth became mine. "Things will get better, don't you worry about that. They always do, don't they?" He would smile down at me and tell me he had "a lot of faith in me." Whatever troubles came along, he was sure that I could handle them.

That part was always important. If my dad knew that I could handle things, then he was right—I could.

Sometimes I would cry, and he would hold me, and sometimes he just talked until I was feeling better.

If the crisis was one of my own creation, he would tell me a story about himself, and how "One time…" things had been similar for him. It helped me understand that it was my perception, not the reality that was the problem.

What a gift he had been to me, although he hadn't seen it that way. When my distress was over and I was feeling optimistic again, he would always say, "I'm so lucky to have a daughter like you."

And I would tell him I loved him.

I forced air into my lungs, past the terrible ache in my throat, and looked down again on Dr. Bill's tranquil face. Then to his folded hands. Hands that, like my father's, had never been still. Hands that had healed, and held, and soothed.

Those hands would never soothe again. I reached down into

the coffin to touch the wrinkled skin of Dr. Bill's hands and felt the chilling coldness of death.

What if there was nothing beyond death? No heaven, no hell, just an end? The thought almost overwhelmed me, and I turned around and hurried out into the hallway.

Diane was waiting for me. "Are you ready?" Her voice was soft and concerned. "Are you okay?"

I lifted my head, stepping toward her. "I'm fine," I said. There were others watching. I nodded toward them.

Diane introduced me to Gretchen's sister, Lorena. She looked fierce. Her words didn't penetrate my own sorrow-induced fog, but I understood that her only reason for being in Purple Sage was to take care of Gretchen.

Diane and I signed the guest book and started down the hall toward the front door.

The number of people visiting Rose Campbell was just as large as before. As we approached them I felt no small-town familiarity. I was encased in a coldness of my own making, and far outside the gathering of mourners visiting Ms. Campbell.

Diane smiled, and said quietly to me, "I need to pay my respects to Rose." It was only right; Diane was the mayor's wife.

While she slipped into the viewing room I stood outside, hardly aware of anything but the hurt inside of me. When a hand touched my arm, I jumped. It was Gretchen's sister.

"Excuse me," she said. "I didn't mean to startle you. I just thought you might know where the ladies' room is."

It took a moment for the question to reach me, and when it did I pointed toward the doors next to the office. "Just down there," I said.

"Thank you." She hurried off and I became aware of the other voices creating a web of conversation around me. One voice, piercing and severe, stood out.

It was an elderly woman speaking from somewhere behind me and she said, "We oughtn't be talking to her. That woman. Gretchen's sister."

A gentler woman's voice responded, "I don't reckon she's any happier about Dr. Bill committing suicide than we are."

There was no softening the smug superiority in the first voice. "Burning in hell, that's where he is right now, and like Brother Binder said, we don't want nothing more to do with that kind."

I turned. The woman had a wrinkled crone face, and thin curly white hair.

"I beg your pardon?" I said.

Black eyes took in my face, and from her tight mouth words spat at me like an epithet. "Suicide is a sin."

It was so vicious I couldn't take it in. "Dr. Bill did many wonderful things for the people of your church."

"A man has to be judged by his last act, not what he did in the past."

"No," I said, shaking my head. That was wrong, so very wrong. "That's not the way it is. None of us has the right to judge, isn't that true? Isn't it only God who is allowed to judge?"

Her thin chin with its pokey gray whiskers went up. "All who are righteous know about the wages of sin."

"Righteous? Don't you mean self—"

"Jolie!" It was Diane. She slid her arm through mine, nodded toward the woman, and headed us toward the door. On the way she said over her shoulder, "Lovely seeing you, Ms. Edgely."

Once outside she continued to hold my arm until she had the Mercedes unlocked and me deposited in the passenger seat. The day was gray. I hated the weather. I hated death and I hated that old woman. She was cruel and stupid.

Diane was in the car, starting the engine. She looked straight at me, sympathy thick on her face and in her voice. "I'm so sorry you're having such a hard day."

"I'm not," I said. "I'm fine. I'm really fine. It's just that I'm lonely and I need to talk to my dad. I'm so…so…" And then I broke down and cried.

The deep sobs focused the pain.

TWENTY

I CRIED OVER the loss of my dad, and then at the changes taking place in my life. Over Jeremy growing up, the gentle shift in my relationship with Matt from the honeymoon stage to a stable tranquillity, and the stress of facing my mother. I cried at the aging of my friends and my own mortality.

My sorrows were nothing more than the constant movement that is a given in this world, but I had held it in too long, and the events of the past week had pushed me to a catharsis I hadn't seen coming. When I finally slowed, a dozen tissues were scattered across my lap, and my face was the mottled red that only comes after a deep, cleansing cry. I was more at peace than I had been in months.

"I'm sorry," I said to Diane, after blowing my nose. "I didn't mean to fall apart on you."

We were driving, had been driving for a while, because Diane didn't want all the people at Jackson's Funeral Home to walk past us and see me. I was grateful. My facade of strength might be fragile at times, but it was my facade.

"That's okay," she said. "I cried myself to sleep last night over Dr. Bill and my house and everything else that's going on."

"Wise of you; you beat the rush."

She glanced over at me and smiled, "Now there's the Jolie that I know and love." Her eyes were back on the road. "So, are you feeling better? And what are you up for? A cup of hot tea, or could I interest you in something a little more physical?"

"I'm fine," I said, then blew my nose hard. "I don't think I have any tears left. What did you have in mind?"

"First, I want to run by the house and check on the carpet—they should be installing it about now. Then I'd like us to get the galoshes and take a look at Cavalry Creek."

I looked out the windshield; the skies were still gray but it was a lighter color. Then I glanced down at my clothes. I was in my good black flannel slacks, not appropriate attire for a tromp through mud at Cavalry Creek.

"Do you have some spare jeans that I could borrow?"

"I've got some that Rand outgrew. I keep meaning to give them to Goodwill, but I never get around to it. I bet they'll fit you."

"Okay. Next question: what are we expecting to see at the creek?"

She took her time before saying, "Whatever is there."

DIANE AND I took off our shoes and slid across the glorious champagne-colored carpet. It was only in place in two rooms, and while I changed into Randy's old clothes, I could hear Diane having a discussion, half in English, half in Spanish, with the installers. When I came out of the bathroom I stepped onto the plush carpet and said, "Lovely." Then I realized she was standing hands on hips, a thoroughly annoyed look on her face. "Not lovely?" I asked.

"Oh, the carpet is fine—what there is of it. Unfortunately, the salesman was a little exuberant in his estimate of their supply, which means it will be next Thursday by the time I have the rest of my house finished."

"What a pisser."

"Isn't it? So, we'll just have to move back in and work around—"

"Not happening," I said. "You are staying at my house until everything is complete. End of discussion."

"Are you sure?" she asked.

"Very sure." I had followed her to the utility room, where

we found a whole row of heavy rubber boots, neatly lined up in a closet.

"Okay, then pick your size," she said.

I did just that, and came up with some that weren't going to be too large. "What are all these for?" I asked.

"When we go out to Mom's ranch. Goats and pigs can be very messy."

"Why don't you leave them out there?"

"My dad can be very messy, too, so they aren't there when I go back."

"Ah. I see."

From the refrigerator she took a couple of bottles of water, handed them to me, and asked if I wanted anything to snack on. I said no, wondering how long and what kind of an expedition she had in mind. I was going to ask but my cell phone rang. I dropped everything on the washing machine and dug the phone out of my purse. "Hello?"

"Jolie, it's Sheriff Donelly. I have some news and thought you'd want to hear it right away. From the horse's mouth, as they say."

"Of course. What's up?"

"I got a phone call from Web Koker over at the DPS lab. They found some things in the preliminary exam of Dr. Bill that I thought you'd want to know." Mac took a breath. "They found some water in the lungs, so he did drown. All of the bruises and contusions on Dr. Bill's body were consistent with the accident. Some injuries occurred before death, some after."

"I see."

"Which means," Mac went on, "no bullet holes, no rope burns."

"I'm so sorry to hear that," I said, but in one sense, of course, I wasn't.

Diane turned to face me. "What?" she mouthed.

I put my hand over the phone and whispered, "Dr. Bill's autopsy report."

All along I had fought the idea of Dr. Bill committing suicide, and had told anyone who would listen that he couldn't and wouldn't take his own life, but there was no official support for my position.

"I want to be clear," I said to Mac. "Does this give any indication that he didn't commit suicide?"

"Is it important?"

"Well, it would put a stop to Brother Binder and his Band of Bigots. I'd like that."

Mac said, "Sorry, I can't officially say that for sure."

My shoulders slumped. "Damn."

"Can't officially say that, either."

It almost made me smile. "Thanks, Mac."

"You're welcome. Oh, and Jolie. Your mom was kind of upset about all this—"

"Is she still there? I'll—"

"No, that's what I was going to tell you. Your sister was coming up to pay you all a surprise visit. She's with your mom, so you don't have to worry about her."

"Oh. Elise is here. I see." I took the open water bottle that Diane was holding out to me and took a sip. "Well, thanks, for calling, Mac."

"It's your payback for getting me the names of Faith Melman's boyfriends. Now I don't owe you." He hung up and I slumped against the wall.

Diane asked, "Is it bad?"

I shook my head. "No. At least not unexpected. All of Dr. Bill's injuries are consistent with being in the creek. Nothing that would confirm another person had inflicted them."

"I see. So, who's at your house? Which Elise? Your sister?"

"She drove up to surprise us. Let me call and see if they're around. I may beg out of our trip to the creek."

I called and waited through half a dozen rings until the answering machine picked up. "Hi, it's me, Jolie," I said. "I'm with Diane and I should be home in an hour or so. Love you." I turned to Diane. "No one is home, so there's no need for me to rush off."

"We'll hurry."

I followed Diane out to the Mercedes. She had both pairs of galoshes with her, several large plastic sacks, and my water. As I settled myself in the passenger seat the vehicle parked in Tom Greer's driveway—a dark green minivan—caught my attention. As we went past I could see that it was a Dodge Caravan, the same one that we had searched for on Thursday night. It belonged to Beverly Kendall.

"Diane, look," I said, pointing.

She glanced over at the car. "Exes can be friends."

"Right, and some exes even date and get back together, but not right now. It doesn't look good." The gossips of Purple Sage would have a field day with it.

"You can't be thinking anything underhanded of Bev."

"No, no. I adore Bev. She's been angelic when I would have been downright evil, but I'm not the one who will be judging."

"You're right. Let's just hope the busybodies stay home out of the rain."

We drove through the inclement weather toward the creek. I felt pressured to get home, yet there wasn't anyone there.

Everything would be just fine if it weren't for Brother Binder. If he would just change his mind…

"You know," I said. "When we're done here I think we ought to take some extra time and talk to the minister of the Lakeside church."

Diane was driving carefully, easing us off the highway onto the sticky white caliche mud that formed an unofficial parking lot in the dry months of summer. Now it was slick and treacherous. "You think he could tell us something?"

"No, but I have a few things to say to him."

"Really?"

"Actually, as the mayor's wife, maybe you should do the talking. You know, the old 'for the betterment of the community' kind of thing. Get him to back off on this suicide thing. Then, depending on how things go, I would like to tell him that he's a bigot."

"That sounds workable, but how come you get the fun part?" She parked the car and we looked out. "Well?"

"What a muddy mess," I said.

Diane reached behind her and pulled up the trash bag with the boots. "You don't have to come with me if you don't want to."

"I'll come."

We put on the huge rubber boots and started toward the creek. The thick mud sucked at our feet, making walking difficult. I lagged behind, not for physical reasons, but because even as a part of me wanted to know what happened to Dr. Bill, another part of me hurt at the thought of what he went through.

The water was the color of mocha latte, with debris whipping past. The water was eroding the banks, so that they were no longer stable. Surely Dr. Bill would have stayed back, and yet, this is where he went in the creek.

I stared at the spot, long and hard, trying to take it in.

"This way," Diane said, moving off to our right.

With reluctance, I followed her over the slippery ground. There was a small path, probably used mostly by kids and animals, although it was overgrown, with leafless twigs that poked at us.

The stream was on our left, swift and swirling around a large tree that had gone down with the flooding. If it had been me in the creek, I would have grabbed at it. I'm sure Dr. Bill would have tried to get a handhold, too, there, on that outstretched branch, but with the water moving so quickly it must have pulled him on.

Just beyond was a whirlpool, and an elderly man, cold and weighed down with his wet clothes, wouldn't have been able to fight the swirling water. Even if he had still been conscious, the power of the creek and the pain had to have pulled him under here. It must have been terrifying.

Had he come up? Had he fought on to the next moment of hope?

I couldn't help but think back to a time in high school when almost all my friends were either Catholic or Jewish. With the irreverence of youth we called ourselves the Cashews, and even had our own special invocation that ended with, "What are you, some kind of a nut?" That same spring Jody Taylor, Bruce Tenen, and I wanted to go to some concert of long-forgotten bands. Jody's mom was adamant that Jody had to go to church first to make her Easter duty. Although neither of us was Catholic, Bruce and I went with her.

Inside the huge, solemn church, we walked with Jody through the Stations of the Cross. She explained to us what each one meant, and the prayer that went with it. Halfway through it stopped being a curious exercise, and Christ became a real person to me, just as his mother became a real mother who must have bled for her son. I remember starting to cry, and by the time we left the church Jody and I were sobbing, with Bruce trying to console us both.

Walking along the creek felt like walking those Stations of the Cross so many years ago. Here was where Dr. Bill went into the water. Here was where he fought to hold on to the tree.

"Are you okay?" Diane asked.

I nodded, swallowing hard. "I can't think, though. This is too hard."

She reached back and touched my arm. "Think about the brush." She bent down and a feathery twig snapped toward me.

"Thanks, that helped."

I focused on the ground beneath my feet. The path took a turn and we were on mud; I was stepping carefully so as not to slip. In the distance a rumble of thunder echoed, and the only other sound was the surging of the creek. Then there was a flash of lightning that struck nearby followed by another crash of thunder.

"That was close," I said.

It felt as if someone had turned nature loose, angry elements that were determined to get back at mankind for all the destruction and hurt we had caused. Hard rain would follow soon.

"Damn," Diane said. "Do you want to go back?"

"How much farther?" I asked.

"Not much."

"Then let's go on. Maybe the rain won't catch up to the special effects."

We walked another fifty feet or so. The creek turned sharply away from us. Here was a downed tree and a sandy bank covered with debris that had come from the lake. I saw tangled fishing net and pieces of Styrofoam. As I stepped closer I even saw a fish—a huge fish, bloated and white.

Diane gasped and swung around, her hand over her mouth. Then she was retching and finally she vomited several times in a row.

"Are you—?"

"Don't look at it," she said between heaves.

I turned back around and stared at the large tangled fish, only this time I saw the blond hair matted to the head, and the form that was a body—swollen, white, with marks where something had nibbled at the bloated flesh.

We had found Leigh Greer.

TWENTY-ONE

THE CAR HEATER was on, and our galoshes were in one of the trash bags. The other bag was spread across the floor in the back seat, a good thing, because as Mac climbed in I noticed his western boots were coated with mud. Diane and I faced him as best we could. She was still pale, but doing better. I was cold and queasy in a way that was going to last awhile.

Mac looked us over, and said, "You want to tell me why you were out here?"

It was fortunate that we were outside the city limits so it was Mac who was interviewing us and not the chief of police, who wasn't as quick and wasn't as friendly.

"It was my idea," Diane said. "I asked Jolie to come with me."

"I understand that, but I want to know why you chose to come out in this weather? I know you had a good reason."

Diane nodded. "As soon as Jolie told me about the green bag going through the drawdown tube, I thought that, well, if—" she stopped. "I thought I might find something of Leigh's. Maybe the bag, if we were lucky. I also thought that perhaps Leigh was..." She stopped again, to lick her sickly white lips. "You understand."

"I do." He took off his hat with its plastic rain covering, and rubbed his forehead. "That was good thinking on your part, which doesn't surprise me, but I am a little curious as to why you didn't call us to check it out, rather than coming out here in the rain yourself."

"It was a long shot," Diane said. "And I didn't want to bother you if it didn't pan out."

"Ma'am, we have followed a lot more tenuous leads than this, including one from a woman who said she and her cat were reading the Tarot cards and saw Leigh in a castle. I will always welcome your ideas for many reasons, one of which is that you are the mayor's wife. Not that it's the most important."

Diane gave him a shaky smile. "Thanks, Mac."

"Well, you could have saved yourself some real unpleasantness." He was grumbling, but not unkindly. "Now, I have a few more questions if you're up to them."

We were, but we didn't have any answers that were helpful. We simply hadn't seen anything except Leigh's almost unrecognizable body. We hadn't touched, or even looked at the body, while calling the sheriff, and waiting for him to arrive.

A DPS mobile van pulled up and two young men got out and came toward us.

"I understand you have some work for us," the youngest-looking of the two said.

I thought how delicately he had phrased his comment, and how instead of a trooper looking for a body, he might be a hired hand looking to run a tractor or a combine.

Mac climbed out of the car before turning to say to us, "I think y'all need to go home and get on some dry clothes. Drinking something hot wouldn't hurt, either. If I have any more questions I know where to find you." He adjusted his hat before asking Diane, "Are you okay to drive?"

She nodded her head. "I'm fine."

She started the car and drove to the radio station in silence. There simply wasn't anything to say. Being right is usually a good thing, but not when it results in finding a person dead.

Once we were in the parking lot I climbed out of the car, my movements slow and deliberate. My joints hurt with the cold and my muscles were stiff with shock. This was only the third time in my life that I had seen the effects of death before a mortician had done his work. Leigh looked especially bad because of the water, and the damage caused by the debris. I was working very hard not to remember the sight of her.

"I'll see you at the house," I said.

"I'm going to try and find Trey first, so don't expect me right away."

I nodded agreement, and stood there as she drove off.

TWENTY MINUTES LATER I was on the road again, my depression replaced by my sense of urgency.

I had called around trying to locate the various members of my family, but I couldn't find my mom, sister, or even Jeremy. The only one I'd been able to talk with had been Matt. He already knew about Leigh being found—the sheriff had called him and requested his presence when the news was given to Tom. Matt was on his way to Tom's house, and his voice was heavy with dread.

"There's not much to say to a man when he's lost the woman he loves." He paused and swallowed so hard I could hear it over the phone line. "There would be nothing anyone could say to comfort me if I lost you."

"You never will," I said. "I'll be here forever."

"I wish you could promise that." He let out a breath. "I'll be home as soon as I can, but it might be late."

"I know."

He finished the conversation with, "I love you."

"I love you, too," I responded before we hung up.

It was then I remembered another person who cared greatly about Leigh Greer, and that was Linda Beaman. It wasn't likely anyone was going to drive out to give her the news, or even phone her. She would hear it from a newscast, and I couldn't let that happen. She needed someone with her—and with Travis out of town, who was there?

The least I could do was break the news to Linda myself.

There were no deputies on the road between the station and Linda's house, and that was a very good thing, as I was well over the speed limit.

When I stopped on the muddy drive in front of the house,

the dogs ignored me. Maybe they sensed the importance of my mission. They stayed behind me, slinking until I reached the porch. Linda opened the door as I raised my hand to knock.

She stared at me, her face impassive.

Driving over I had thought and thought of what to say but none of it had been right, and in the end, I had hoped the words would come when I needed them. Now that the time was here, no words came at all. We faced each other in silence across the doorway.

Linda's lower lip trembled, and she spoke. "They found her, didn't they? She's dead, isn't she?"

Slowly, I nodded, still in silence.

"I knew it. I knew she wouldn't just go off like that." Her voice cracked, and sobs began to shake her body. "I knew she was dead. We were just kidding ourselves—"

She stopped and the tears poured in earnest. I reached out my arms to her, and then she was holding on to me, enveloping me, as her body heaved with sobs.

LINDA WAS making tea.

I have heard it said that during a wedding the food should be prepared so that there is nothing for the guests to do but eat and party, but at a funeral, you should always give people food that needed assembling. Now, I could see the value in that. Linda was taking comfort in preparing tea, and it was keeping her mind from focusing totally on her pain.

She didn't set out the elegant tea strainers or the fancy napkins, and she used the microwave to get the liquid hot quickly.

"I'm sorry I broke down like that," Linda said, putting two sturdy mugs of hot water on the table. Then she went to the cupboard for tea bags, and placed one in each of our cups before sitting across from me. "I don't truck much with women who carry on like that."

"You didn't carry on; you just cried. We all cry when we lose someone we love," I said. "I'm so sorry that you...that Leigh is...gone."

"I know."

"And I feel so bad about what I said to her. And to you and—"

She didn't let me get any further. "But you came out here to tell me about her being found, which was more than anyone else did. So now, I feel bad 'cuz I've been rude to you ever since you came to Purple Sage. I had no call to be that way."

"And I've been rude right back. I judged Leigh, too. I never gave her a chance."

Linda's eyes turned watery, but her voice was strong. "She was a real fine person. She was smarter than people gave her credit for, too. Sometimes she'd hide behind that little girl attitude, but she was sharp." Linda sniffed hard, then blew her nose. "She was so troubled about seeing Dr. Bill at the creek."

"And people saying it was suicide?"

A slow nod. "I just wish Leigh had been one hundred percent sure of what she saw that night. I don't blame her, what with the rain and all, it was hard to see that far, and she was tired after the party."

"You wish she was sure about what Dr. Bill was doing?"

"Partly, and partly about that shadow."

"You think that 'shadow' she saw was a second car?"

"I always say go with your first instinct, and that was hers. But there's something else I've wondered about. You know, she said she saw Dr. Bill in the headlights, but she didn't see his face. What if it was someone else? The person who killed him?"

I couldn't believe I hadn't thought of that. She said she'd seen Dr. Bill in his raincoat with his back to her, which wasn't at all conclusive. "How did she describe the coat to you? Something about a spy coat, I think she said to me."

"It was one of them London Fog type trench coats. You know the kind I mean? Beige and kind of long."

"And she saw an umbrella."

"But she never said what color it was, or anything. That night at the reception most everyone had an umbrella and lots of people had coats like that. Gretchen even wore one. It was *after* Leigh heard that Dr. Bill was dead that she assumed it was him she'd seen. But I think it could have been anyone.''

''But she saw his car, remember? And that big white thing is hard to mistake for anything else.'' It was a huge Suburban that I had kiddingly called the starship *Enterprise*.

''I'm sure there's more than one in town. But, I reckon you're right.'' Linda lifted her teacup, and sipped. After she swallowed, she said, ''You know what I think? I think Leigh saw whoever killed Dr. Bill, because she said he was facing away from the creek, like he was walking back to his car. So, I think she got there after Dr. Bill was already in the water, and the person who pushed him was getting out of there.''

''And Leigh was a danger, so the murderer went after her, too?''

Linda nodded, then her lip quivered. ''I don't like to think of that part, but yes.'' A shaky sigh and then, ''Leigh must have known who it was, too, because she met him out at the lake.'' Tears slipped from her eyes. ''I sure hope they catch him and give him what he deserves.''

I STAYED UNTIL Linda stopped crying and Travis, Sr., got home. Once she was in his capable care, I left, my car on automatic pilot and my mind on Dr. Bill and Leigh. I was becoming obsessed by that dark night at the creek.

If Linda was right, then Leigh had actually seen Dr. Bill's murderer, as well as the vehicle the murderer had driven to the creek. So what might that have been? What would look like the shadow of a Suburban? Obviously something large, perhaps an SUV or a minivan, and it would have to be dark. A dark green minivan.

An image of Brother Binder's and Ute's matching Windstars came to mind, followed by Bev's dark green Caravan, and then Matt's dark blue Explorer. And Jeremy's Midnight Blue Beast.

There were probably hundreds of cars that could pass for a shadow beside the hulking Suburban, and the sheriff had better access to information in that arena than I did. Then there was the coat. Or perhaps there were issues even more vital than that, such as who and why.

Who would feel pressured to go out into a stormy night to kill a man who had done so much good and worked so hard for his patients? What could possibly drive a person to that?

It was clearer with Leigh's murder, since there was fear of exposure, but with Dr. Bill, there wasn't a reason I could see. The man was retiring from practice. He had never been embroiled in public controversies or malpractice suits. He took unbelievably good care of his patients, and his personal life was quiet and simple. He spent most of his time working, either at his office or at the hospital. He donated his time and expertise when people couldn't afford to pay him. In the few hours a week when he wasn't practicing medicine he had liked to work in his yard and flower garden.

It was Gretchen who had been the driving force in the remodeling of their house. She had told me it was more about repair than anything else and she was the one who worked with the contractor. She'd confided in me that it took all but an act of Congress to get Dr. Bill to say anything more than "Fine; I like them all" when she asked his preference on samples of tile and paint.

And yet someone had killed him.

I turned into our drive, letting out a long sigh that neither eased my unhappiness nor solved the seeming impossibility of Dr. Bill's murder. The sky was almost dark, and ahead of me I could see the house lights blazing out. Several vehicles were lined up in front; I recognized my mother's rental car and Jeremy's blue truck, but not the red BMW sports car. It was shining even in these weather conditions, and only the wheels were marred by our white caliche mud.

I parked the car and had started toward the porch before I realized whose it was. It belonged to my sister.

TWENTY-TWO

THE HOUSE SMELLED warm and wonderful, like food cooking. My mom was stretched out in Matt's recliner and Elise was sitting on the hearth, the fire reflecting off her short curly hair. Her clear blue eyes were bright with laughter, and the red of her sweater matched the car outside.

"Elise!" I said. "I can't believe you're here. You look beautiful."

"Hi, sweetie." Elise rose and gave me a hug, then pulled away. "Jolie, you're soaked."

"Oh, sorry." I released her and we both stepped back to brush off water. "I didn't mean to get you wet. It's not part of the standard greeting package." I removed my coat. "Let me hang this up." I went into the foyer and threw it over a doorknob.

"I don't mind; I was too warm by the fire, anyway. You see, Mom, and you thought she'd been kidnapped by aliens."

"Hey, Mom," I said, returning to the living room. "How was your day?"

Elise was smiling at me. "Where'd you get that outfit? I thought the grunge look went out. At least, I'd hoped so."

I looked down and realized that I was still wearing Randy's things. The jeans were baggy with the tattered cuffs rolled up. I had on two of his shirts—a T-shirt topped by a faded concert sweatshirt.

"And," my mother added, "where have you been? Your sister has been here for hours and we tried to call you on your cell phone but you didn't answer."

"My cell?" I shook my head, remembering that I'd turned it off after Mac's call. "I'm sorry, I turned it off. Damn."

Mom raised one eyebrow, as Elise said, "Aren't they the most obnoxious things? I swear, if I leave mine turned on the battery runs out, and if I turn it off, I forget to check messages."

"That's me," I said. My mother grunted softly, perhaps mollified. I sat on the other side of the hearth from Elise. "So, what have I missed? It's so good to have you here. And where is everyone else?"

"Diane and Trey moved out," my mother said. "Randy came by and got their things." She swiveled the recliner to get a better view of us.

"But why? I just saw Diane a little bit ago." I looked at my watch. "Not much more than two hours ago."

"They found more carpet," Elise said. "Or the dealer did. A remnant, but it's enough to finish their house, so she wanted to be on hand to oversee the whole thing. This is on a Sunday, no less. She must have some clout."

"Oh, it's Trey, not Diane," I said. "He's like Matt, he can work miracles."

"Which reminds me," Mom said, "Matt is at Tom's, did you know that?"

"I knew. I talked with him. So, where have you two been?" I asked. "Did you do anything exciting?"

Elise said, "No, we were just knocking around. Before he got the news Matt gave us a tour of the ranch. There were already several calves—they are so darling. And then we went into town and Mom took me by the shelter, and showed me some of the flooded areas. What a mess. Oh, and we ran into a friend of yours at the grocery store."

"Who was that?" I asked.

"Beverly Kendall," my mother said. "She recognized me, and I remembered her as soon as she started talking. She ended up inviting all of us to lunch tomorrow, and I accepted."

"That should be fun," I said.

"Which brings us to you," my mother said, more pointedly

than necessary. "Where have you been? We looked for you for some time."

"Sorry, I wasn't actually in Purple Sage; I was at Linda Beaman's house. She was a close friend of Leigh's, and I went to break the news about Leigh's death in person. I didn't want her to be alone."

"That was sweet of you," Elise said, tipping her head so that the light caught her shining curls.

"How did you hear about Leigh's body being found?" my mother asked. "It hasn't been on the news yet."

My feet were tapping the floor of their own accord, and I felt the rest of my body stiffen. My mother was not going to be pleased with me. "I was there. I found Leigh."

"What in the world were you doing out at the creek in the rain?" my mother demanded. "Mac told me that she was nearly a mile from the highway. Did you walk way out there? And why? Why would you do that?"

"Because," I said, drawing in a large breath. "Diane asked me to go with her. I told her about seeing Leigh's craft bag go down the drawdown tube and she thought, well, she suspected that if Leigh drowned, she might also have…be in the creek."

"Jolie, I still have absolutely no idea why you would do such a thing. Mac Donelly is a wonderful sheriff and he is perfectly capable of doing his job, so why you would even consider poking—"

"He is not investigating Dr. Bill's death, okay? That's the first thing. And number two, Diane and I didn't know for sure that we'd find anything. She just had this idea, and she asked me to come along, and I agreed."

"You are not twelve and you don't have to do everything that your friends ask you to."

"You're right. I'm not twelve, so why are you treating me like I am?"

"I hate this," Elise said, jumping up. "Jolie, you haven't been here ten minutes and you two have already gotten into an argument."

"I didn't start it!" I said.

"Besides, it's not an argument," my mother snapped. "I'm merely appalled at some of the things that Jolie does. I will never understand—"

"Truer words were never spoken," I said.

Elise made a sound. "There you go again. Can't you two just be nice to each other?"

"Of course we can," I said, forcing myself to breathe. "I'm sorry, I shouldn't have snapped."

My mother was watching me closely for signs of sincerity, and when she saw them she said, "That's all right, and I'm sorry, too."

"It's just been a hard day and I'm hungry," I said. "Let me go fix something for all of us."

"That's not necessary," my mother said, rising. "Elise and I made a wonderful shepherd's pie. It's a recipe I got when I was in England, and no matter what they say, there are some wonderful English cooks."

"I love shepherd's pie," I said. "That was really nice of you. What can I fix to go with it? Salad? We have that. And wine, and bread."

All three of us were up and moving, doing what women have done for years—bonding in the kitchen.

"We already made the salad," Elise was saying, "and the pie just needs reheating, but shouldn't we wait for Matt?"

"No. He could be gone all evening." I didn't even know where Jeremy was, which would be another sin in my mother's eyes. I'd seen his pickup out front, but that didn't mean that he was here.

She didn't comment on that; she was busy moving around the kitchen with proprietary control. First she turned on the oven, then took one of the pies from a cooling rack and put it back inside. Meanwhile, Elise was getting wine from the refrigerator.

"I brought this with me. You'll love it. It's a wonderfully fruity white, with just enough oak to save it from being too sweet. Not really a sharp edge, but a tad crisp."

"Great." At that moment I didn't trust myself around any-thing with a sharp edge. "There's some giabatta bread in—"

"Yes, I know," said my mother, turning the second oven up to three-fifty. "I wish Mac had the time to come out here and have dinner with us."

Elise grinned. "I didn't think you were putting all that effort into a dinner for us. It was really for Mac." She looked at me. "Sheriff Mac Donelly has been quite the topic of conversation this afternoon."

My mother almost blushed. "Oh, Elise, he was not."

"He was supposed to come for dinner, but Mom got a call from someone—"

"The dispatcher," Mom said.

"She even knows the lingo—"

They reminded me of junior high girls, teasing each other about boys. "It was just a courtesy call," Mom said. "Mac had apparently found out about Leigh and he wasn't able to join us."

"I didn't even know you knew Mac," I said.

"I met him at your wedding. When you and Matt renewed your vows last summer in front of the courthouse. We danced a lot that day."

"I met him that day, too," Elise said, "but he didn't make quite the impression on me that he did on Mom. That's why I made this trip up here to check him out."

"I don't think that was necessary," I said. "I've known Mac for years, and we all adore him. Ask Jeremy about him. Or did you?"

"Not yet."

"Well, he's great."

"Good enough for our mother?" Elise asked, tilting her head and giving me the impish look that is her trademark.

"Oh, yes. He's almost too good to—"

"To what?" My mother snapped, dropping the dish towel on the floor. "Too good to go out with me?"

"No! I wasn't going to say that. Too good for our family. For us. Elise and me. I was teasing."

"Well, it wasn't very funny." She picked up the towel and threw it on the counter.

"You didn't even let me finish the sentence before you started yelling at me."

"I didn't yell."

Elise said, "You're both yelling. I don't know what's with you two, but I'm going upstairs, and I hope when I get back we can have a little fun. Remember that word?" She stared at me before she left the room.

I turned to my mother. "I'm sorry," I said. "If you want the whole truth, I think Mac is an incredible man, and I'm thrilled that he's found someone to go out with. I just don't want to lose him as a sheriff. Now, does that satisfy you?"

My mother leaned up against the counter. "It's all about protecting Mac, and losing Mac. You don't give a damn what I do. You were always such a little daddy's girl and then you transferred that affection to Dr. Bill, and now, I suppose it's to Mac."

"Mother, that's not fair—"

"No it wasn't. I gave birth to this beautiful little girl, and I don't think you liked me from the day you were born."

"That's not the way it went. You had Win." My older brother had always been her pet. "Smart Win", "Big boy Win", "so athletic." And then Elise came along and she was talented and beautiful. "You never even noticed I was around."

"You *weren't* around. You acted like you were too good for us—no, too good for me—from the time you were a baby. When you weren't even two years old I went in the dining room to set the table and you know what I found? You. Moving your high chair. And do you know what you said to me? You said, 'I'm sitting by my daddy. Forever.' Quite articulate and quite emphatic."

"Well, thank God I was at least articulate."

The door opened and Jeremy walked in. He looked as if he'd just woken up. "What's all the noise? Are you two arguing again?"

"No," I said. "Go to your room. We're talking."

"Jolene Berenski," Mom snapped. "You apologize to him. He didn't do anything wrong, and you had no right to speak to him that way."

"I'm sorry," I said to Jeremy through a tight jaw. "I didn't mean to be rude, but we were having a private conversation." I thought of Linda Beaman saying that about her and Leigh.

He threw up his arms as if in surrender. "Then I'll go out; I just thought you might need a referee." He turned and left.

"You see how you are?" my mother demanded. "Do you have PMS? If not, you should have your hormones checked."

"Why? According to you I've been this way all my life."

"You've been that way to me...not everyone else."

"Wait," I said, taking in a breath. "Let's be very clear on something. You decided that I was a brat when I was under two years old. I was just a baby, and you're still holding it against me that I moved my high chair. That's ridiculous. Besides, you must have done something to make me mad."

"That's right, blame it on me."

"I'm not." I was trying, without much success, to bring this conversation under control. I had the feeling that this could alter our relationship for years to come, but then I'd thought that before. And maybe I'd been right before. Maybe that's why we were still arguing. "Mom," I said, holding my tone as level as possible. "What I'm saying is that a one-year-old doesn't do things without reason. And it could have been a stupid reason. Maybe you told me no cookies, or spanked me for something."

"I only mentioned that incident because it seems to epitomize our entire relationship." She turned to the drawer and began counting out silverware for the table.

"Is that why you cared so much more for Elise and Win than you did for me?"

She turned, her expression incredulous. "Is that what you think? That I loved them more? That's completely wrong."

"Why? I'm sure there are plenty of mothers who love one child more than another."

Her voice went soft. "Honey, every mother feels that way, but the child she loves most changes all the time. Usually it's the one who's sick or hurt or farthest away."

Tears pricked my eyes. That meant I had been the one she'd loved most some of the time. I'd never known.

I swallowed air. "I always thought that Win or Elise...you spent so much time with Elise."

"I did. A great deal of time, but I didn't know you minded. You know why."

"No. Or maybe, yes, I do. I thought because you liked her better."

"Honey, when Elise was born, she stayed in the birth canal too long; there were complications because of it. She didn't get the air she needed, so the doctors were very worried about brain damage. We didn't know any of the things we know today, but by instinct, I guess, I knew that if I could help her study, she would learn—so that's what I did. You're right, I spent hours and hours working with her."

"I never knew that. You never said anything—"

"We never talked about it. I guess your father and I hoped if it wasn't discussed, it wouldn't be true."

Another family secret.

My mother's eyes went to the floor and a great sadness moved across her face. I don't think that I have ever seen her appear so vulnerable, and it surprised and saddened me. Why had I always pictured her as a Valkyrie who brooked no nonsense and took no prisoners, when in truth, she was just a woman like I was?

Perhaps not like me in all ways, but fundamentally, her concerns were for her family. That touched me.

She looked up. "You see," she said, "in some ways Elise was slow. I don't know what they call it today, but her analytical powers didn't develop well, and she had trouble memorizing. That's all the first several years of school are, so it was difficult." She paused. "You didn't realize that?"

"No." Children don't view the world clinically.

"You told her she wasn't smart."

It wasn't clinical, just cruel. I felt sick. I didn't recall the incident, but it was obviously memorable to my mother. I wondered if Elise remembered, too. "I'm sorry—it was a kid thing."

"And more than once you called Win a big moron."

I had called Winthrop a lot of things, and few were flattering, but it never mattered, since Win was so far above the fray. He was big, three years older than I was, and he was an incredible athlete. He always seemed to hit the winning home run or make the game-saving tackle. Everyone adored Win, and if an adult stopped me on the street it was invariably to talk about Win and what a champ he was. How he made the home team great. And while people seemed to think I would be thrilled to listen to their exclamations over my wonderful brother, nothing could have been further from the truth. Hearing of his greatness, I always felt myself turning into a little brown mouse in comparison, with no personality, no power, and no distinguishing characteristics. I did remain polite, but then I would walk home, my whole psyche slinking. Calling him stupid was my only defense. It was like saying Tom Cruise had the start of a pimple—who cared? My comments hadn't diminished Win in the slightest.

"Win didn't care; I was invisible to him." Yet, I was the one gazing at the floor as I began to take in the truth. "Elise was so talented. And beautiful. She still is."

"Yes—and in high school when she was tested she was slightly above normal. And she is talented, too. Your father and I were thrilled when Elise started playing the piano—it was like a new world for her where she could excel. Music is wonderful for her."

I said, "I didn't have a world like that."

"Jolie! You were clever, inquisitive, and there was nothing that you couldn't figure out or accomplish when you put your mind to it. You were like a brilliant quasar, shooting through life, with abundant energy and intelligence. You hardly needed parents." She paused, then added, "And it didn't appear that you wanted them, either. At least not this one."

"What was the point of wanting?" I asked. "I couldn't have you. You were always too busy with Win or Elise, and after that came your charities. Even this weekend—I seem to come in last." My throat tightened and my eyes began to sting. I closed them quickly, but it was too late. Tears were already slipping out. "I'm sorry…it's just that sometimes I'm jealous of the way that you and Elise are, and sometimes I just feel lonely and…and left out. So, I don't even come around. And now you have the shelter and Mac. That puts me last again…."

"Oh, honey." She put her arms around me, and I started to cry even harder.

I couldn't remember the last time my mother had held me. I was embarrassed that I was so emotional, and yet it felt so good to have her touching me. To smell her perfume up close, and know her warmth.

"I didn't mean to cry," I said, still sobbing. "I just missed having you."

"And I've missed you, too." She ran her hand over my hair, rocking her body slightly. "You've always been so independent."

"That doesn't mean I always wanted to be."

"I know, honey, now I know."

"I'm sorry, I'm still crying."

"I'm not." She rubbed her hand along my arm. "It's almost like you moved the high chair back."

I gave a little laugh, and tasted the salt of my tears. "Then maybe you could help me keep it beside you. Apparently I'm not too good at this."

She held me tightly; it was unprecedented, at least in my memory. "I certainly will. We'll learn together."

TWENTY-THREE

LIKE A SKI RUN, the evening was filled with moguls and dips, some hidden until I was right on them, so I was always off balance. First was dinner, with its tentative beginning. Jeremy and Elise were unsure of how my mother and I were going to act, particularly, I suppose, in light of my red and blotchy tear-stained face.

"Everything is fine," I said, taking my place at the table. "Just fine. Really."

"Yes, so come and eat." Mom was shooing them into chairs, then she smiled at me. "We're going to have a wonderful meal."

And for the most part, we did, with lots of laughter and telling of stories. Jeremy was more animated than I had seen him in months, and my mother was absolutely charming. There were moments when I would catch myself about to say something to my mother that was questionable—it never went beyond that, and I'm sure she caught herself, too. Then things smoothed out, and I remember looking around at them thinking, it doesn't get much better than this.

We stayed at the table for hours. I was afraid that if we moved into the living room the spell might be broken, and the others must have had the same thought. By the time we finished cleaning the kitchen it was almost eleven, and everyone headed for bed.

"'Night, sweetie," I said to Jeremy, giving him a quick hug.

"'Night, Mom." Then he hugged my mother. "'Night, Grams. 'Night, Aunt Elise."

He started up and my mother hugged me. "Good night, honey." Then she brushed my hair back from my face with the palm of her hand. "You sleep well, you've had a rough day."

"I will. You, too."

Then Elise and I hugged. I was so warm and happy, like Pollyanna at the Waltons, that I wondered if I was dreaming. And once upstairs in bed, I thought of all the things we could do as a family, if I took some time off in the coming week. I had the same giddiness as the first flush of falling in love.

I was finally dozing when Matt slipped into bed with me. "Jolie? Are you awake?"

"Almost. How are you? Are you okay?" I rolled over to be closer to him. "How's Tom doing?"

Matt enveloped me in his hug, his body cool and taut next to mine. "Tom is doing as well as you could expect." He took a breath. "God, I've missed you. I may never leave your side again."

I snuggled closer. "This has been so hard for you."

"Only because I knew how it would be if I lost you. I don't think I could live through that." He kissed my nose, then moved his lips down to mine. It began softly, then the kiss turned deep and serious. "Jolie, I love you."

"Thank you," I said.

"For?"

"For everything; especially for letting me love you back."

I LEFT THE STATION shortly after I finished the news, walking toward the *Trib* building, swinging my arms both to keep warm and to use up the excess energy. Last night had been like a vacation, but now I was back to the real world, and I was worried, particularly about Dr. Bill's funeral.

First, I was going to see Ute, to find out why she had been acting oddly yesterday afternoon. I had this feeling that she was keeping silent on something, and it hadn't started until after Jessika went to see the sheriff. If there was anything that could add to our knowledge of Dr. Bill's death, then I needed to know now, although in truth, my forward momentum was slowing only to be replaced by dread. Nothing short of a miracle was going to change people's opinions on how he died.

Perhaps in concession to that I had decided that as soon as Katharine came into the station I was going to ask for the week off. Charity starts at home, as I had always believed, and it was time for me to do some nice things for my mother and sister. When I left KSGE it would be around noon, just in time to join them at Beverly's for lunch. The final thing on my agenda was attending Dr. Bill's funeral at two-thirty.

I had it all planned out, but as we've heard, the best laid plans of mice and men and Jolie Wyatt oft times go awry. I should have expected it.

The *Sage Tribune* building is an ugly square three-story building that always smells faintly of bat guano. I used the side entrance and inside found a large scaffold in an area that used to house office supplies; bright blue tarps were strung over the walls, and they might have been festive under other circumstances.

A teenage girl was standing behind the counter, playing solitaire on an old computer. "Hi," I said. "Looks like you've had a leak."

She glanced up quickly and then moved a red jack to a black queen. "Lot's of leaks. Morris is all freaked out about it, too. Is there something I can do for you?"

"I was looking for Ute. Is she around?"

"She isn't in yet, but I expect her any time. How about Rhonda Hargis? Could she help?" Rhonda Hargis is the ace reporter for the *Trib,* and a former member of my writers group. Like any good reporter, Rhonda has her own special sources and often knows things that aren't general knowledge.

I considered that. "Well, maybe she can help me."

"She's in the back." The young woman pointed without looking up. "Go around the scaffold. Can't miss her." She moved a black ten to the jack.

I skirted the scaffolding and found the closed door to Morris Pratt's office. The door sign said, "Editor," but it's almost always where I found Rhonda. The office is small and painted in that particularly unattractive shade of green that was once considered soothing for schools and hospitals. Luckily the walls are covered with clippings and articles from other newspapers, so that the green is now an accent color, rather than the primary.

I knocked on the doorjamb.

"What? I'm busy in here."

"Sorry," I said. "The girl sent me back—"

Rhonda swung away from the computer to face me. "Jolie, I'm sorry. I thought you were Tiffany out there. She's been driving me crazy all morning. She couldn't get the games to work on the damn computer! Like it's my job to fix it for her. Can you believe that? Come on in." Rhonda has blond streaky hair and the athletic body of someone who works out constantly. She used to ride a bike and wear Lycra; these days she's into bare navels and power lifting. "Like I don't have enough to do without catering to her, but she is Morris's niece, so we all have to be nice to the little twit." She sat forward in the chair. "So, what can I do you for?"

"This isn't a good time."

"Yeah, well until it stops flooding or we're all in the ark, there isn't going to be a good time." The ark jokes had been prevalent of late. "You know how many buildings in this town have sustained damage? Some have had high water coming in from the streets, and others have water coming through the roof, and they all want their picture in the paper. And they want to make sure we get pictures of every single little problem. Not my idea of a claim to fame."

"Me, neither."

She pulled out a chair for me, scrapping it across the battered linoleum. "Here. Have a seat. What's up?"

I sat down. "I wanted to ask you about Dr. Bill Marchak and the way he died. Have you heard anything that isn't public knowledge?"

Rhonda shook her head. "Jolie, if I did have any additional

information I couldn't tell you. We're competitors. You'd have to read it when the *Trib* comes out."

I can never convince Rhonda that we aren't rivals for readers or listeners. She deals in written history and pictures, while I offer short bits of the immediate. But she sees it differently.

"It's not about the radio station," I said. "I want to know for me."

"Meaning?"

I leaned toward her. "Rhonda, Dr. Bill took care of my dad when he was dying of cancer. All I want to find out is why he was in that stupid creek. It's personal."

Rhonda's expression showed more emotion than usual. "I'm bummed about Dr. Bill, too. He shouldn't have died."

"Did Morris see anything when he found Dr. Bill? Anything at all? I mean, like how Dr. Bill got in the water?"

"I've seen the pictures," she said, "but there wasn't anything, anything—" She took a breath. "Jolie, it was awful. You don't want to see the pictures, honest."

I believed her. I had seen Leigh's body, and that was more than enough for me. "I understand. But what about Morris? Did he see anything?"

"No. I don't think he was even looking through the viewfinder when he took the pictures. It really shook him up. Why Dr. Bill went down there is a mystery."

I nodded and stood up. "Thanks, Rhonda."

"For nothing," she said. Then she added, "Hey, Jolie, the reception you gave for Dr. Bill—that was really nice."

"Thanks."

There were so many questions and there didn't seem to be a single person who could supply the answers. The more people I talked to, the more negatives I found. My biggest hope was that Mac would solve Leigh's murder, if that's what it was, and the answer to that one would also get us the answer to Dr. Bill's death.

I was just leaving the *Trib* office when the door opened in front of me and it was Ute.

"Excuse me—" she said. "Oh, Jolie. It's you."

"Ute. Just the person I was looking for."

"For me? Now?"

"Why? Isn't this a good time?"

She appeared to be searching for a direction to run. "Actually, I'm a little late and I have a great deal to do. You know the paper comes out tomorrow, so we have deadlines...."

"I just wanted to find out..." I glanced over to see Tiffany, the teenager at the computer, watching us with great fascination. Perhaps this wasn't the best time or place. "How about if I stop by later? Would that be better?"

"Today is not really a good day."

"It will just take five minutes. Promise."

Ute was already moving away from me. "I cannot say right now. I will have to see how the day goes." And then, with a quick wave of her hand, she slipped behind a door and was gone.

I looked over at Tiffany and shrugged, then stepped outside. Parked at the curb was Ute's green Windstar. I couldn't see Ute murdering Dr. Bill or Leigh Greer, but there was definitely something going on.

As I walked past the car I wondered if there might be someone else in her family who drove it. Interesting thought. Kevin was way too young and Jessika didn't have her license. Franzi might drive the family car at times, but she was even less feasible as a murderer than her mother. Which left Wolfgang, Ute's husband, until I remembered that he'd been out of town all last week, in Germany, no less. Not much possibility there, so why was Ute running from me?

I headed back to the station to get my final morning chore complete. As always the building pulsed with sound—at that moment there was an old Dolly Parton song setting a fast pace and a happy mood.

Our news director, Katharine, was coming down the hall toward me, her movements rhythmic, as usual, more like dancing than walking.

"Well, lady, how are you doing?" came her greeting.

"Fine. Please tell me you have five minutes to talk to me."

"Sure. Why wouldn't I? Or have they found another

body?'' She looked at my face. ''You didn't find another body, did you?''

''No; nor do I ever intend to.''

''It isn't something I'd want to make a habit of, either. Let's go in the office, shall we?'' She led me into the news office and we sat in chairs opposite each other at the partner's desk. ''So, what's up?''

''Actually, it's good news. I have family in town this week, and if it's not going to cause a problem, I'd like to take the whole week off.''

There was a pause as she considered my request. ''That's nice. And, my first instinct is to be selfish and say no, but you've covered for me too many times. I'm in your debt,'' she said. ''Do you even get vacations?''

I wasn't surprised at her question. We change news directors pretty often, since Purple Sage is not considered a choice spot on the career ladder, and she had only been at the station for a few months. ''Actually, Lewis gives me a couple of weeks at half pay, but this would just be free time. Go play; no pay.''

She smiled. ''Sure, take the time off. Although, I do request that if things get hectic with more flooding, or whatever, that you are available.''

''Oh, sure, that's not a problem. I'll still be in town. We're going to have a family week.''

''Have fun.''

''I intend to.''

I glanced at my watch—my timing was excellent. It was almost noon, leaving me just enough time to drive to Beverly's and meet everyone for lunch.

It didn't take more than five minutes to get there, and when I did, I parked on the street, then hurried along the sidewalk to the house.

Bev opened the door immediately, her expression distraught, her eyes darting beyond me to the street, then back to my face. ''Oh, Jolie, it's you.''

''What's wrong?'' I asked.

She swallowed hard, her chest heaving, then said, ''It's my dad again.''

TWENTY-FOUR

"Is HE HURT? Did he fall?"

"No, no. I'm sorry, I shouldn't panic, but his dementia seems to be getting worse." She took in a big breath and ushered me into the house. "Yesterday he drove to the store and then walked back an hour later. He'd forgotten where he'd gone, why, and even that he had a car. It must have been some homing instinct that got him back here."

"Oh, Bev, I'm so sorry. Where is he now?"

"That's what I don't know. He said he was going to the senior citizens center, but when I called to see if he'd made it, the person who answered the phone said he wasn't there. I have no idea where he might have gone."

"How long ago did you call?"

"Just a few minutes ago. I didn't want to leave, since you were coming."

"I'll wait here for my family. As soon as they get here, we'll all go search."

She put a hand to her face. "I'm so sorry to have to do this. It's just—" She dropped her hand and stopped to breathe. "I think the stress is getting to me."

"Of course it is. Look, find your dad and then we'll see what we can do about you."

"Okay." She grabbed her purse and keys off the piano and whirled back toward the door.

"Have you got your cell phone?" I asked.

"Yes. Oh, and go ahead and answer this phone, just in case someone calls about him."

"Will do." I watched her run to her car and get in. She was too distracted to notice that I waved good-bye, but I could hardly blame her. The role reversal from child to adult is difficult under the best of circumstances; I had watched it with my father, as he grew too weak to do much more than lie in bed. He had been testy at his loss of strength and health, but at least he had remained sane. With Bev, watching a once-powerful male like her father slipping in and out of reality had to be almost unendurable.

Confusing too, because he'd been so normal at the reception. He'd been irritable that evening, but for the most part, he seemed aware of everything around him. Except for that comment about Dolph Briscoe being governor. Dolph Briscoe had been in office more than twenty years ago, something Henry Kendall should have remembered, since he'd been a mover and a shaker in the Democratic Party until only four years ago. But then he'd forgotten his car just yesterday.

Like Matt was always losing his keys? Half the time I couldn't remember what I was looking for in the midst of a search. Did that mean that dementia was what we could all look forward to? Gaps in both our memories and our realities?

I closed the door and stood near the window, watching for my mother and sister. I would take them to the Red Roof B&B for lunch to make it up to them.

Then I remembered that my mom and the sheriff had a dinner date there just the other night, and it might be a special place for them. One that she didn't want to revisit with her two grown daughters.

I was beginning to think it was nice that my mother was dating Mac—another role reversal, although this one I could adjust to.

The phone rang, and after one more look out the window to assure myself that no one had arrived, I went to the kitchen to answer it.

"Kendall residence," I said. On the chipped, pale green counter was a large quiche, along with a plate of homemade cookies.

"Bev? Is that you?" asked a male voice.

"No, this is Jolie Wyatt. Bev isn't here right now."

"Jolie, hi, this is Tom. Tom Greer. What are you doing there?"

And why are you calling? I wanted to ask. Instead I explained what had happened and where Bev was at that moment.

"Jolie, maybe you're the perfect person for me to talk to. You know about Leigh?"

"Yes. I'm so sorry, Tom."

"Thanks, I appreciate it. Matt's been a real help. He went with me to the funeral home yesterday; the services are set for tomorrow at two o'clock. The problem is that Beverly won't attend the services with me. Even the girls don't want to go. Teri says she hardly knew Leigh and it would be hypocritical to sit in the family pew. Tammy says she doesn't have time right now, but I think it's because she never liked Leigh. I can't get them to see that this isn't about Leigh, it's about me."

If a woman had expressed those thoughts it would be labeled whining, but with Tom it translated into self-righteous indignation. He was angry at the lack of support and sure that he was justified. I wasn't. I did think that perhaps he was still in shock and not thinking clearly.

"I'm sorry you're having so many problems at once," I said.

"It's hell. Beverly could persuade the girls to come, I know she could, if she wanted to."

"She probably feels awkward—"

"Why? I asked her to do it. I want all of us there together. All four of us. Tammy, Teri, Beverly, and me. The whole family needs to be together."

I held the phone out, fighting the temptation to smack it into the tile, creating a few more chips. He was oblivious to the reality of the situation. As my mother used to say, the man needed to have his head examined.

"Tom," I said with all the patience I could, "Leigh was

your family. This is for Leigh and you. What would people say if Beverly was in the family pew? You'd have gossip flying—''

"Oh, who cares what the old biddies say? I don't. Help me out, Jolie, won't you? Talk with Beverly. Convince her to support me on this."

"This is between you and Bev. I'm not getting involved." I heard a car door slam. "Tom, someone's here—I need to go. I'll tell Bev that you called."

"Just do what you can for me, okay?"

"I don't think it will amount to much," I said, and hung up the telephone.

There must be a protocol for dealing with a friend who is on the lunatic fringe, but I didn't know it. I didn't seem to know the protocols for much of anything. Except for funerals. The clock chimed in the other room—it was noon, just two and a half hours until Dr. Bill's funeral.

The front door opened and I stepped into the living room expecting to find Bev. Instead, her father stood there, his hair tousled, and his face sagging.

I was startled for a moment and my only response at seeing him was, "Oh."

He squinted his eyes. "I thought this was my house." He looked around the room. "You're not my daughter, but that's my piano. Where am I?"

"This is your home. I'm Bev's friend Jolie. I didn't mean to startle you—Bev went out, uh, for a minute and asked me to wait for her."

He looked me over, recognition sliding on and off his face. Then he opened the door and stepped outside. Before I could catch him, or panic, he looked at the house numbers beside the door, then apparently satisfied, stepped back inside.

"This is my house." He spoke with authority. "Is my lunch going to be ready soon?"

"Five minutes," I said.

"Good. Thank you." And like an aging king he nodded briefly, then used his cane to walk toward his bedroom.

I was trying to call Bev when she came flying in the door. "Hi! I followed him half the way home, then I lost him at a light! I was terrified that he was going to disappear again."

"He's in the bedroom, I think, but he's hungry and wants his lunch."

She was pulling off her coat. "That I can handle." She gave me a quick hug. "Thanks for covering for me. We'll be eating on the back porch—go ahead and make yourself comfortable. I'll set Dad up in the kitchen."

Bev was a whirlwind, doing all the last-minute things that a good hostess has to do when her preparation has been disrupted. In the meantime, I answered the door and let in my mother and sister, then escorted them to the back porch. Here the reminders of the fifties had been updated and refurbished to make it a charming area that any magazine editor would love to photograph.

The floor was a buffed and polished concrete, and the tablecloth and chair pillows were predominantly pale blue, with bright red and yellow flowers. Touches of white, and lots of plants, including a brilliant orange-red blooming geranium made it look as if Beverly had spent years creating the decor.

The best part was that this area had gone from the traditional screened porch to one with actual panes of glass that made it warm and cozy.

"Isn't this lovely," my mother said. She moved to the table and picked up a china plate. "What a pretty pattern."

Bev delivered drinks on a tray, and a few minutes later lunch began.

"DR. BILL WAS almost too good," Elise was saying as she looked at her watch. I checked mine as well, and there was still over an hour to go before Dr. Bill's funeral.

I wasn't the one who brought up the topic of Dr. Bill; it had been my sister, who quite naturally wanted to discuss his death, since she had so little information on it. She also wanted to discuss his life, which we had done for a good fifteen minutes.

"Such a kind man," my mother said, summing up the conversation, then sipping some tea.

Elise added, "The hours he spent at the hospital when Dad was dying, well, it just amazed me. He always seemed to do a little more than you expected."

Beverly had been quiet, nodding in agreement like a good hostess.

My mother said, "It appears that he made his mark here in Purple Sage, as well. Oh, we stopped by Gretchen's on the way over. I think she's doing some better."

"I liked her sister," Elise added.

"Were a lot of people there? At her house?" I asked. "This thing about suicide will keep people away."

"Jolie, you don't know—" My mother stopped, and swallowed as if she were literally holding back her words, just the way I was suddenly holding my breath. We'd both been so careful toward each other. At least half a dozen times I had clamped my jaw and smiled in an effort to keep our relationship smooth. Now she was doing it. She went on, "I suppose the rumor of suicide could have done that. People do talk in small towns."

Bev spoke for the first time in several minutes. "That was my biggest reservation about coming back to Purple Sage. I liked being anonymous in Dallas, and not having people judging me by their rigid standards."

Elise wiped her hands a final time and placed her napkin on the table beside her plate. "Well I hate that anyone judged Dr. Bill. He was a saint."

Beverly jumped up. "Let me bring fresh coffee to go with our dessert."

"I'll help," Mom said.

"No, no. I can do this myself. I insist." She was already stacking plates.

Mom looked out toward the backyard. "Then if you don't mind, I'd like to take a look at your flower garden. I know it's not the season for flowers, but you do have things blooming.

It reminds me of some of the places I visited in England and Scotland last year. Really lovely.''

Bev laughed. ''That garden is the one thing my father and I have always agreed on.''

Every time Dr. Bill's name came up, Bev shifted the conversation just slightly.

As soon as she had taken the first load of dishes into the kitchen and could no longer see me, I scooped up the remaining items and followed her.

''This is the last of things,'' I said, placing them in the kitchen sink, which was already filled with dishwater.

''Oh, Jolie, I could have brought them.''

''I know, but you need to check on your dad. Besides, I have to tell you something.''

Her face paled as she turned toward me, and her voice was soft with dread. ''What?''

''Tom called while you were gone.'' I barely had the words out before she uttered a groan. I said, ''I'm sorry, I didn't mean to upset you.''

''Let me guess—you're supposed to talk me into getting the girls down for Leigh's funeral.''

''Yes.''

''What else? There was more, I can see it on your face.''

''He wanted me to talk you into attending, too. With him.''

She was shaking her head like someone fighting entrapment. ''Do you ever feel like it just isn't working? Nothing; not any of it. Like with my dad, he either gets mad because I'm hovering over him, or I stop hovering and he disappears.

''And Tom acts like I've abandoned him in his hour of need. But, damn it, Jolie, he divorced me.''

''And you don't owe him a thing.''

''I wish it were that cut and dried. You see, there was a time when I wanted him back and I did everything short of beg him. It seems impossible that I said the things I did, but I wanted our family together, and nothing felt too extreme to make that happen. And, now, all of a sudden, he wants that, too, but we can't. I don't…he's off the deep end! If you only knew…'' She stopped and seemed to get control of herself.

I watched, waiting. I wanted to ask what Tom had done—had he killed Leigh?

She wiped her face on a dish towel and shook her head. ''Sometimes it's overwhelming.''

I nodded, hoping, but not really, that she would say more. She didn't. With an effort she pulled herself upright, both mentally and physically. ''I'm sorry.''

''Don't worry,'' I said. ''There's a lot of it going around.''

''Maybe it's just a moon phase.''

''Or hormones. Look, I'm going to take my family out for dessert, so you can have some time to yourself. Or you're more than welcome to join us—''

''I won't hear of it! You have to stay. I made cookies and chocolate-dipped strawberries just for you. Of course, I want to eat my share, but not everybody else's.''

''Then at least let me help with the dishes.''

She protested, but I had most of the luncheon plates washed and in the drain board before she had tea glasses refilled and the dessert ready to go on the table.

She gave me a hug as I finished the last plate. ''I owe you for this.''

''I intend to collect,'' I said, watching her reach for fresh napkins. ''Bev, would you answer just one question for me?''

She closed the drawer. ''As payment?''

''I guess. And I suppose if you don't want to tell me, you don't have to.''

''I feel like I'm on some TV show. Go for it.''

''Okay.'' I took my time, bringing out the words. ''Do you still love Tom?''

The answer was even slower in coming. Bev looked off to some distant place, focusing as if the response was there. Perhaps it was, because when she finally looked back at me her expression appeared to hold all the hurt she had suffered over the last several years. ''Yes,'' she said quietly. ''I think I'll always love Tom.'' Her eyes dropped down as if to close out the sadness. "There are so many different kinds of love. I don't know which one I feel right now."

I patted her arm. "I can understand that."

"I feel like all these elements from my past have come up and they need to be dealt with. First my father's illness, then Tom, well, you know. I'm not sure I'm up to it."

"It's just the combination that's so overwhelming; I have faith in you," I said, thinking of my own life. "Last Christmas we were in Austin and my past was...well...prominent, so, like you, I had a lot to deal with. I told Diane that it felt like the skeletons in my closet were dancing."

Bev shuddered, then said softly, "I think it's a little worse around here. The skeletons in my closet are dying."

TWENTY-FIVE

"I JUST FEEL SO sorry for Bev," I said, as we walked toward our cars.

Elise is the one who responded, but I'd heard the words a hundred times before from my mother. "We all do what we have to do. I guess Bev still has to take care of her father or she wouldn't be doing it."

"I know," I said, "but...oh, I don't know."

It was now half an hour until Dr. Bill's funeral and that was the real source of my frustration. I wished I'd been able to talk with Brother Binder. "Why don't we just take one car? We can leave yours at the radio station."

"That's fine," Mom said, getting into her little rental vehicle.

They pulled out behind me, and I started thinking more about Beverly and the problems she faced. Those with her father would be long over if Dr. Bill had let him die.

DNR. Do not resuscitate. I was sure I'd heard the term before—someone had probably issued one for my father when he was at the end. He was withered and ill, without hope of recovery. Certainly there had been no hope for quality of life.

Henry Kendall's DNR seemed different. Yes, he had a terminal illness, but he hadn't been in pain and his body had to have been functioning pretty well back then. Even now, two years later, he was up and about, creating problems for Bev, going to the senior citizens center, and in some respects, living a good life. Maybe Dr. Bill had known that was probable and that there were years ahead for Bev's dad.

And yet, it was Mr. Kendall's prerogative to die in peace without anyone trying to save him. I wasn't sure how I felt about that. I did believe that he had the right to make that decision, just as I want to make the decision for myself. If Dr. Bill had tried to save my father at the last minute with more painful treatments and expensive machines that would only keep his heart beating, I would have objected. In Texas the law is clear that when the brain dies, the body is dead as well. I like that law—it's a safeguard for all of us and takes a painful decision away from a suffering family.

I had to wonder if Dr. Bill saved Henry Kendall because it was what he knew to do. The will to live, as well as the desire to preserve life, seems strong in all of us—perhaps it comes from some primal need to perpetuate the species.

It may have been that Dr. Bill just didn't have the heart to let Mr. Kendall die. I wondered what I would have done in that same position?

I turned up the radio to drown out my thoughts. Katharine was speaking, "...according to Skip Jackson it could take several weeks before the building is repaired, however, he is confident that services can be held tomorrow.

"Again, a partial roof cave-in at Jackson Funeral Home means all services scheduled for today are being postponed until tomorrow in new locations. For more information, tune to our regularly scheduled newscast at five o'clock.

"I'm Katharine Kimbriel for KSGE news."

I almost stopped the car in the middle of the road. I had just been given a second chance to stop the rumors in time for Dr. Bill's services, and if I ignored it, it would put me in the *Guinness Book of World Records* for cowardice.

I pulled into the station parking lot, and jumped out of the car. Mom pulled in beside me.

"How can you look so happy?" Elise asked.

"The services have been postponed! The roof caved in at Jackson's Funeral Home."

"I still don't get why you're pleased."

"Elise, Dr. Bill did a lot of charity work for a fundamentalist church here in town and those people are not going to show up at the funeral because he committed suicide. They believe that's a sin, or whatever they call it—''

''You don't know that,'' my mother said.

''Yes, I do. Their minister has preached about it. I was told that by his secretary. He even told them not to associate—''

''That is bullshit,'' she said.

''Yes, it is. Which is why I want to do something about it—''

''That is Mac's job, and I don't understand why you can't—''

''I've told you—because Mac isn't investigating Dr. Bill's death!''

Elise cut in, ''Are you two arguing again?''

''No,'' Mom said.

''Besides,'' I added, ''I just want to talk to Brother Binder. Why not? We don't have anything to lose.''

'' 'We'?'' Mom said. ''You want us to come with you?''

''There's nothing all that great to see in Purple Sage, and this way we might even be helping someone.''

My mother was breathing noisily, not quite huffing, but obviously thinking. At last she said, ''We'll go with you, but only to keep you calm.''

''I'll be calm,'' I said, climbing into the car.

''Then we'll go to keep you company.''

''THAT'S THE CHURCH.'' I pointed as it came into view.

Elise seemed puzzled by it. ''It's odd. I don't know what it is, but it's not quite right. What's the minister like? Besides a hell-and-damnation kind of guy?''

''I don't know,'' I said. ''I've never met the man. I don't think I've ever seen him. He hasn't been here all that long, and apparently we don't frequent the same places.''

I pulled into the gravel lot and parked toward the back. There were empty spaces on both sides of us, with Brother Binder's minivan closer to the outbuilding where the offices were housed. My ability to stay calm, which had concerned my mother, wasn't worrying me. I was more concerned that I could say anything that would make a difference. If I hadn't had the audience of my sister and my mother I might have backed out.

"I'm not going in," Elise said.

"Here. Keep the keys," I said, handing them to her. "You can turn on the heater if you get cold."

She came up to sit in the passenger seat, and my mother stood to the side, waiting for me. "Well. Are you coming?" she asked.

"Of course. I have to do this—no one else will." I started toward the office.

"What are you going to say to the man?"

"I don't know—I'm hoping something brilliant will come to me."

We passed by his Windstar. It seemed a big vehicle for a single man, and I knew that he was single. I wondered if he might need it for the church baseball team or for Sunday school outings. I was curious about other things, too. Could he be young and handsome, and could he have been having an affair with Leigh? One that went wrong, and so he killed her? It was an unkind thought to have about a minister, but, then, I was prejudiced against this man without ever having met him.

When we stepped inside the building the same woman as yesterday was behind the same cheap desk. She saw us and smiled congenially, then her eyes widened in recognition as she looked at me more carefully. The welcoming expression disappeared. Her chin came up and the eyes narrowed, so that this nice, normal middle-aged lady transformed into something like the troll who guarded the gate.

She was, however, determined to be civil. "You've come back," she said. "I assume you still want to see Brother Binder."

"Yes, we do," I said.

"I need to tell him who you are."

"Of course you do," I agreed. "This is my mother, Irene Berenski, and I'm Jolie Wyatt."

In Purple Sage my name often gets a reaction from people. Old-timers ask if I'm related to Will and Betty Wyatt, Matt's parents, or if I'm Matt Wyatt's new wife. Those who haven't been around as long mention KSGE and how they've heard me on the air. This woman appeared not to recognize my name at all. She simply wrote it down, and added a few more words that I couldn't see.

"I'll be right back." She stood up and took a second look at her desk, perhaps wondering if there was something she should put away so we wouldn't steal it. Then she looked at us again and reluctantly turned and made her way down the bare hallway.

"What was that about?" Mom asked.

"Remember I told you that someone said these people really believe that Dr. Bill is in hell and his name shouldn't be mentioned? Well, that's the woman who told me."

"Obviously there was something more to the conversation."

"I was with Ute Roesner. You don't know her—she is absolutely charming. Even with three kids she looks like a schoolgirl; her skin glows and she has this wonderful air of sweet innocence. However, Ute was a fan of Dr. Bill's and doesn't think much of bigots. She might have pushed her point with this woman."

"I can see how that could happen."

The secretary returned, her footfalls audible on the flat, gray industrial carpeting.

"Brother Binder will see you." She made it sound like an audience. "His office is the final door on the left."

My mother smiled. "Thank you so much," she said, with such sweetness that I recognized where my Pollyanna streak came from.

We started down the hallway, with its plain white sheetrock and cheap plastic molding around hollow core doors. The only decorations were pictures—my least favorite kind—Christ hanging on the cross, and next to it a bloodied Christ wearing a crown of thorns. Why would anyone want to see that horrible suffering every day? Surely there are joyous moments in the life of Christ that would uplift the spirit and offer hope for the future? Apparently this group liked to wallow in the torture of Christ's last moments.

I shuddered, reminded again of the Stations of the Cross. Maybe this hadn't been a good idea.

The door to Brother Binder's office was open, and my mother stepped through first, with me behind. The room wasn't huge, but large enough to hold a solid wood desk with two palomino leather chairs in front of it, a matching credenza, and a glass-fronted bookcase filled with what looked like leather-bound books.

Across from the door there were large windows that gave a view not of the church, but of the rolling hills.

The man behind the desk appeared to be in his early forties, with grizzly brown-and-gray hair that was too bushy to be proper. His skin was rough, as if it had once suffered acne, and he wore large plastic brown glasses. His suit, which fit well, did nothing to hide his narrow shoulders. In high school, I'd bet he'd been a skinny runt.

Brother Binder remained seated as he gestured somewhat magnanimously to the chairs. "Come right on in. Please have a seat." His voice was deep and smooth, the kind that wraps around you and tickles all sorts of senses. I'll admit, it threw me.

"Thank you," I muttered, sitting near the door.

Once we were seated he said, "I understand that you've been here before, Miz Wyatt." He half smiled, and raised one eyebrow slightly as if this was a joke between us. "Quite the rabble-rouser, according to Ms. Finch out there."

It was like going into the ring for a heavyweight fight to find your opponent making a daisy chain. "That wasn't my intention…" I looked to my mother but she said nothing. "I just wanted to talk to you," I said. "Get you to…"

He waited. "Yes?"

I had to look at the desk to gather both thoughts and courage, but then I could face him and make all the words come out. "Brother Binder, I want to talk to you about Dr. Bill Marchak. He was a friend of our family's. When my father was dying of cancer, Dr. Bill took great care of him. He supported our family, too. Morally, I mean. He and Gretchen both offered moral support." Brother Binder was listening with that slight smile touching his mouth. I went on, "Also, Dr. Bill did many wonderful things for this community. He even gave up his time to offer free medical care to the members of this church. At least...I heard that he did." I hadn't actually seen his records.

Brother Binder spoke without particular emphasis, letting his rich voice carry the persuasion. "Ours is a fairly new church—just under a year old. My mission has always been to serve those who needed me most, and it appeared that the greatest need was here, in Purple Sage. A number of our congregation are on the lower end of the socioeconomic scale. We don't discriminate against people who don't have money."

"No, of course not. Neither did Dr. Bill. He gave so much to your church that this is a chance for all the members to give back. By going to the funeral and supporting Gretchen."

"How versed are you in religious matters?" he asked.

Surprised, I said, "Somewhat."

"Did you study it in college? Attend a seminary? Teach a Bible-school class?"

"Well, no. I'm spiritual, but not really religious."

"Which means?"

I brought my chin up and said, "That I have a deep faith in God, but I don't attend church all that regularly..."

"Exodus 20:8. Remember the Sabbath day, to keep it holy." When I didn't respond he added, "In Exodus 31 the Bible also says, 'Six days shall work be done, but the seventh day is a Sabbath of solemn rest, holy to the Lord; whoever does any work on the Sabbath day shall be put to death.'"

His words stunned me. Was he advocating my death as a sinner? I tried to smile. "Luckily those were only the laws back then."

"God's laws," he said, softly, pityingly.

There had to be something to say in my defense. It finally came to me. "But you work on the Sabbath. All ministers do."

"What I do is not work—it is pure joy to offer the word of God to my congregation."

It was my mother who answered him. "Brother Binder, we recognize your knowledge, but we didn't come to talk about Jolie or about you. We have concerns about Gretchen Marchak. Dr. Bill did many good things for your parishioners, making it only kind to offer thanks. Since Dr. Bill is dead, Jolie wants to make sure that his funeral is well attended."

"A celebration of his life," I added.

Brother Binder nodded, the half smile no longer visible. "As Shakespeare said, 'Aye, there's the rub....' You see, we cannot celebrate a man who sinned so blatantly. It would be worse than idolizing a false god."

"How can you say—"

"I don't say," he offered. "It is the Bible, the word of God that says. 'Do not yield your members to sin as instruments of wickedness, but yield yourselves to God as men who have been brought from death to life, and your members to God as instruments of righteousness.' It is from Romans 6."

He had some evil quote—a quote taken out of context—for everything. They created a viscous web that tangled me up and left me fighting to maintain my equilibrium. I couldn't see how to cut through it.

My mother said in a deceptively gentle manner, "I'm not a biblical scholar, either, Brother Binder, however, I have studied the Bible for many years. One phrase that has helped me through many moments like this is the very simple, 'Judge not, that you be not judged.' I believe that is from Mathew."

"Very nice," he said tipping his head slightly. "And, yes, it is from Mathew, with a longer explanation in Luke, 'Judge not, and you will not be judged; condemn not, and you will not be condemned; forgive, and you will be forgiven.' It's a favorite of mine as well." He waited a beat, then smiled like a man forced to trump her ace. "However, God has chosen some of us to be protectors of others, just as there were shepherds to care for the flocks of sheep. In that role, it's my duty to determine what to protect my flock from. In Leviticus, we are even given guidelines. These were initially offered to the judges of the day, but it is my belief that they are wisdom for ministers as well. 'You shall do no injustice in judgment; you shall not be partial to the poor or defer to the great, but in righteousness shall you judge your neighbor.'"

My mother said, "I'm not sure how that applies to the case of Dr. Bill."

"Perhaps Deuteronomy will help you see my purpose here. 'The man who acts presumptuously, by not obeying the priest who stands to minister there before the Lord your God, or the judge, that man shall die; so you shall purge the evil from Israel.' I assume Purple Sage could be substituted for Israel, and I am merely trying to purge the evil."

I wasn't convinced of that, but I was clear that Brother Ray Binder put himself above man's laws.

His light brown eyes were watching me from behind his large glasses. Was I looking into the face of a murderer? I asked, "What if you make a mistake? What if Dr. Bill didn't kill himself? There isn't any proof that he did."

"There was a witness, who unfortunately now is dead." The minister seemed regretful.

"It was dark and it was raining, and all Leigh saw was the back of a man in a raincoat. It could have been anyone, doing almost anything."

"I was told that he was alone, and she did recognize his car." He paused for emphasis. "Unless you know of someone else who was there? Perhaps yourself?" he asked.

"Me? I wasn't there. If someone else was at the creek it was the person who killed Dr. Bill. Doesn't that make more sense? That someone murdered Dr. Bill?"

He was nodding, taking his time, playing with my words in his mind. "I see your point of view, but you have to admit you have a great deal of investment in your supposition. Your rejection of suicide could be based entirely on emotion."

"Fine. But, what if you are making a mistake? You'd be hurting Gretchen and Dr. Bill, and all the people who loved him."

Brother Binder smiled serenely, not quite able to keep the self-righteousness off his face. "I will take it under advisement, although I don't feel concerned, as you do. The Bible says in Deuteronomy, 'Consider what you do, for you judge not for man but for the Lord; he is with you in giving judgment.' God is with me in all things concerning this church. However, to please you I will do some additional praying on it."

My mother was up, gently pushing me toward the door. "Please do that," she said. "Dr. Bill deserves to be honored."

"And please, let your congregation know your answer," I said, as if assuming that he would come to his senses.

"Yes, I will. Thank you for coming." He stayed in his chair, watching us leave.

There are certain rules of etiquette in the South: When a woman enters or leaves a room, particularly my mother, a man is supposed to stand up. Brother Binder had not stood either time. It was a subtle way of dishonoring us. It made me angry, but there was more about Brother Binder that concerned me.

For thousands of years evil men have twisted scriptural excerpts from the Torah to the Koran to the Bible. They have been used to cause wars and kill good and innocent people. It's nothing new, but I had never stood face-to-face with someone who did it so cleverly. And not only had he used his quotes against me, he also used them to sway the members of his congregation, so that they, too, became his weapon.

We were in the car, and driving away as quickly as could be managed without throwing gravel behind us. I didn't want Brother Binder to have any additional reason for wishing us harm.

"Elise," my mother said from the back seat, "would you turn up the heater? I'm freezing."

I was, too, but I was sure the cold came from inside us.

I got the car onto the highway, gratefully putting space between the Lakeside Fundamental Church of God and us. "That man is evil," I said.

"The minister?" Elise sounded surprised.

"Yes." My mother's voice contained the anger she had held back in Brother Binder's office. "He was dangerously close to threatening Jolie. And he played with Bible quotes, like some all-knowing minion of the devil." I could hear her shudder. "We have to do something. He is poisoning people's minds, and he's not going to stop here."

"But, why?" Elise asked. "He's a minister, for God's sake." She suppressed what could have been a laugh. "Sorry. I'm just not understanding; why would a minister hurt people?"

"It's nothing new. Leaders of religious congregations have hurt people almost since the founding of religion," Mom said. "Not all, of course, but it seems that there is a great temptation to use the name of God to claim power and wealth. Think of the Crusades or as recently as Osama Bin Laden and his jihad."

In eighth grade I had been on the debate team, taking on the topic of capital punishment. I had spent hours in the library researching quotes to support our arguments. What I had considered our big gun was the biblical "an eye for an eye and a tooth for a tooth." We had planned to use that when we were arguing for capital punishment, and when switched to the other side we would finish the quote, "but only God shall wreak the vengeance." Our first time putting it to the test we were told by the judge in firm terms that quoting God was unfair and not to be done again. She gave us two contradictory reasons. The first was that God is the highest authority, so quoting him allows no room for counterargument; and second that there are many interpretations of God's word and no human was the final authority on that.

As the debate judge she was *our* final authority, so I took her words to heart, sowing the seeds of skepticism in a thirteen-year-old. In this instance I had gone far beyond that doubtful curiosity.

My mother's voice mirrored my own emotions. "What a horrible, horrible, man. That quote he used about being *appointed by God* positions him above other people, and that is wrong. When I think of all those who consider him their leader, I'm appalled. I wish there were a way to discredit him."

His drinking would certainly do the trick, but it would be Ute's word against his.

"I'm trying to picture this man; what did he look like?" Elise asked.

I answered her. "He's not handsome; I suspect when he was younger he had terrible acne and probably wasn't very popular."

"Jolie's being polite," my mother said. "He's a skinny little runt with a sexy voice. He probably grew up looking for his own power and a way to get revenge on the rest of the world. Children like that are often bullies, but Brother Binder is too intelligent to use anything brutish to conquer other people. He's set himself up like an all-wise holy man, and people who aren't as intelligent follow his lead."

"And that voice of his just pulls you in—it's magical."

We were almost away from the lake now, and I glanced in the rearview mirror at my mother. Her expression was quizzical. She said, "To get people to build him a church the way they have, Brother Binder must be a whole lot better with his congregation than he was with us. For some reason he let us see him for what he really is."

"You think so?"

"Oh, yes. He didn't try to sweet-talk us; he just drowned us in quotes. Well, no, at first he tried to enlist our support. He was almost flirting with Jolie, and that surprised me."

"No!" I said. "You think he was, really? I just thought that he was trying to be clever and smarmy."

Elise said, "Jolie, you're so nuts over Matt you don't even notice when someone is flirting with you."

"Maybe." But that wasn't the issue. This was about Dr. Bill. "Brother Binder was using that as a tool, besides he wasn't relinquishing his power. That's what this is about. I'm guessing that Dr. Bill was revered by the congregation of the Lakeside church, and for Brother Binder that would mean sharing the limelight. I'll bet he resented that all along, and now he's not even going to let the members honor Dr. Bill in death. It's a petty little revenge.''

Elise's blue eyes grew large. ''Mom, do you think that, too?''

''Yes, I'm afraid I do,'' she said. ''But there's more. Worse.'' She let out a frustrated breath, and I looked in the mirror to see her shaking her head.

''Go ahead, Mom, just say it.''

She let out another breath. ''I don't even like to think things like this, but it just makes sense. He was off his stride with us today, in retrospect that seems obvious, which makes me think he's nervous about something. And that leads to the real question: What if he was so jealous of Dr. Bill that he killed him?''

''His own personal jihad?''

''Something like that.'' She sounded so frustrated. ''It makes me so angry. Someone should do something.''

''Who?'' I asked. ''Mac is busy investigating Leigh's death, and the chief of police never does anything, at least not very well. Besides, this is not an official matter; it's suicide.''

She said, ''You've made your point. So, if you're so smart, what do you think we can do?''

''Well, I wanted to talk with Ute, again. It might not help, but something's going on there. You might talk with the sheriff. I hear you have some pull with him.''

She was silent for about thirty seconds and then she said, ''Drop me off at my car; I'm going to see Mac Donelly and get his official insight on this.''

TWENTY-SIX

ELISE WENT WITH my mother while I dashed into the radio station to call Ute. Katharine was at the partner's desk in the newsroom, scowling at the computer screen.

"Hi," I said.

Her head came up. "Hey, lady, what are you doing back here? Did you change your mind?"

"No, No. I'm just going to use the telephone." I reached for the thin booklet that held phone numbers for both residents and businesses in Purple Sage. "Anything new on the murder of Leigh Greer?"

"It's not really murder."

"What?"

"The coroner, so far, has no ruling on cause of death."

"They think she jumped in the lake? Like Dr. Bill jumped in the creek?"

"Skip is being very quiet on this one," she said.

We all have our favorite sources for information, even in a small place like Purple Sage, and Katharine is well wired with Skip Jackson from the funeral home.

"Why so quiet?" I asked.

"For one thing they're doing the autopsy in Austin, and those take forever, but I think there's something more." She looked thoughtful. "It's the rumors about Dr. Bill. They've been so damaging that Skip and the sheriff are doing everything to prevent a repeat."

"That makes sense."

She pointed to some pink messages. "You've had a couple of phone calls; I don't think they're business."

"Thanks." One was from Bev, and one was from Ute. Now there was a nice coincidence. I picked up the phone and dialed the number. It was the *Trib* office. I was told that Ute was out but expected back any minute.

"I'll be right over," I said. After I hung up, I said to Katharine, "I've got my cell phone with me—would you call me if you hear anything on Leigh's death?"

"Sure. Hey, I thought you were going to have some time with your family. Where are they?"

"My mom and sister are at the sheriff's office. We're meeting back up in about an hour, or whenever Mom calls me."

"Which is why your cell phone is turned on, and charged. Your mother must be a powerful woman."

"Well, I didn't want her to ground me." I picked up my purse. "Oh, what's the latest on the weather? Is that new front still coming in?"

"In about four hours we are supposed to be inundated again. But, you know what they say about bad weather—wait a while and it will change. Or if that doesn't work, get a new preacher."

"That appeals to me." I was already headed out. "'Bye."

"Ciao."

Rather than walking the few blocks to the *Trib* office, I drove because it was starting to sprinkle again, and because when Mom called I wanted to be ready to roll, literally. I had barely stepped inside the building before Ute was beside me. "Oh, Jolie. They told me you were coming and I'm so glad. I must talk to you right now."

"Sure. Of course."

She had her hands outstretched, pulling me toward the press room, which was quiet and empty. "I owe you an apology," she said once we were inside and the door was closed. "Have you seen the paper?"

"No? Is it out?"

"Yes, and there are almost no pictures of Dr. Bill's reception. I feel so bad. It's all my fault—"

"Wait, wait. There are no pictures because Morris decided to use flood pictures instead? That's not your fault."

"No." She stood straight now, her words firm. "Because there are no pictures from the reception. They are gone. I hurried so to print the shots of the drawdown tube and go to the sheriff's office that I forgot the disk and left it beside the computer here. After I picked up Kevin I finally remembered it, but too late."

My heart began to hurt. "Someone else used the disk and erased all the pictures?" I guessed.

She nodded solemnly and I felt my shoulders slump in response. It felt like every link to Dr. Bill, and in turn my father, was being taken away.

"Who did it?" I asked, thinking the disk could have been erased on purpose because there was something incriminating on it.

"It was Tiffany."

Morris Pratt's niece, the sullen teenager at the front desk who spent her working hours playing computer games. "And there's nothing left?"

"Nothing. She saved a game on the disk, but she is particular about her games, so she was careful to erase it first."

Which ruled out an insidious plot. Whatever the reason, I wouldn't be seeing the last pictures taken of Dr. Bill.

Ute saw my disappointment. "I did get a few pictures from the video, for the *Tribune,* but they are not high quality."

"I'm sure you did your best."

"Yes, but there is more. I was not polite when you came to my house. I am so sorry. I did not want to tell you what had happened, so I did not invite you in."

"It's not a big deal," I said. And in the grand scheme of life I supposed it wasn't, but I was disappointed.

"I have only one thing to make it up to you." She pulled open the heavy door and led me out to her desk, where she picked up a videotape. "This is a copy for you. I haven't seen it yet, and if my memory is correct it is not much more than the end of the reception, but there is a good moment with you and Dr. Bill.''

She held it out and I must have stared at it too long because she thrust it into my hands. I wanted to view this more than anything, and I was excited to have it, but another piece of me was holding back. It was going to hurt to watch it, I was sure of that.

"It is okay?'' she asked.

"It's wonderful,'' I said. "It's so nice of you to do this.'' Now I was clutching the tape to my chest as if for solace. "Thank you so much.''

"It's nothing. I have one for Beverly as well, and for Diane. Those I will put in the mail.''

"No, don't do that. Just put a little note on each one, and I'll drop them off for you.''

"Are you sure?''

I looked at my watch. I still had forty minutes before I was meeting my mother, and if I took the tape to Bev's I might have the chance to watch a little of it with her. "Absolutely.''

Ute had notecards in her desk drawer, small ones with a Texas star on the front, and she wrote out two messages, put them in envelopes, and slid one inside each tape box.

"Again,'' she said, "I am so sorry about the pictures.''

"It could have happened to any of us. In fact, I think it has happened to me at least once or twice.''

I hurried outside with the tapes inside my jacket to shield them from the rain. The huge drops would ruin the boxes.

It didn't take but a few minutes to get to Bev's and the whole way I was conscious of the tapes on the seat next to me, like three little presents that might hurt or heal, or a little of both. When I got to Bev's house I slid one tape in my purse, and actually considered locking my car to protect the other two, which is unnecessary in Purple Sage. They seemed so valuable, as if they held not just the image of Dr. Bill, but his essence as well.

After a quick dash through the rain I arrived on the front

porch. Bev already had the door open and she seemed thrilled to see me. "I saw you drive up," she said. "Can you believe this weather? I feel like I'm living in a rain forest without the benefits."

"The benefits being naked natives running through your trees?"

She laughed and gave me a hug, pulling me inside. "Exactly! Naked natives on my lawn. Wouldn't that make me popular in Purple Sage. Do you want to come in the kitchen? Can I make you some tea?"

"No thanks. I have something for you," I said, digging in my purse. "How are things going? How's your dad?"

"Oh, fine. Everything's fine. Just a little cabin fever, I guess, in this little house. My kingdom for a kingdom."

"You're always welcome at the ranch, and if there's one thing we've got, it's space." I brought out the tape. "I'm delivering this for Ute, you remember the lady who took pictures at the reception?" I explained about the disk and the loss of all the stills. "This is from the end of the reception, if I understood correctly."

Bev took the box from me and slid the tape out, fingering it. She looked like a kid. "Do you want to take a peek at what's on it? Do you have time?"

"I'd love to see some of it." While Bev went to the VCR, I made myself comfortable on the couch. "I hardly remember Ute using the video camera, but then I guess it's not as formal as stills where she was asking everyone to pose."

Bev punched buttons until the TV screen lit up and there was a full shot of the inside of her old living room. She straightened. "Can you see it okay?"

"Just fine, don't worry about me. Come and sit down."

She sat beside me, her eyes already fixed on the television. The camera panned the room and I felt myself tensing. The world had changed dramatically since the reception, and viewing the tape was like peeking back through time. I wanted the tape to move quickly to the moment when I would see Dr. Bill again, and yet I dreaded it, too.

Ute had been modest when she'd said that it wasn't much more than the end. The governor came into view with Trey on one side of him and Bev on the other. Bev was talking and then all three laughed. The laughter was far in the background and the words were lost in the jumble of music and voices that filled the room.

Even without hearing the conversation, the body language spoke volumes. The governor touched Bev's arm as if they were old friends and Trey was nodding agreement at whatever had been said. Beverly had woven her homespun magic on the governor as well as she did on everyone else.

"I should get my dad to see this," Bev said, jumping up. "Do you mind?"

"Of course not. I'll stop the tape." After I did, I could hear her father querulously demanding to know why he should go in the living room where it was stuffy and hot. Apparently he was on the back porch watching the rain.

"It's a tape of the party they gave for me; do you remember that? Don't you want to see? Come on, Dad, it will be fun." Her voice held laughter in it, and apparently Henry Kendall could resist anything but his daughter. With just a little more grumbling he followed her into the house.

"You know Jolie," she said to him.

He nodded and gave a little grunt at seeing me on the couch. "I'll just set back here so you girls can stay up front." He eased himself down slowly into the antique rocker. I remembered my grandmother saying that old bones and rain are a painful combination.

Bev started the tape again. Ute was a wonderful photographer. Her candid shots always seemed to capture the mood of the moment, and her video did the same, but there was the added bonus of Ute's wonderful eye for the whole picture, and the steady hand of a professional.

On the tape Bev continued her conversation with the governor, then the camera slowly slid away, moving down the line of well-wishers. There was tiny IdaMae Dorfman from the Bakery. When she saw that she was being photographed she waved. As the camera continued moving, Leigh Greer came into view. At first I didn't recognize her, and when I did I caught my breath. She was extremely photogenic, so much so that she looked like a movie star, with her delicate face and slender shape. I hadn't thought about seeing Leigh on the video.

Sadness washed through me, as well as guilt for not being kinder to her. I could have been more understanding, especially with what she'd been going through. But I hadn't. I'd only seen her surface, a beautiful and vibrant young woman who had hurt my friend. And then she'd been hurt, ending all her potential.

Tom stepped through the background of the tape; he appeared to be looking for someone. Would Tom have divorced Leigh to be with Beverly? And I wondered again if Tom could have killed Leigh.

A large gap of time was missing from the tape; Ute must have put down the video recorder to use the other camera and picked it up again much later. There was a shot of me talking to someone and I saw that it was Leigh and Henry Kendall.

"There you are, Daddy," Bev said. "And Jolie and Leigh. You're still the lady killer."

He snorted.

The picture wobbled as if someone had jostled the camera and our view shifted to the other side of the room. In the center, full screen, was Dr. Bill. My heart tightened. Someone slipped into the frame from the side and Dr. Bill put his arm around her—it was me. The camera stayed on us, coming in even closer to catch our expressions as we laughed and teased each other. The background noise was still too loud to catch our words, but I remembered he had complimented me on the party.

I was jerked back to the present by the phone ringing in the kitchen.

"Oh, damn," Bev muttered. "I'll get it."

"Do you want me to stop the tape?" I asked.

"No, that's okay. Whatever I miss I can catch later." She

scooted around me, and I turned my attention back to the television.

On the tape the crowd in the family room had thinned, so there must have been an edit that I missed. We were seeing a slow pan of all the guests who were left. Linda Beaman was talking with Leigh, nodding seriously, using her hands to explain something. A new craft project?

Gretchen was sitting on the settee with IdaMae Dorfman, having what looked like a serious conversation. An errant thought popped into my mind, and I shook my head to send it away. Gretchen Marchak would not kill her husband. After all the years of marriage she had obviously loved and admired Dr. Bill.

Bev was still on the phone, and I checked my watch. It was almost time to leave. I was about to do just that when the camera moved again and I saw Dr. Bill. This time he was seated beside Henry Kendall, with Beverly standing to the side, her back to the camera. Dr. Bill looked tired. His head came up and he spoke to Bev. There was a smile on his face, that teasing expression he used often. They seemed to freeze in tableau. After a long moment, Dr. Bill said something else. It wasn't received well, either. Henry Kendall clutched his cane as if he wanted to strike out with it. Beverly's body went rigid and she leaned forward so that I could only faintly hear, "It was wrong of you." Dr. Bill looked surprised. He said something that I couldn't quite catch, going on for several seconds. I thought the last words were, "...it again."

Henry Kendall snapped a response and Dr. Bill leaned back as if to take a blow. At the same time Bev whirled away; oblivious to the camera she mouthed, "Son of a bitch." I'd never seen such rage in her.

Dr. Bill looked shocked and it was Henry Kendall who leaned closer to him, perhaps to explain the cause of Bev's anger.

I wished that part hadn't been caught on film. I knew that Bev didn't want to hear Gretchen brag about Dr. Bill, and I knew that she believed Dr. Bill had overstepped his rights in bringing her father back to life, but I couldn't judge right and wrong on this. I wasn't sure how Beverly could.

Not that Bev would have harmed Dr. Bill. She hadn't even spoken out against him; never publicly, and not even privately that I was aware of.

The only person she might have shared her anger with was Tom. Tom Greer. Whose wife was now also dead.

I jumped up from the couch, clutching my purse to my side. "I have to go," I called to Bev who had just hung up the phone.

"Are you sure?" she asked. "I can fix some tea."

I shook my head. "I have to meet my mom. She's expecting me. But thanks." I was running from my own thoughts, almost out the door before I added, "And thanks for letting me see the tape."

TWENTY-SEVEN

"THE SHERIFF SAID he doesn't have any conclusive information, and didn't think he would have any in time for the funeral." My mother said it curtly after she'd climbed into my car.

Lately her conversations were liberally sprinkled with "Mac says," but this time she didn't use his first name, and her voice held no affection. Whatever else had gone on was festering under my mother's calm surface and I suspected it wouldn't be pleasant when it erupted.

"Oh, okay," I said, as I pulled out of the parking lot.

I was suffering my own thoughts. Bev's behavior at the reception didn't seem right. Once her initial response at seeing the house was over, Bev had settled in as comfortably as lady of the manor. She hadn't appeared jealous of Leigh or upset about being thrown into Leigh's domain. It could have been because Bev no longer had feelings for Tom, but the other explanation was that she knew Leigh wouldn't be around much longer. Through divorce or death.

"I'm starved," Mom said. "Is there someplace where we can get a good cup of coffee and something sweet? And not the Sage Café. I know, I know, you go there all the time, but I can't face it right now. I don't know if it's because of the dead deer on the walls, or that I think the health department should have shut the place down years ago."

"We have other places," I said. "There's the Red Roof B&B, or we can go to the Bakery."

"I vote for the Bakery," Elise said.

I turned the car and headed up the hill. "What else did Mac have to say about Dr. Bill's death? Did he know any more about how Leigh died?"

Elise sucked in air and said, "Bad topic. Might want to change the subject."

"Really?" I glanced at my mother's face in the rearview mirror. The annoyance still showed and I didn't push any further. I said, "IdaMae has put in a couple of tables and is offering coffee. I think that's new since either of you was here."

"Perfect," Mom said.

The Bakery building was white, with a new patio on the side covered by a bright blue awning; there were several small tables, used primarily by tourists. The rest of us knew that anything said on that patio would be circulating around town in a matter of minutes.

With the rain, the patio was empty, and two tables had been moved inside. Mom and Elise skirted them deftly to get to the glass cases of goodies.

"I could die happily here," Elise said. "I'd be quite a bit fatter, but very happy."

"I'll go get IdaMae," I said.

"No rush," Mom said. "Looks like we've got to make some vital decisions. Elise, did you see the cream puffs? And the pecan pie?"

Whatever was going on with her she was going to drown it in sugar.

I stepped back through the *employees only* door and called, "IdaMae?" It always concerns me when she's not out front, since by her own admission she's older than the dirt in Purple Sage. I turned the corner and found her in her tiny office, feet resting on a half-open drawer, a cigarette in her gnarled right hand. She's also more resilient than dirt. "Are you still smoking?" I asked.

"You still eating shortbread cookies?"

"Yes, but they won't kill me. Unless you're slipping in a secret ingredient you aren't telling us about."

"People keep harping on my smoking and I might." She stubbed out the cigarette and dumped the ashes in a large coffee can before replacing the lid and sliding the can under the desk. "Where's your momma? Didn't I hear she was in town?"

Some towns have a beauty parlor that serves as a vital link on the grapevine; in Purple Sage we have the Sage Café, a beauty parlor, and the Bakery.

"She's out front with my sister."

"Then why are you holding me up if I got customers and you got family to tend to?" She shook her head and pushed her chair back, but I stopped her.

"IdaMae, wait. I need just two minutes of your time. I wanted to ask you something."

She let out a self-satisfied snort. "I knew you was up to something the minute I saw you. What is it this time?"

"I'm not up to anything. It's just that tomorrow is Dr. Bill's funeral, and with that rumor about suicide, the people from Lakeside church won't attend."

"Them hypocrites. Who needs 'em? I don't want them coming to my funeral, but then I don't imagine any of them will still be around by the time I die."

I smiled, but it was short-lived. The topic was serious to me. "So, what have you heard about Dr. Bill's death?"

"You want fact or rumor?"

"Facts would be nice if you have any. I'll take rumor if you don't."

She pointed to the green plastic chairs practically crammed against the wall across from her. "Set down, you make me nervous." I sat. "I know Dr. Bill was a friend of your family's, and I know this is hurtin' you, so I'm real sorry about that." I mumbled a thank you. "That Faith Melman girl that works for me has been doing some talkin'. I don't like her, but she's smart and she can do her work. At least the till comes up right when she's here. I overheard her saying that Dr. Bill committed suicide because he was too old to practice medicine and folks booted him out."

"That's just—"

"You don't need to lecture me; I know it's crazy talk. She's a big talker, and I'm guessin' she made it up."

"Great. Of course she could have heard it from Brother Binder. What do you know about him?"

"Man's a prick. The kind ought to be tarred and feathered, but nowadays, they get to be some kind of a hero. Like rock stars with just about as much talent." She rose. "I got to go out front—"

"No, wait. What about Leigh's death, have there been any rumors about that?"

"There's always rumors." She started for the door.

I jumped up and banged a knee on the metal desk. "Damn. Ouch. Then you have heard something?"

"Some folks in this town don't have enough to do."

"Which folks and what are they saying?"

She gave me a long look, followed by a sigh. "Beverly Kendall was a friend of yours from back when she lived here, isn't that right?"

I felt a wave of dread. "Yes."

"You might ought to take into account that people change, and you should act accordingly."

"You sound like some biblical prophet. What are you talking about? You think that Beverly killed Leigh? Why? Why would you think that?"

IdaMae looked old and sad. "I got customers out front and you got family; we got to go."

I wasn't upset that she'd heard a rumor about Bev. Small towns hold some of the finest people on Earth, but they're also a breeding place for petty minds. What concerned me was that IdaMae wouldn't talk about the rumor. I took that to mean she also believed it.

A circumstantial case against Bev. It made sense that she didn't like Leigh. Who could be fond of the woman who took your husband, your house, and even your town? Still, Beverly had been kind. She had used her Southern charm to deal with Leigh and it had allowed Beverly to come out the winner.

Or had she won?

Perhaps IdaMae meant that Beverly had been married to a man who was...

My thoughts were like hamsters running on a wheel that went no place but back to the start. Circumstances, and even facts, be damned, I could not in my heart believe that Beverly or even Tom had killed anyone.

I went out front where my sister and mother were paying for a huge slice of chocolate icebox pie, a piece of chocolate cake, and various other goodies.

"IdaMae said you like shortbread cookies, so we got you some," Elise said. "And hot tea."

"Thanks." We picked a table and I invited IdaMae to join us, but after just a moment she waited on some newly arrived customers, then ducked into the back room. She wasn't averse to visiting with my family, so I could only conclude that she didn't want to talk to me. IdaMae and I like each other, and I knew it wasn't about me personally, it was about what was going on in Purple Sage.

I swallowed the final bite of a cookie and shook my head in desperation. "I hate feeling so useless," I said. "Rumors are flying, and I can't think of a thing to do to determine how Dr. Bill died. Damn. Mom, what do you think?"

"Nothing," she said. "I think you need to drop it and just enjoy life."

I looked from her to my sister. "This is important; I thought you agreed with me on that."

Mom waved away the comment without speaking.

"Are you all right?" I asked.

"It's about the sheriff," Elise said, in that hushed voice that our family uses to keep secrets. "He doesn't want her to do anything, and he said some things that upset her."

I don't believe in family secrets. If you can talk about an issue you can move beyond it, which is surely a better way to live. "Like what?" I asked. "What did Mac say?"

Elise raised an eyebrow. "Let's change the subject to something else."

"No," I persisted. "Mom, I'm sorry you're upset, especially if it was Mac who upset you. In a way I feel responsible, since you met at my wedding—"

"Oh, Jolie," Mom said with a snap, "just let it alone."

"Fine, if that's what you want." I finished the last of my tea, which by now was too cool to be good. "And when no one shows up at Dr. Bill's funeral, I assume that's okay. After all, we can't do anything because of a remark that Mac made, which you can't tell me. Well, as I have said at least a hundred times, Mac is not investigating Dr. Bill's death. And I do believe in getting involved."

My mother turned on me with a look that I knew from my childhood. I had pushed her too far. "Would you like to know what Mac said?" she asked. When I didn't answer she said, "Well? Would you?"

"Yes, certainly." It was a lie; at that point I didn't really want to know anything.

"Good, because he said that I reminded him of my daughter, one Jolie Wyatt. He went on to say that she was like a cat with her curiosity and that I was a lot like her."

"Oh." My mouth opened, closed, and opened again. "And that's what upset you?"

"There are many ramifications of the conversation, none of which I want to discuss."

"I see." I crumpled my napkin and shoved it in my empty cup. "I meant it when I said that I was sorry you were upset; I want you to have a good time in Purple Sage so you'll come back. And, Mac was right; I am a curious person. Maybe that's why I like doing news and writing books. I get to ask questions."

"You go far beyond asking questions. You get involved in things that are none of your business."

"It seems to me most of the world *is* our business. If they are beating women in Afghanistan or children are starving in Ruwanda, it's our responsibility to do something about it. Give food or money or demand that our government step in. Or go there ourselves."

"I've heard all this before," my sister said, rising to throw away our plates.

"Well, pardon me, but I'm right. Minding your own business doesn't help those who need it—"

"Give it up, Jolie," Elise said. "That's Mom's soapbox and she's had more practice than you."

I looked at my mother who was staring right back. Then, with great deliberation, she picked up her purse and stood. "I think it's time we get to the house. Jolie, you need to drop us at my car."

"Sure."

I could and would do that. What I couldn't do was understand why my own mother resented being told that she was like me. But did we talk about it? No. That would have broken the unspoken family code of pushing things away and stomping off. The more mature version was to keep your voice level and your tone cold, saying, "That's not something I choose to discuss."

As a child there had been times when I would come home only to have my father take me aside and whisper to me, "Your mother is upset about—whatever—so don't bring it up." It could have been the dog dying or the roof leaking or a neighbor gossiping, but in my family it became a secret that isolated us from each other.

I was good at avoidance; in fact, I was so good that I had almost ended my marriage to Matt in just that way. Eventually he had called me on it, and so had Diane when I used that technique on her. Since then I have painstakingly unlearned the automatic response in order to keep my relationships intact and the people I love close to me.

Meanwhile, my mother has gone forward to perfect it to a high art form, far beyond the example she had been when Elise, Win, and I had learned from her.

And now, with the wisdom of age and maturity I saw one thing very clearly—her practice of staving off issues by refusing to discuss them still hurt. I was hurting just the way I had as a child.

TWENTY-EIGHT

I PICKED UP some groceries, then swung by Diane's, but she wasn't home. After leaving a sappy note about how she was missed, I drove out to the ranch. I thought I had bought myself some time to figure out what to say to my mom; instead it bought her and my sister the time to stomp off silently.

By the time I got home it was twilight, the sky made even darker by ominous clouds. It had turned colder again, and I had to trundle the groceries into the house by myself. There were notes of explanation on the kitchen table. Jeremy and Elise were out riding. We have three horses and Elise is on a first-name basis with all of them, plus every other animal she's ever met. My mother had gone upstairs to rest and asked that I not disturb her, even if there was a phone call for her.

I translated that to mean that if Mac called she was not available.

By the time I had a roast and vegetables in the oven and the table set, the sky was dark and the wind was beginning to pick up. I went out on the back deck to see if I could spot Elise and Jeremy, but there was no sign of them.

"Well, damn." I said it out loud but the wind snatched up my words and whirled them away.

From inside the house came the ringing of the telephone. I swore again and raced in just in time to catch it before the machine picked up. "Hello?"

"Oh, Jolie, thank God." It was Bev and she sounded like she was about to cry. "I'm so glad you're there."

"What is it? What's wrong?" Her father was dead; that had to be it.

"My dad—he left again. I went outside to bring in the towels and sheets that were on the line, and when I came back in he was gone."

"Is he walking?" I asked.

"He's in his car and a storm is coming." The words were followed by a half moan, half cry. "I'm just about to lose it. I went looking for him, but I can't stay out, what if he comes back? And when he does, I'm going to have to put him in a home. I hate that thought, but there's nothing else I can do."

"Wait a minute—slow down. You're getting ahead of yourself," I said, then took a breath, too. "I'm so sorry. You've been through such hell with this."

"It's not about me—I can take it, but I'm so worried. It's going to rain hard, and then it will flood again. I don't want him to die like that—"

"Bev, it's okay. We'll find him. I'll help. Did you call Mac?"

"Yes, but he doesn't have any deputies available."

"Okay, then there are other means to get help. Faster, better. I'll call the radio station and we'll put it on the air. We'll ask—"

"K-Sage has been off the air for over twenty minutes."

That meant our engineer had gone to the transmitter and whatever had knocked us off was not an immediate fix. We could be off the air for hours or days.

"Then I'll start looking," I said.

"Would you? Oh, Jolie, you don't know how much that would help. I'm going to call some other people, too, but I think I needed someone to listen to me. Thank you so much."

"Not a problem. Where do you want me to go?"

"Mac gave me a list of areas. Would you take the section near the lake road? Oh, wait, I'll fax you the map and you can see it."

The miracle of modern conveniences. "Consider it done. And please try not to worry; we'll find him."

I looked outside again, but there was no sign of my sister or Jeremy. I raced back into the house and scribbled out a note saying that I'd gone to help Bev look for her dad and would be back as soon as possible. I added a P.S. asking that someone get the roast on the table and see that everyone was fed. Then I ran upstairs to my office and waited impatiently for the map. Our fax machine, not quite as modern as the best of them, rang once, started to whir, then cut off.

Rather than swear, I called Bev. "It didn't come through— would you try again?"

"Sure."

The phone wasn't even in its cradle when the fax started printing out. I had been too hasty. I had my hands on the paper, ripping it out of the machine as soon as it was printed. It looked like about the same area that Leigh had covered during our last search for Bev's dad.

I left the second copy printing and hurried down the hall.

The guest bedroom door was closed and no sound emanated from the room. I made my way downstairs, and grabbed my purse, a heavy windbreaker from the closet, a flashlight, and my cell phone before I dashed out.

Halfway along the lengthy drive I spotted Jeremy and Elise on horseback heading toward the barn. Jeremy had a large electric lantern, and they were trotting along, laughing at something. I wasn't close enough to talk to them, but they saw the car and waved. Jeremy pointed to the barn to let me know that they were on their way in. At least I needn't worry about them.

At the road I turned right and stepped on the gas. It wasn't raining yet, and I wanted to get closer to the lake before the roads got slick and I had to slow down. At the stop sign I noticed that another car was about half a mile behind me. I wondered if it was Linda Beaman or Travis, Sr., coming out to help with the hunt. The more eyes and cars, the faster we would find Henry Kendall, and the better Beverly would feel.

Just a few minutes later as I drove through the edge of town, the thunder and lightning started. I shivered at the sound. I don't like storms, and I like having to be out in them even less. Several orange and white barriers, reminders of the previous week's rains, prevented me from taking my first choice of cutoff road to the lake. I slowed down, waited for the next one, and turned off. It was almost the same way, in reverse, that Ute had taken from the lake.

The rain began with splatters of large drops on the windshield and I slowed to take a better look at the brush on either side of the road. There was no sign of a car or a person. As the rain came harder, visibility lessened.

The road rose up and I could only see the two streetlights illuminating the bridge ahead of me. Beyond that, barely in the pool of light, I thought I saw a vehicle. I strained forward to see better and between swipes of the fast-moving wiper blades I spotted it again. Was it the one that Henry Kendall was driving? It was large—probably a minivan or SUV. Was it dark aqua? It could have been, but it could have been green, too; there was too much rain to tell.

Something like a chill prickled my skin, and rather than continuing to the bridge, I slowed. The rain was pounding down now and the windshield wipers weren't helping much. A solid sheet of water blurred my vision.

The van didn't appear to be moving—but why would it be parked there? It didn't look like an accident. Could it be a breakdown? Perhaps the driver was waiting to meet someone. Or waiting for the rain to slow?

A thought caught at me—Beverly had said that Mr. Kendall was in his car. His is an older, dark blue Lincoln, which meant that I wasn't seeing a confused Henry Kendall up ahead.

I turned the steering wheel more quickly than I'd intended and sent the car sliding in a circle.

"Shit!" I tapped the brakes and counterspun the wheel; the car slowed, and I was facing back the way I'd come. A horn honked and another car swerved past, barely missing me.

I saw the lights of the minivan come on. Someone in a dark minivan had killed Leigh Greer. It spooked me. With more speed than care I headed out of the rural lake area.

So, who could it be in that van? Bev? Ute? Brother Binder? Someone I didn't even know?

What if it was Tom Greer and he had murdered Leigh and Dr. Bill? Then he had somehow conned Beverly into sending me out into the dark rainy night, alone, so that he could kill me, too.

I was frightened and I wasn't thinking clearly. Yes, Tom could have killed his wife, but why would he want me dead? I neared the highway, where there were lights and other cars; I slowed.

Why? Why? Why? Because I'd said repeatedly that I didn't believe Dr. Bill had committed suicide? I'd even said I was going to find out how he really died, and who helped him into the creek that night. I'd said it to Bev, and she could have repeated it to Tom.

I pulled the car to the side of the highway. It was too crazy, thinking Bev would send me out here when I could easily call someone and find out if Henry Kendall was really missing.

I picked up my cell phone and dialed the sheriff's number.

"Wilmot County Sheriff's Office." It was Relda.

Her warm voice calmed me. "What are you doing there so late?"

"We've got the search for Henry Kendall going; I didn't think I should leave."

I let out a breath, enjoying the relief, even while I felt incredibly foolish. "I'm helping, too," I said. "But, I need to know what Mr. Kendall is driving."

"His dark blue Lincoln Town Car." Then she gave me the license number.

"Thanks, I've got it," I said. "Oh, and Relda, I just saw something you might want to have checked out. There was a dark minivan stopped on the far side of the bridge. They could have broken down or something. The lights did come on, but they still might be out of gas."

"I've got a deputy out at Sage Lake Estates—he can check. Oh, wait, hold on, I've got another call—"

"No need. I'll talk to you later."

I took another breath and placed the phone on the console. When there was a break in the stream of oncoming headlights I swung the car around and headed back to the lake road.

My mother had asked about my hormones. If they were out of balance that could have caused my fear tonight. It might also account for my most recent troubles with her. I tried to laugh but it was barely more than a croak. I don't like being scared, and I don't like feeling out of control. Tonight had been a mix of the two. My consolation was that if hormones were the problem, they could be fixed or at least adjusted.

I turned onto the dark lake road. There were no streetlights here, and the pavement was worn and slick. Bushes moved in the wind, although the rain had eased off enough that I could see my surroundings. A tree branch lay across the road and I swerved carefully, avoiding the muddy shoulder. Just a few more minutes and the bridge came into view. I strained to see beyond it, and I was pretty sure that the van was no longer there.

The car continued to climb until I was almost on level with the bridge. That's when I spotted another vehicle—lower, darker—in the same place the van had been. I wasn't sure I was seeing right—I blinked and continued to stare. Yes, it was there, almost hidden by the bridge railing and the trees.

It really was a dark blue Lincoln.

TWENTY-NINE

THE TEMPTATION WAS to grab the phone and call Bev immediately, but I wanted to make sure it was her father, and that he was all right.

I drove toward the bridge slowly, tapping the brakes when I spotted him. He was standing in the middle of the bridge, no umbrella, staring down at the drawdown tube. Why was he doing that? Was he thinking about jumping?

He looked up and saw me, starting as if frightened by my presence. I parked the car on the near side of the bridge and stepped out into the rain. The rain was colder than I'd expected, and I fumbled to zip my windbreaker as I eased toward him.

"Mr. Kendall," I called. "I'm so glad I found you." He stared at me saying nothing as I moved closer. "It's awfully cold out here, isn't it? The temperature must have dropped twenty degrees in the last couple of hours. Aren't you chilly?" Again he merely stared and I wondered if he understood my words. "I'm practically freezing and I just got here. How about you? Would you like me to drive you home? My car is warmed up and dry. That sounds pretty good, doesn't it?"

If he had made any movement I'm not sure what I would have done, but he was still not responding to me. I drew closer so that I was less than ten feet from him. "I wish I'd dressed more warmly. Actually, I wish I were in the Bahamas, but I guess we're stuck with Purple Sage." I wasn't even making sense, but the words were rolling out of my mouth of their own accord, while my concentration remained solely on him, and the rushing water below him. "Beverly is worried about you. She called me and asked if I'd come out here. You know how much she loves you. She didn't come herself because she was afraid you'd go home and get worried if she wasn't there." I tried to laugh, like that was funny, but a crack of thunder overhead made me jump. Mr. Kendall seemed not to hear it.

"This is some storm, isn't it?" I said.

He was leaning on his cane, his thin hair plastered to his shiny head, his beige raincoat so wet it had turned a dark khaki color. I reached out a hand toward him. "Mr. Kendall, I'd really like to get us both out of this rain. Wouldn't you like something warm to drink and some dry clothes?" I was sliding closer and closer, treating him like a horse that might bolt at any sudden movement. "Are you hungry? I think I have some shortbread cookies in the car. They're my favorites; how about you?" I was so close that I could see his eyes behind his glasses. Water was running down into them, but he seemed not to notice.

As I reached to take his arm, he stepped back. I didn't know whether to grab him or not. In that moment of hesitation, Henry Kendall lifted his cane, and swung it down fast and hard. I flinched, and it struck my shoulder instead of my head.

I gasped and he pulled back the cane. It came down a second time and I grabbed it.

"Are you crazy?" I jerked the cane, throwing him off balance. He held on to stay steady. I took a breath. "Don't you know who I am? I'm Jolie Wyatt—Beverly's friend. I came to help you."

Once again I tried to reach for his arm, but as soon as I released the cane he pulled it back.

"I won't hurt you," I said. "I'm your friend."

This time he hit me in the chest and the air rushed out of me in a *whoosh*.

I stared, terrified, as the cane went back again. I tried to scream but no sound came. I raised my hands for protection. The light reflected off the cane as it hit me again. Pain shot all the way up my arm.

I turned and ran toward my car. I was bent double, clutching my arm. He was crazy, his mind gone, and I couldn't help him. When I stepped off the end of the bridge I slipped on the slick mud and my feet went out from under me. My hip hit first, and I groaned aloud. I braced just in time to save my head from crashing on the edge of the sidewalk. I wanted to cry from the pain and the cold, but there wasn't time. A couple of breaths and I rolled over, got to my knees, and saw that Henry Kendall was only a few feet away. He was moving quickly, murderous intent on his face.

"You know me," I said. "I'm Jolie. Bev is my friend. She sent me for you."

"Bitch!" He swung the cane and I barely had time to dodge. That's when I understood. Henry Kendall had killed Dr. Bill. Beverly hadn't driven her van that night, her father had taken it at the reception, and somehow he had convinced Dr. Bill to meet him at the creek. Did he threaten suicide? That would be enough and then he walked with Dr. Bill to the creek's edge and—what?—hit him with the cane and shoved him in?

He was the one Leigh had seen in his trench coat. He had killed Leigh Greer, as well. And now he was going to kill me.

The cane was practically in my face. I heard a tiny click and a knife slid out of its base.

"You can't use that," I said. "They'll see it during the autopsy—they'll figure out what happened."

He barked out a sound meant as a laugh. "I am old and sick," he rasped. "But not as weak as they think, and not as demented as I pretend. I'll be dead by the time anyone figures it out."

"Why are you killing me? I didn't hurt you."

"You hurt Beverly, just like Leigh did. You made her go back to her old house—that was mean-spirited. And then you decided that she'd killed Dr. Bill. I saw it on your face the day you watched the tape."

I had forgotten he was even in the room. How invisible the old and the feeble can be, not that he was feeble. "But why? Why would you kill Dr. Bill?"

"Why? Because he was an arrogant son of a bitch, that's why! Thought he was some great savior, doing me a favor, bringing me back to life. I signed legal documents so that I could die naturally, in peace, without some sorry-ass doctor beating on me and pumping me full of artificial life. It was my right to die. Do you hear me? My right, and he took that away, so I took his life. We were even.''

I had always heard that Henry Kendall was a ruthless businessman and a demanding tyrant, but I never would have believed how far he would push it. The arrogance Henry Kendall saw in Dr. Bill was his own reflection.

My cold muscles shook as I warily got up on one knee. I had to make it to my car, then I would be safe and I could get him help. But if he struck out again, I had to have a defense; I knew I couldn't run anymore.

He stood on the edge of the sidewalk, holding the railing for support. I was two steps away, at the top of the slope that went down to the lake. If I could get a small head start, the slickness of the mud combined with his own imbalance would slow him enough to allow me to get into the car.

He pushed the knife gently against my neck. ''You have to go in the lake, there's no other way.''

''Three accidental drownings? No one will believe that.'' I was shifting my weight slowly so that when the time was right, I could stand quickly. ''It's too late, it isn't going to work.''

He brought the cane down on my head. ''Don't you talk to me like that.''

I shot upward, and grabbed the cane. ''Stop that! You killed Dr. Bill! You're a murderer.'' I shoved backward, but the slick wood slid through my palm, hardly moving him.

''Don't you call me names.''

I grasped the cane and tried to wrench it from him. He fell forward, crumpled on the ground, and I had the cane. ''Get up.'' I held it out, knife blade toward him. ''Get up!''

I think he tried, but the mud defeated him and suddenly he was sliding downward.

''No!'' I dropped the cane and reached out.

''Get away.'' He fought off my hand. ''I don't need you.'' He was struggling against the slope and the mud, gasping for air even as he went down. He rolled, hit a rock, and then I heard only a splash.

"No!" I grabbed the cane and tried to control my slide as I followed him down. "I'll get you out. Hang on—" There was the rock, and several more. I sat, using my entire body to cling to the wet ground. I could see him, up to his chest in the cold water. He was gasping, his face white in the streetlights. "Don't thrash around," I said. "I've got the cane. Get ahold of the crook. Can you see it?"

"Get away." He was going deeper, the water up to his shoulders.

"I can help. Here." I held out the cane, but it didn't reach. I slid both hands down the shaft. My left hand caught on the knife blade and I bit back a gasp. "Oh, no, oh, God." I looked down. Fresh blood rushed out to rinse away the mud. I doubled over, fighting to stay useful. "It's okay, it's okay." I was talking to both of us. "We can do this."

"No. I don't want help."

I let myself slip farther down the bank. "Don't worry, it will work." I was afraid to use my left hand, but I couldn't let Bev's father die. Not here, not now. He had floated closer to me and I held out the cane, intent on getting it to him. He reached out a hand and batted it away.

I was suddenly aware of the mud and the rain and the dark night. I could feel mud plastered to my arms, caked on my hands. My hair was wet to my scalp and the cold penetrated to my bones. I wanted to turn over and cry, but Henry Kendall was still there, and for everything he'd said, he looked scared. Scared the way my father had looked when he first got sick.

This might be Henry Kendall's time to die but I didn't know that for a fact, and I wasn't letting him go without a fight.

I lifted the cane again, wiping off mud so that I could hold it with my right hand. Then I aimed. I was going to hook it around his neck and pull him in. The cane went out, and fell into the water. He struggled, and somehow, miraculously, it caught in his coat.

I pulled with everything I had. "Hang on, you son of a bitch, I'm going to get you out."

He was too weak to fight me and I was too determined to be stopped. I jerked and slipped and grasped tighter until I could pull him up on land. When I did I saw that he wasn't fighting anymore.

"Don't you dare die on me! Don't you dare!" I rolled him on his back, grabbed the collar of his coat, and began hauling him up the bank. "I mean it, if you die you'll be sorry. You have no right to die, do you hear me?" I fell, but got to my knees and pulled some more. "We're almost there. A few more feet and I can get you some help."

I heard a voice call my name. "Jolie!" The voice sounded relieved and scared. I thought it was a dream, but when I looked up I saw headlights shining on us. There were people, only silhouettes in the light, running toward me. I turned to Henry Kendall, "I told you we'd make it."

He made a sound; he was alive.

"Jolie. Oh, my God, honey, look at you." It was my mother. Even in my muddy, bloody state she threw her arms around me. "Oh, honey." She was crying as she held me.

I hugged her back, "I'm okay. It's Mr. Kendall—he killed Dr. Bill and Leigh Greer."

"I know," Mac said. Gently he wrapped a blanket around Henry Kendall. "Beverly realized that a day or two ago; that's why she was so scared tonight. She thought he was going to kill himself."

"Instead he tried to kill me." I held my hand up.

"Oh, Jolie." My mother pulled a delicate silk scarf out of her pocket and wrapped it around my wound. "At least that will stop the bleeding."

The scarf had been shades of pale green and soft yellows, but it was now dark with mud, and staining with blood. "I'm ruining your scarf," I said.

She shook her head, then reached up and wiped mud off my face with her clean, soft hands. "Honey, it's just a scarf. You're far more important."

THIRTY

WE SAT AROUND my dining room table and I was finally warm, and as my mother would say, "squeaky clean," courtesy of the nurses at the Wilmot County Hospital. They saw to it that I had a shower and fresh clothes while we waited for Dr. Baxter to finish working on Mr. Kendall. I was still wearing the clothes, an incredibly frayed hospital gown and non-matching robe with plastic sandals, but I didn't care. I seemed destined for the grunge look in all its forms.

"More tea?" my mother asked me.

I shook my head and yawned. "No thank you. I'm fine."

"How about you, Mac? More coffee? Another brownie?"

He reached over and patted her arm, which wasn't hard to do, since they were sitting inches apart. "We're all fine; you just sit back and rest a bit, Irene. You've been waiting on us since we got in the door."

They were cute together, happy.

"I could use another brownie," Jeremy said. Since he was up against the window, and couldn't get out without disturbing everyone, Matt got him one. "Elise?" he asked.

"No thanks. This whole town seems fattening."

The phone rang and Matt got it. "Hello?" He nodded a couple of times and made nondescript comments before saying thank you and hanging up. "That was the hospital," he said, sitting back down. "Henry Kendall is resting comfortably and Beverly is with him. They are calling his condition guarded but stable."

"What in the world does that mean?" Elise asked.

The sheriff knew. "They're hedging their bets," Mac said.

I shook my head. "I feel so sorry for Bev. She's such a good person, and she just keeps having terrible things happen to her. First Tom leaving, and then having to come back here—and now this." The *this* I was referring to was knowing that her father had committed two murders and had plans for more. She had found a list in his drawer when she was cleaning the house. Dr. Bill Marchak was right at the top, along with both Leigh and Tom Greer. There were other names, as well, but not mine, which is why she hadn't worried about sending me to look for him. Little did she know that I had been added quite recently.

"What happens to Mr. Kendall if he lives?" Jeremy asked.

Mac shook his head. "Can't rightly say. I figure the grand jury would indict him, but he's pretty tough, so I'm thinking he'd commit suicide before he went to trial. Or just up and die out of sheer cussedness."

I wondered how Mr. Kendall felt about me right now. I had been instrumental in saving him from death. I had no illusions of great heroism about that, after all, Mac and mom might have arrived in time to do the honors if I hadn't. Still, would Henry Kendall hate me? He had hated Dr. Bill for saving him. I had been operating on sheer instinct, without any conscious thoughts or decisions about the rights or wrongs of what I was doing. I wondered if Dr. Bill had been that way, too.

I do believe in the right to die—but the mistake was in forcing another human being to participate. I pushed that thought away, saving the concern for another time.

I had other questions to ask. "Mac," I said. "What was the story on that van by the bridge? Did the deputy see it? I'd hate to think I was hallucinating."

"Oh, it was real. Wiley was almost run off the road by it."

"You're kidding. Why?"

"DWI. Brother Binder's blood alcohol level was well over the legal limit. He'd been sitting by the side of the road with a bottle of vodka and he should have slept it off right there.

Instead he is now a guest of the county for the night. That's the third time, so the consequences are going to be severe.''

"Brother Binder was in it? Drunk? And it was the third time?" I said.

Mac nodded. "Didn't need any publicity the first two times—he kept promising he'd quit drinking and the judge believed him. Brother Binder is a minister, so he ought to have been trustworthy. Guess we know better now."

I looked at Mom and grinned. "There's our miracle." I stood up. "I'll just call the station and make sure it's the lead story for tomorrow's newscasts."

"No need," Mac said. "Katharine already got a full report from me. I believe it's going to be on the front page of the newspaper, too. Rhonda Hargis said she was real tired of flood stories, and this was much more interesting."

Mom smiled. "It's almost a happy ending, don't you think?"

"As close as we'll get. I just feel sorry for poor Gretchen. And poor Bev," I said.

Matt slid an arm around me. "How about poor Jolie?"

"Me? I'm fine." I raised my bandaged hand with its seven stitches. "No permanent damage and I can't do dishes for a while. I think that's great."

"As usual," Elise said, "Jolie comes out the winner. It's always been that way."

I said. "Are you nuts?"

"No. You have a great house, a great husband, you only work part-time, and you wrote a book that's actually going to be published. Do you know how many people would love to have your life?"

"And she has me," Jeremy added. "Don't forget that."

"You see?" Elise said. "And one perfect son. You have it all."

Matt winked at me. "Actually, I have it all—I have Jeremy *and* Jolie."

"And I'm getting my hormones checked," I said. "You

will have a kinder, gentler, and more secure Jolie Wyatt. I promise.''

My mom nodded. ''You are at that age, so it's a good idea. I wonder who suggested it?''

''You.'' Along with the rest of the world. I had no illusions about my mother, or my relationship with her, but I wasn't giving up, either. The way things were going she'd be around for us to work on it.

''Think that will help how headstrong you are?'' Mac asked. ''And will it keep you from gettin' involved in things you shouldn't? You're a lot like your mom in that way, and I have to tell you, I knew one of you was going to get yourself hurt over this thing. Driving out to the lake tonight I was scared spitless we'd find you dead, or hurt real bad.''

''I had no idea it was going to be dangerous,'' I said. ''I was just trying to help out a friend.''

''It's a family trait,'' my mother said.

Mac looked at her with such affection my breath caught in my throat. ''I'll buy that,'' he said to her. ''I'll definitely buy that.''

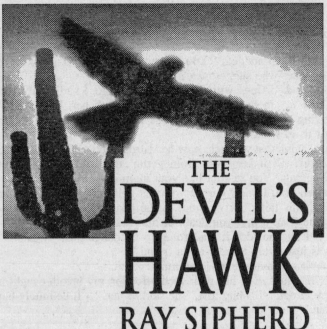

THE
DEVIL'S
HAWK

RAY SIPHERD

A JONATHAN WILDER MYSTERY

Artist Jonathan Wilder is drawn into the ruthless human smuggling enterprise run by "The Hawk," who charges outrageous fees to transport illegals over the border, only to leave them in the desert to die.

Helping a friend whose relatives were victims, Wilder passes himself off as a desperate "chicken"—a move that will lead him directly to the Hawk's aerie, where the identity of The Hawk may be a secret he takes to his grave.

> "...will draw crime fans interested in the New West,
> particularly Hillerman devotees."
> —*Booklist*

Available January 2004 at your favorite retail outlet.

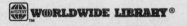

WORLDWIDE LIBRARY ®

WRS480

SCAVENGERS

A Posadas County Mystery

Steven F. Havill

A man's body is found in the
unforgiving New Mexico desert,
the beginning of a brutal murder
spree that has roots on both
sides of the border.

Retired sheriff Bill Gastner
offers unerring logic and
horse sense to new undersheriff
Estelle Reyes-Guzman in her
attempts to identify the "Juan" Doe.
When another body turns up in a
shallow grave and a suspicious fire
takes a third life, the terrible twist
finally offers the break Estelle has
been looking for, one that will lead
her back into a harsh, merciless
desert where death welcomes all.

"…there's solid pleasure to be derived
from Havill's consistently good writing,
colorful cast, and dead-on sense of place."
—*Kirkus Reviews*

Available February 2004 at your favorite retail outlet.

UP
AND
DOWN

AN INSPECTOR DON PACKHAM MYSTERY
Mat Coward

A man is found pitchforked to death in his garden, and
Constable Frank Mitchell finds himself paired with the
legendary Inspector Don Packham. Unfortunately, Mitchell
is never sure whether he'll be working with the upbeat,
jovial Packham or his manic-depressive alter ego.

Why would anyone murder an old man who did little but tend
his beans? The answer, Packham is certain, lies with the
other gardeners in the allotment where the victim toiled daily.
Digging into the lives of the other "plotters," the two uncover
the real dirt surrounding a garden-variety killer.

**"...impressive...will remind readers of long-suffering
Lewis and moody Morse in the Colin Dexter series."**
—Booklist

Available February 2004 at your favorite retail outlet.

WMC484